Kathy

A Loving Family

Acceptance

Published by Completely Novel
Printed by Lightning Source International.

Front cover art work by Eve Harrison.

To Paul,
For always believing in me.
To my Librarians,
For your friendship and encouragement.
To my small band of readers,
For walking the path with me.
To Eve,
For the wonderful art work.

Thank You
x

Chapter 1

Naomi stopped, with her hands still in the soapy water and sighed deeply. She looked out of her kitchen window at the garden she loved so well. She sighed once more and, lifting her hands, wiped them on her apron. Something was wrong. She couldn't put her finger on what it was; but there was definitely something. The feeling had been growing since the weekend, and now it was Tuesday evening, and the feeling was like a solid lump inside her. As her eyes took in each area of the garden they stopped on the greenhouse.

Bernard loved his greenhouse, loved to potter in it for hours, and it was there the boys, her precious sons, went when they had something they wanted to talk through with him. Naomi smiled; maybe she should go there herself to talk to him. But she knew what Bernard would say.

'If the boys have a problem they know they can come to us. They are grown men, Naomi, let them work things out for themselves. Trust them to know when they need our advice. Don't look for problems where there might not be any.'

Fine for him to say, but she was a mother, and mothers knew when something was wrong. Bernard was her rock, the love of her life, but there were times when even he didn't understand her and he never understood mothers' instinct!

Something brushed against her leg, and Naomi looked down to see which of her babies was gently trying to remind her that they hadn't been fed yet. It was Basil, the tabby kitten, though kitten was beginning to stretch the mark now, he was eight months old. Naomi moved from the sink with yet another sigh and bent down to pick him up.

'Ok my baby,' she murmured into his soft, furry neck. 'Are you hungry? Well come on then let's call your brother and put your food out.'

Basil purred his response. He loved being petted by his owner, and took advantage of her regularly. Bernard and the boys teased her about the two kittens she had brought home a few months back being her babies, making up for the fact that her two real babies had grown up and no longer needed constant mothering. Not that that stopped her trying.

Naomi loved her family more than anything else. It was what she had ached for as a child – to be a part of a loving family. From the day Bernard had rescued her and shown her true love she had vowed that their family would be different. They would love, show love, give and take love. Her children would know how precious they were to her, would be able to bring friends home, talk to her about anything - and they did.

From the time they could talk, both Paul and Peter openly asked for cuddles, brought her their fears, triumphs and hurts, and had the confidence to open the cupboard as soon as they came in the house and help themselves to some of her home baking. She had gone to every school concert, every football and rugby match, every parents evening, school fete, PTA meeting, and she had loved every minute of it. Her only regret was that she had never had a third child.

Bernard's sister Jennifer had four girls, so there had always been plenty of children around at family gatherings, and soon the next generation would start arriving as Eve and Abe's baby was due in a few months, but part of Naomi had always wanted another baby of her own, hopefully a daughter who would become a friend. Still, she was blessed with two wonderful boys and she wasn't one to waste time on regrets.

She thought about them in turn. Paul, her first-born son, tall, athletic, handsome, and quickly becoming a successful businessman. She just wished he hadn't married that girl. Oh, she knew all mothers struggled to accept another woman taking first place in their son's life, but this was more than that. Felicity was a mistake. She knew it. Even before they married, Naomi had cried many tears at the thought of Paul getting hurt. Bernard told her to hold her tongue, just wait, but Paul had married her, and had looked more and more unhappy ever since.

Peter, her youngest son, was equally tall and good-looking. Working hard to follow in his father's footsteps and become a doctor. A quieter boy than his brother, who at four years older, had always been the leader. It was even his brother who had chosen his name – his favourite nursery rhyme at the time being two little dicky birds because it had his own name in it; he had insisted that the new baby should be the other one. Peter (though everyone but Naomi now called him Pete) was often lost in his own thoughts. He didn't seem to notice the many girls, and now nurses, who batted their eyelashes at him. He studied so hard. Perhaps that was what was wrong Naomi thought now. Perhaps it was the studying and the exams and the hospital work. Maybe he was just tired, but she had a gut feeling it was more than that. Something was bothering him, and it hurt her to see it in him. Something in the last three or four weeks had changed in her son.

She shook her head, and with a final stroke of both cats, Alfred, the black one, having arrived as soon as he heard the tin open, she returned to the washing up. She had a dishwasher, it was another thing she was teased about, but sometimes, when she needed to think, she preferred to wash up by hand. Perhaps it was a memory thing, hours spent washing up when the boys were little and there was no dishwasher. Perhaps it was another of those 'being the perfect housewife' things that meant so much to her. Whatever it was, Naomi just knew it met a need inside her, and tonight that need was great.

Upstairs in his bedroom, Peter was also sighing. Lying on his bed, music on, he stared up at the ceiling. He should be getting ready for rehearsals, but so far he hadn't motivated himself to move. He could text the director and tell him he was ill, but Mum would be sure to notice, and as she had already started giving him little looks that meant she knew something was up, he didn't want to raise her suspicions further so he wasn't going to do that.

It wasn't that he kept secrets from his parents. He and Paul often joked together that they must have carried out some really heroic deeds in a previous life to get such wonderful parents. They had had a few arguments in their teenage years, but nothing compared to any of their friends, all of whom told them regularly how lucky they were. He sighed again. No it wasn't about keeping secrets.

It was just that he didn't know what was wrong himself. How could one moment make you feel as though you had found the secret you had always been looking for, yet leave you so confused at the same time? Well, the answer wasn't on his bedroom ceiling, he thought with a grin, sat up and swung his feet off the bed. The only thing to do was go to the rehearsal and see what happened tonight.

He grinned to himself at the memory of the time, after a lovely family outing, he had told his parents he was going to run away with the circus and become a trapeze artist. They had coped so well, said they would support him, but thought he should wait until he had finished junior school and high school before he left home. His parents were so cool, and seemed to cope with anything he threw at them, but this could be the ultimate test and the trouble was he wasn't feeling cool about it himself yet.

Peter hurried into the bathroom, washed, brushed his teeth, looked at himself in the mirror, without seeing how gorgeous he was, and then ran down the stairs, grabbed his car keys, shouted his goodbyes and rushed out of the door. He was running late, and nothing made Phil, the director, mad easier than actors being late for rehearsals. He seemed to forget they were the local amateur society and think he was running a West End blockbuster.

Peter turned the CD player up to an ear splitting level and drove carefully to the hall. Late or not, he was always a careful driver, thanks to his mother, who constantly told him and his brother to drive carefully because she worried. He pulled up outside, turned the engine off, took a few deep breathes and felt his stomach lurch at the thought of going inside. With a look of determination he opened the car door, got out and locked it. Then pulled himself up straight, gulped and walked into the hall.

Across town, in the house his father-in-law had insisted on putting a huge deposit on as a wedding present, Paul had just finished his evening meal. There were only the two of them there, but still the table had been set with cloth, napkins, crystal glasses, and the best cutlery. Paul often wondered why they had a second set of cutlery, because Felicity would never use it when they had a silver set. He rose from the table, muttered thanks for the meal and claimed he had a business meeting to attend. Felicity didn't acknowledge that he had spoken, but wouldn't question a business meeting anyway, because that would hopefully bring in more money for her to spend on her very spoiled life style.

Paul wondered how he had never seen how spoiled she was before he married her. He guessed it was because Daddy had met her every whim, so she had never needed to complain. Now he only had to say no to something and the tantrums started. Then the threat that she would ´ask

Daddy' came into play. She knew he hated the amount of input into their lives her darling Daddy had and, that if he possibly could, he would, then give in to avoid the comments from his in-laws.

He got into his car, intending to go to his best mate's house. Abe, married to Paul's favourite cousin, had been his best friend since infant school. The two had always been inseparable, and nobody had been more pleased than Paul when he got together with Eve. He loved both of them totally, but as he drove tonight, he knew that going there would be a mistake. They were so loved up and glowing now that the baby was due, that they would simply make him more depressed.

He changed direction to go to his parent's house, and then thought better of that too. His mother was sure to pick up on his mood. He smiled thinking of the times he and Peter had seriously discussed whether or not their mother could be a witch, as she always seemed to know what they were thinking, what they had done, or even what they were thinking of doing. Of course they had made her a white witch, because there was nothing evil about their mother.

Thinking of her now increased the pain he felt. He knew she was aware of how unhappy he was, and he knew that she was hurting for him. He would give anything to take that hurt away but he was at a loss to see how he could.

He stopped the car while he tried to decide where to go. Peter was at rehearsal so he couldn't talk him into coming out. It wouldn't be fair to laden his younger brother anyway. The pub was an option, but he didn't think drink would help. He might get totally bladdered, and that would lead to another row when he got home. He would have to leave the car somewhere too, which would be a problem in the morning as then he really did have a business meeting to get to.

He smiled at the thought of turning up to his meeting with the puritanical Mr Blowings with the mother of all hangovers. That would lose him the contract – not that he had much confidence in getting it anyway. It was a contact his Father-in-law had got him, and Mr Blowings knew what his Father-in-law thought of Paul, so he treated him like an idiot at every meeting.

In the end he drove to the nature reserve and just sat in the car, looking at the lake and thinking. Life wasn't meant to be like this, but Paul couldn't see a way out. One thing was for certain though, he knew he had to find a way, because he couldn't go on much longer with things as they were.

Chapter 2

The rehearsal had ended, and Peter heaved a sigh of relief. He had forgotten his lines, missed his cues, walked on at the wrong time and generally messed up the whole thing. Now all he needed to do was to get out of the hall before Phil caught him. Almost at a run, but not quite, so as not to draw attention to himself, Peter made his way to the door. He was almost out of it when that dreaded booming voice stopped him.

'Peter! I think a chat is in order don't you?'

Biting his lip, and knowing he was rapidly going red, Peter turned and walked back into the room. Some of the others gave him encouraging smiles as they passed him, glad it was him and not them being yelled at tonight. One or two patted his arm, and they all had the decency to leave quickly, keeping his embarrassment to a minimum.

'Petey, Petey, Petey. Have you an explanation for your performance – or rather lack of one – tonight?' Phil's voice was icy cold.

'Not really, no,' murmured Peter lifting his eyes heavenward.

'You are one of the best members of this team. I rely on you and now this! It's only days 'til the performance and suddenly you don't know your lines, you seemed to have no idea of when and where you should be on stage, and you made other people make mistakes.'

Peter wasn't sure how to answer. He knew it was all true. He was about to shout back when he realised the scenery crew were still working and most of them were hanging onto every word. Peter, Phil's blue-eyed boy, the one Phil regularly said should be a professional actor and the others should watch and learn from, was getting a rocket. That was worth hearing!

Peter rubbed his hands over his face. He took a deep breath and thought about his reply. 'Phil, I'm sorry. Let's just put it down to a bad day. I'll be back to normal by Thursday I promise. Just got a lot on my mind, you know how it is.'

'Oh yes. I know very well how it is. Do you not think *I* have a lot on *my* mind? Sometimes I think it's a miracle that I haven't got ulcers the way you lot mess about and fail to see the importance of rehearsals. And why we are on the topic of rehearsals you were late as well this evening!'

'No way! You hadn't even started when I walked in.'

'Because we had to wait for you,' Phil thundered.

'I don't need this tonight Phil, either accept it was just one bad rehearsal or fire me – I don't really care anymore. I have enough to deal with and think about, and if you are going to be another headache to deal with I'll just back out and the understudy and take my part.'

'Now Pete, there's no need to get so defensive,' stammered Phil, backtracking quickly. 'I'm just doing my job as director. Just because you are the best actor I have here, doesn't mean you are above the rules. I can't be seen to have favourites. And you never know who might come to watch the play – it could be your big break.'

'If that's supposed to make me back down, it failed. I've said all I'm going to say, and now I'm going home. If I don't hear from you, I'll be here on Thursday. If you don't want me to come just ring me or leave a message for me.'

Peter turned and walked briskly to the door. As he got outside his shoulders slumped, and by the time he got to the car door his hands were shaking. He didn't want to leave the company, he loved acting, always had. Why had he said all that? He groaned and banged his fist on the roof.

'I wouldn't worry about it Pete.' He turned to see Jason walking across the road towards him. 'He is in such a

9

panic in there. He would be lost without you. Terry is now getting it in the neck because the scenery isn't as good as Phil thinks it should be. I left them having the mother of all rows. But you were not yourself at all tonight. If you need someone to talk to I'm a good listener.'

Peter could feel a headache coming on. He was feeling hot and didn't trust himself to speak. After a minute he realised that Jason was waiting for a response.

'Oh, hmmmm, not sure I know what's up myself really,' Peter grinned apologetically.

'It's ok, it was only a thought.'

'No, a drink sounds good to be honest. Do you have a car?'

'Porsche round the corner,' laughed Jason. 'No, sorry, not that rich a student, and a father that won't trust me with his!'

'Hop in then. Do you mind if we go nearer home for me? I never drink and drive and I don't want to have far to walk to the car in the morning. Unless that's too far from home for you?'

'Not sure where you live, but I'm sure it will be fine. Buses are quite regular'

Peter opened the car and they got in. The CD was playing loudly, so there was no need to talk on the way. Peter parked the car at home and they walked back to the King's Arms at the bottom of the road.

It was becoming quite dark Paul suddenly realised. Other cars had started to come into the car park. Paul's guess was that they would be couples, and as he had no desire to be labelled a pervert, he decided it was time to move. He checked his watch, half nine. Too early to go home and straight to bed, but the rehearsal might have finished. Maybe he should ring Peter and see if he fancied meeting up for a drink. He picked up his phone and clicked on Peter's number. He answered after the third ring.

'Hi Pete, wondered if you wanted to meet for a drink after rehearsal?'

'Hiya, I'm in the pub actually with a friend from rehearsals.'

'Oh, doesn't matter then,' Paul replied, trying to sound casual, but feeling let down even though it wasn't Peter's fault.

'No, no, come and join us, if you don't mind not being on our own that is.' Peter pulled a face at Jason and mouthed, 'You don't mind do you?' Jason shook his head and smiled.

'Are you sure?' Paul asked, 'Where are you, the King's Arms as usual?'

'Yeah, see you in a bit.'

Paul put the phone down, turned the key and reversed out of the car park. He drove off towards the pub, feeling better at the idea of some company before facing home. It didn't take him long to get there and he parked and walked in. He saw Peter straight away, and thought he looked stressed.

'How goes it little brother?' he asked, 'you look like you have had a bad day.'

'No, just a bad rehearsal.'

'Oh I don't know,' laughed Jason, 'it was quite a good rehearsal for everyone else. It's not often we hear the great actor Peter Smedley yelled at. It made a nice change!' Peter and Paul both laughed, and checking what they were drinking, Paul went to get more drinks.

They stayed until closing time, chatting, joking and generally making each other feel better, without knowing they were doing it. Paul offered Jason a lift home, and Peter said goodbye to them at the door and walked down the road.

'Is that you love?' Naomi called as she heard the door close.

'No, it's a burglar,' called Peter, using the old familiar family joke. He poked his head round the door and gave his mum a smile. She smiled back; pleased to see he looked calmer than he had earlier. Bernard walked in with two mugs of tea.

'I see he heard the kettle as usual,' he commented, winking at his wife. 'If you want any supper its whiskers for you and me,' he added looking at his son. Seeing Peter's confused look he laughed and explained. 'You missed the fun earlier. Our two little Lords didn't want to come in, and your mum couldn't cope with that. Tried shaking the box of dried food, but they weren't interested. So she decided to offer them my Brussels pate!'

'It worked!' stated Naomi defensively.

'Of course it did. They have good taste; I'll say that for them. But, like I said Pete, its whiskers for you and me. I think those cats have replaced us in her affections. They climb on my bed, get more cuddles than I do, and now they are fed on my favourite supper!'

Peter laughed at Bernard's hurt look. Life was so simple here at home. Sometimes he wished he could just stay here and not go outside. All his life had been this warm and comfortable, and he wished he was still a little boy, listening to his parents tease each other and laugh together, being welcomed into their closeness and knowing nothing could hurt you.

After dropping Jason off, Paul drove slowly home. He pulled onto the drive and grimaced at the thought of what awaited him. Locking the car he went into the house. Downstairs was in darkness. That meant a row because he was so late home, and however quiet he was, he was sure to wake Felicity, which was another hanging offence in her mind.

He crept up the stairs and was startled to hear soft music coming from their room. He entered, and only just stopped himself from exclaiming at the scene that greeted him. The room was lit by candles, soft music playing, and Felicity lying on their bed looking utterly gorgeous in what was, he guessed, a new negligee. Paul stood and looked at her, and hated himself for the immediate reaction she caused in him. He didn't trust himself to speak, but wet his lips and let out a long breath. She smiled up at him seductively.

'I take it you like what you see, Mr Smedley?' she purred, then beckoned him towards her, and with trembling hands he joined her on the bed.

Paul gazed up at the ceiling, feeling tears sting his eyes. Felicity was snoring gently next to him. She had gone to sleep quickly, after spending nearly an hour in the bathroom, obviously washing any scent of him off her. Unable to sleep, Paul left the room quietly and went downstairs for a glass of water. He wondered what it would be this time. For a few minutes, when he first saw her, he thought that maybe Eve and Abe's news had stirred her into realising that a baby would be lovely.

Now, in the cold kitchen, he knew that was a vain hope. So what would it be? There had to be a reason for her to behave like that. Felicity wasn't like other women. Tonight was only the third time, in nearly two years of marriage, that they had made love. They had waited before marriage, as they both had strong religious views. In fact, they had never gone very far at all, Felicity claiming she didn't want them to be tempted.

13

Paul had accepted that, felt it was respecting her, even though he knew Abe got a lot further – and he was at Theology College, training to be a vicar for goodness sake. He said he didn't mind. It would make the honeymoon all the more special. He gave a bitter laugh as he remembered how wrong that thought had been.

On their wedding night, Felicity claimed she was tired. Although very disappointed, Paul knew it had been a long day, and she did look tired, so he tried to be patient. As the days went by, he realised she was nervous. He didn't want to push her, didn't want to row on honeymoon, but in the end he demanded they talked about it.

It was then, with cold eyes and an, 'it's not up for discussion' look on her face, Felicity told him she considered sex just to be for procreation, and had no intention of it being a regular part of their relationship.

Even now, thinking back on it, it still caused the same reaction in Paul. He felt cheated, as though he had been trapped and as though the bottom had dropped out of his world. He was a red-blooded man, and Felicity was one of the most beautiful women he had ever seen. There were only so many cold showers a man could stand!

For the next two days they had hardly spoken, until Paul had given her an ultimatum. Either they made love, or he would have the marriage annulled as soon as they got back to England. With a look of horror Felicity realised he meant it. He got his own way, but it was not the close loving act he had wanted it to be.

The second time had been a few months later. As had happened tonight, Paul had come home to find her waiting for him. His pleasure at her change of mind had been complete. For the first time, he felt that the problems in their marriage could be overcome. The joy lasted until the next morning, when Felicity announced that she 'needed' a new car. A brand new car, no less, and that she expected Paul to pay for it!

Now he stood leaning against the kitchen sink feeling foolish. He had no doubt that tomorrow morning over breakfast he would be told what it was she thought she had paid for by being nice to him tonight.

He could kick himself for being so weak. All she had to do was give him the slightest encouragement and he was powerless to resist. This was no way to conduct a marriage. He thought of his parents, his Aunt and Uncle and Eve and Abe. All of them had such strong marriages. They were obviously in love, had respect for each other, and most of all they had companionship.

Even if sex was a rarity, Paul could have coped if he and Felicity had that closeness and companionship, but they didn't even have that. She had never forgiven him for threatening the annulment. He knew that by making that demand on honeymoon he had dug his own grave. Now the marriage couldn't be annulled, he was against divorce, and she could keep him at arms length for the rest of his life. With a groan Paul sank to the floor and crouched there weeping.

Naomi awoke with a start. She lay very still trying to work out what had woken her. Was there a noise downstairs? She listened, but the house was silent. She looked over to the cats' basket. They were curled up together both sleeping, so it wasn't them that had disturbed her. She switched on her bedside lamp, and quietly, not wanting to disturb Bernard, she went into their bathroom.

She stood looking at her reflection in the mirror. She had a feeling of dread. Something was wrong, she knew it. But what? She crept out of their room and along the landing. She listened at Peter's door. She could hear him breathing deeply, obviously asleep.

15

She turned on the landing light and made her way down the stairs. Going into the kitchen, she filled the kettle and put it on to boil. Two cats padded into the kitchen. They seemed to sense she was upset, and had come to join her. She smiled at them, opened the fridge and gave them the last of the pate. She would buy some more for Bernard tomorrow.

Cup of tea in hand she sat at the breakfast bar. Something had woken her, and she still couldn't put her finger on it. There was nothing she could do at this hour, but as soon as it was morning she would have to check everyone was ok. Naomi seemed to have a sixth sense that told her when something was wrong. Could it be Bernard's parents? Eve? Paul? Someone needed her. She closed her eyes in prayer and took them all to heaven's door with a request for help, and peace, and answers. She finished praying, finished her tea, and feeling calmer decided to return to bed. Naomi was glad she had a strong faith. It helped at moments like this. Now, hopefully she would be able to sleep. Morning would be here soon enough, and she would check on everyone then.

Chapter 3

Bernard woke to the sound of the alarm and was surprised to see Naomi still sleeping. As she looked so peaceful, he left her there, creeping from the room so as not to disturb her. It was unusual for him to make the first cup of tea in a morning, but when he reached the kitchen and saw Naomi's cup on the side, he realised she had been up in the night. He wondered how long for.

Putting the kettle on, he went to feed the cats while he waited for it to boil, collected his paper off the mat, put bread in the toaster and laid a tray ready to take up to Naomi.

Entering their room, he put the tray on the side and went to call Peter. Then he went back into their room, sat on the edge of the bed and gently woke his wife. Naomi was surprised to have slept through the alarm and dismayed that Bernard had had to make his own breakfast.

'You should have woken me sooner. You shouldn't be making your own breakfast before going off to work.' Naomi's strong sense of duty as a wife and mother was kicking in.

'It doesn't hurt for me to spoil you once in a while,' Bernard replied. 'You do far too much for me and the boys, and anyway, I've had a night's sleep which is more than you had isn't it?' A raised eyebrow brought a shy smile in response. 'Mmmm I thought so, so this doctor's orders are for his wonderful wife to pamper herself today. Have breakfast in bed, then rest until it's time to get ready for your lunch with Jen. Us boys can see to ourselves for once, and we'll eat out tonight.'

'We will not! I am not ill, and I am quite capable of cooking for my family.'

'I'm not denying it, just insisting that you let me spoil you for a change. It's not up for discussion, so take that stubborn look off of your face Mrs Smedley, and move over so I can come in for a cuddle before I get ready.'

Passing their bedroom on his way downstairs, Peter shook his head and grinned at the sounds coming from his parents' room. Sometimes they were more like newlyweds than his brother and Felicity. It was good to know that after nearly thirty years of marriage his parents were still so happy.

Reaching the kitchen, Peter got himself a coffee and some cereal. Sitting at the breakfast bar, he planned his day, lectures, then some study if he was going to pass the upcoming exam. But maybe tonight he'd give Paul a ring and meet up for a chat. Although he had been chatty enough last night, he had a feeling he had wanted to talk. Maybe if he could put his confusion into words, Paul would be able to help him work out what was going on in his head as well.

The sharp trill of the telephone interrupted the row over whether or not a two-year-old kitchen needed replacing. Felicity answered it, as she was nearest, and almost threw it at Paul before storming out of the room.

'Hello? Oh hi Mum,' Paul tried to keep his voice light, but knew his mother would see through it.

'Have I called at a bad time honey?' Naomi probed gently. Paul felt tears prick his eyes again at the love flowing down the phone. He felt wretched this morning, tired, drained and very emotional. He had a tough meeting coming up at half past ten this morning and wasn't sure how he was going to get through it.

'It's nothing Mum, honestly. We're both tired and disagreeing over the kitchen. Are you ok?' It was unusual for her to phone him in the morning.

18

'Yes love, just worrying as usual. I woke in the night with a feeling that something was wrong. It's probably nothing, but I'm just ringing round to make sure everyone is okay.'

For a moment, Paul was unable to speak. His mother's intuition was something else. Using every ounce of control he could muster, he managed to say, 'No, I'm fine honestly,' in a fairly calm voice. 'Tell you what, can I come over for dinner tonight?'

'That would be great, but we are eating out. Will it be just you or Felicity as well, so I know how many to book the table for?'

'Just me, the kitchen disagreement is going to drag on, so a few hours apart may help.'

'O.K. darling, our house for seven.'

'Fine, gotta go, Mum, I've an important meeting to get ready for.' Paul ended the call quickly, finished getting ready for work and called up to Felicity that he would be out for dinner tonight. Getting no response he shrugged his shoulders and left.

Coming out of the bathroom after another bout of terrible morning sickness, Eve crawled back into bed wearily. Abe had already rung work and told them she wouldn't be in, and he planned to work at home today. He went and got a cool flannel and mopped her brow.

'I wish I could do this for you darling,' he said.

Smiling Eve replied, 'So do I actually. I won't mind the getting fat bit, but if you could do the sickness and the labour pains, that would be great.' Abe kissed her forehead and left her to get some sleep. They hadn't intended to announce the pregnancy just yet, but Eve had such bad morning sickness, or all day sickness in her case, that everyone had guessed.

Going into his study, Abe began to think about his sermon for the weekend. He was so glad a position as curate had come up so near to home. It meant that both families were not too far away and would be there with plenty of support when the baby came. It also meant he was near enough to offer support to Paul.

Just as he was thinking about his best friend the phone rang. It was Paul. 'Hi mate, wondered if you were free for lunch today? I've a meeting this morning, but it should be over by 12-30.'

'Ermm, yeah that should be fine, say 1 O'clock, usual venue? Eve is bad again this morning, but she will be fine on her own for an hour or two.'

'Are you sure? If she needs you we'll do lunch another day.' Abe could hear the disappointment in Paul's voice, even though he was trying to be thoughtful.

'No, 1 O'clock will be fine. Good luck with your meeting.'

Naomi met Jennifer at their usual spot, a small bistro just off the main shopping street. José, the owner greeted her warmly as she came in. 'Naomi, how wonderful you look today!' He kissed the air both sides of her face, and Naomi smiled at him warmly. She was used to this greeting. 'Now my two favourite customers are here, I will bring coffees to you, on the house, while you decide what you are going to eat today.'

Naomi made her way over to Jennifer. 'Hi Jen. I see José is in good form as always.'

'Of course!' laughed Jennifer. 'How are you feeling? Better than earlier I hope?'

'Well, I've spoken to everyone, and they all claim to be fine, nothing out of the ordinary. But I know things are getting worse for Paul, and Peter is definitely worrying about something at the moment. He has an exam coming up, but I'm sure it's more than that.'

'It'll sort in good time love, try not to worry.'

'It will, and as Bernard keeps reminding me, they'll come to us if they need us. Anyway, how is Eve today?'

'Bad again. Poor thing is having a really rough time of it. I'm going to go and stay with her for a few days. Abe is being wonderful, but I think she wants her mum there. I had a rough few weeks with each of the girls so at least I know how she feels.'

'I remember it well,' said Naomi. 'I sailed through both of my pregnancies and yet never fell again after Peter.'

The women continued to reminisce about their children's younger days. They both chose pasta dishes for lunch and enjoyed their time together as they always did. Lunch here was a weekly event for the two, who were close friends as well as sisters-in-law.

Across town, Paul was running late. His meeting had been dreadful and he had only just managed to control his temper, as Mr Blowings had come up with one awkward objection after another. Eventually they had agreed to both think over the details of the contract and meet again next week.

Finally, finding a parking place, Paul rushed along the road to B.J.'s. B.J.'s had been his and Abe's favourite burger joint since they were teenagers and they still met there whenever they could.

Abe was waiting and had ordered the mega burger meals for them both. He waved Paul over to the table as he arrived. One look at his friend's face told him things were not good. 'Bad morning?'

'Yep, and it followed a bad night.' Paul rubbed his hand across his face. 'Let's eat and then talk, though I don't think I've much appetite today.'

'You will have, you couldn't bear for me to beat you and finish first could you?' Paul smiled at the reminder of the old challenge.

'Aren't we getting a bit old for that now?' he asked.

'Speak for yourself,' grinned Abe unwrapping his burger and starting.

Paul rapidly followed suit, mumbling, 'cheat,' through his first mouthful of burger. Abe finished first, but not by much. Laughing for the first time all day, Paul said, 'You always manage to cheer me up. No matter how bad things seem.'

'That's what best mates are for!' Abe replied, 'Now tell me what's going on.'

For the next half hour, Paul filled him in on the details of the last few days, finishing with the news that after last night, Felicity now expected a new kitchen.

'I know I shouldn't say this, and I certainly wouldn't recommend it mate, but prostitutes are cheaper!' Abe exclaimed. 'There is something seriously wrong with your wife's thinking. But have you ever wondered if there is a reason for all this? Perhaps she thinks nice things have to be paid for in kind?'

'What are you suggesting?' Paul was indignant at Abe's idea. 'You know her family as well as I do, how can you even hint at anything dodgy in her past?'

'I didn't mean it like that necessarily,' countered Abe, 'She has always been given everything she wanted. Perhaps it wasn't given as freely as it seemed. Perhaps she had to be a 'good girl'. It might not have been abuse, just a form of bribery. Maybe she thinks with you the clue is sex.'

'Well sex a bit more willingly and a bit more often would work better,' Paul commented wryly.

'You need to get her to talk about it Paul, use a counsellor if it would help.'

They continued to talk for a while longer, but came to no firm conclusions. They both knew some honest talking had to take place, but also knew that getting Felicity to do that would be the difficult part.

Chapter 4

The Smedley family went to a quiet restaurant on the outskirts of town for their meal that evening. Peter had offered to be the designated driver so that the others could drink. That way, he thought, he would be able to talk to Paul as he drove him home.

Over two bottles of red wine, the family shared some quality time together. Naomi was never happier than when she was surrounded by her men folk. She wished her daughter-in-law felt more like a part of the family and hoped that when Peter found the girl of his dreams she would be easier to get along with. But, for now, she was happy for it to be just the four of them.

Both boys were making a supreme effort to be jovial, keeping the conversation lively and fast flowing. In fact, it was doing both of them good to have some family time, which was becoming much less frequent than it used to be.

Bernard watched his family with pleasure. He was glad to see his sons looking more relaxed than they had of late, but mostly his eyes were fixed on his wife. Naomi had always been the only women for him, and at times the love he felt for her was almost painful. To see her so happy and animated tonight made him happy. As he watched her watching their sons, he thought how beautiful she still was. When they were alone tonight he would show her how much he still loved and desired her. He considered himself to be one very lucky man.

After the meal and coffees the family went home. The happy mood continued and Naomi felt it was just like old times. With one cat on her lap and the other at the side of her, she relaxed and finally began to believe that maybe she had been worrying over nothing.

It was about ten when Paul said he had better return home. He had a feeling that, as much as his father had enjoyed their company this evening, he would like his wife to himself now. He and Peter went out to the car. For a couple of minutes neither spoke. Then Peter asked, 'Did you want to talk last night? I'm sorry I wasn't alone when you called.'

'No problem, I just wanted company really. Are you O.K though? You've seemed really pre-occupied for the last couple of weeks.'

'Oh my head is messed at the moment. Trouble is, I can't even get it straight enough to talk it through with anyone and that isn't helping.'

'Want to try?' Paul smiled encouragingly at his younger brother. Although there were four years between them they had always been close, and Paul had often helped Peter to solve his problems.

'Where do I start?' Peter turned into Paul's road and didn't say anything else until they were parked on the drive. They then sat in the car, both knowing that talking wouldn't be possible inside with Felicity there.

'Something strange happened a couple of weeks back. It's thrown me completely and I keep telling myself it's just the pressure of the play next week and the exam before it even sooner, but the thoughts and feelings won't go away.'

Paul said nothing, knowing his brother just needed to let it all spill out.

'You know how I've never really been bothered by relationships. I mean, I've plenty of mates, male and female, but I've never wanted more than that. I never thought it was a problem. Just thought I had a missing hormone or something. Mates go on about girls and sex all the time. It just never seemed important to me. I just guessed I hadn't met anyone special enough really, that's if I thought about it at all. It didn't really enter my radar as something to think about.'

Peter stopped as the front door opened, Felicity walked to the passenger side and tapped on the window. 'Paul, when you said you wouldn't be home for dinner, I didn't realise you meant the whole night. We have things to discuss. Decisions have to be made on the kitchen.'

'I've made mine. It stays as it is!'

'You are so unreasonable,' Felicity yelled, 'why do you always have to row about everything? Well if you're not in, in the next two minutes, I'm locking the door.' With that she stormed back into the house, leaving the two brothers staring after her.

'Do you think Mum still keeps my old bed made up?'

'Probably.'

'Good. Let's go home then.'

'Do you still think of Mum and Dad's as home?' Peter asked.

'Given a choice between there and this ice palace, which would you choose?'

'Home it is then!' said Peter with a grin.

When they reached home, they found their parents had gone to bed. Peter made more coffee and they sat in the lounge together. 'So,' said Paul, 'before my wife so rudely interrupted us, you were emptying your head of all its confusion.' He raised his eyebrows and waited for Peter to re-gather his thoughts and continue. When he didn't speak, Paul gently encouraged him. 'Pete, whatever it is you can tell me, you know that. I might not have all the answers, but sometimes just saying it all out loud helps. I bent Abe's ear for a good hour at lunchtime."

'I think I might have fallen in love.' Pete said the words in such a rush that it took Paul a minute to digest them. Then he smiled widely at his brother.

'You sound as though you aren't that happy about it,' he said. 'Don't let my marriage put you off. Just because

Felicity wasn't honest with me before we wed, doesn't mean all relationships are doomed. So, come on, what's she like?'

'That's just it,' Peter's voice was no more than a whisper, 'she is a he!'

'Ahh........ That would explain the confusion then. Is it the guy from last night?'

'Oh please tell me it's not that obvious,' begged Peter. 'I don't know what I'm going to do Paul.' He began to cry softly. Paul moved over to him and placed a hand on his arm.

'The first thing to do is to calm down,' he said. 'You're getting yourself in a state and that's not going to help. Why don't you just start at the beginning and tell me it all?'

Taking a deep breath, Peter told his brother how he had met Jason a couple of weeks earlier when the scenery crew came to a rehearsal. He was doing a design degree and had been roped in to help by friends. 'It was like I'd been punched in the stomach and had all the air knocked out of me,' Peter explained.

Although last night had been the first time the two had done more than exchange polite greetings, Peter explained how he couldn't get Jason out of his head. The brothers discussed the situation for a while longer. Then Paul said 'My best advice would be to get to know him better as a friend and just see what happens. If you spend more time with him you will soon know if he feels the same way.'

By the time they had finished talking, and Peter had calmed down, it was half past three in the morning. Paul rang into his office and left messages for his secretary and second in command, saying that he wouldn't be in and to rearrange his appointments. 'I suggest you take the day off too,' he said to Peter. 'We could go out somewhere after a long lie in. Leave mum a note saying not to wake us.'

27

'Sounds good to me,' said Peter. 'Thanks Paul, it's helped having you to turn to.' They made their way quietly upstairs, said goodnight and went into their rooms. Paul sat on his old bed with a sigh. Life had been so simple when he lived here.

Chapter 5

When she woke the next morning, Naomi was surprised to find a note telling her both of her sons were asleep upstairs and wanted to sleep in after a very late night. She set about feeding the cats, and preparing breakfast. Picking up the paper from the doormat, she returned upstairs with tea and toast for herself and Bernard. She sat on their bed, sipping tea and watching him getting ready for work. He winked at her through the mirror as he buttoned his shirt, both of them thinking about the previous night. Then he sat on the edge of the bed for her to straighten his tie.

It was the usual routine of it that made Naomi feel that all was right with her world. Her day lay ahead of her with no worries at all. Washing up, housework, the crossword, with the cats at her side, over her mid morning coffee. To others it might seem mundane, but to her it was perfection. Family life as it should be. She at the helm of her ship, in charge, making sure it all ran smoothly. And when her boys got up, she would cook them breakfast, listen to them laughing and teasing as they ate. For a while she could put all her worries behind her and enjoy time with her men folk.

The day went as she had planned it. The boys appeared mid morning, enjoyed a leisurely breakfast, and then went out together. Both looked more peaceful than they had of late, and although she knew that coming home was not the answer to solve Paul's problems, for today it was helping and that was good enough for Naomi.

When Peter returned he was alone, having dropped Paul at his own house on the way. He greeted his mum with a kiss and asked what was for tea. Naomi smiled at him, 'You are as bad as the cats,' she said, 'all they care about is where the next meal is coming from, and they shower me with affection to get it as well!'

Peter pulled her into his arms and smothered her with kisses, ignoring her pleas for him to stop. 'I do not only love you when there is food on offer, I love you when my washing is done, my ironing is put away, the house is cleaned, and the phone is answered. There is no end to the things I love you for.'

Naomi swatted him away with a smile. 'Dinner will be a while yet,' she said, 'so go and make yourself useful and put the rubbish out for me.' Peter went off and waved to his dad as he drove onto the drive. It wasn't long before the three of them sat down for a pleasant evening meal together, after which Peter went to get ready for rehearsal, leaving his parents to spend a quiet evening in together.

Driving to rehearsal that evening, Peter felt his stomach churning. He tried to control his feelings, but the nerves were beginning to get the better of him. It didn't help that as he arrived he saw Jason walking up the road towards him. He nearly drove on and went home, but then Jason waved at him and he had no choice but to park the car and walk over to him.

'How you feeling?'

'Nervous to be honest,' Peter said with a grin. Jason placed his arm on Peter's shoulder reassuringly. Peter felt the electricity rush through him.

'You'll be fine,' Jason encouraged, 'Fancy going for a drink again afterwards? I really enjoyed it the other night.' Peter suddenly felt more at ease. Maybe it wasn't just him; maybe Jason was feeling it to. At least, he obviously wanted to be friends and that was a start.

'That would be great, thanks. Having something to look forward to might help me get through another session of Phil yelling at me.' Together the two walked into the rehearsal, where everyone else was ready to start.

The evening passed uneventfully. It was the best rehearsal they had had so far, and by the end of it even Phil was smiling. Peter walked over to Jason at the end of it. They smiled at each other, and walked out of the building. Peter unlocked the car and they got in.

'Where d'ya want to go?' Peter asked.

'I don't mind really. That pub the other night was good, but just a drive or something to eat maybe? You're driving, you decide.'

Peter smiled and said, 'Ok, I'll treat you to my favourite burger joint, and a fantastic view over the valley while we eat.'

They drove on, joining in with the cd player, laughing and joking. Peter couldn't believe how much more at ease he was tonight. Having both chosen chicken burgers with large fries and a coke, Pete drove up to the nature reserve and parked in the highest car park.

'It's a good job my mum can't see me now!' laughed Peter.

'Why?' Jason smiled back at him.

'I ate one of her fantastic dinners before I came out, and she would be mortified to think I needed to eat again.'

They both laughed, and it set the atmosphere for the evening. They laughed and joked and swapped silly stories from their past for well over an hour. Eventually Jason sighed and said, 'I hate to say this, but I really should be getting home, I've a long day at college tomorrow.'

Their eyes met and held until Peter, blushing, looked away.

'Penny for your thoughts?' Jason asked, not taking his eyes off of Peter.

'You don't want to know,' laughed Peter, 'I enjoy your company and don't want you to run away from the madman just yet!'

'Try me,' Jason whispered gently. Peter looked at him, their eyes locking again. He tried to speak, but couldn't find the words. Tears began to fill his eyes. Later, Peter could never remember quite how it happened, but suddenly he was in Jason's arms sobbing, great heaving sobs as the emotions of the last few weeks came gushing out. Jason just held him, rocking gently, stroking his hair and making soothing noises until the sobbing subsided.

Eventually Peter calmed himself to pull away. Embarrassed by his behaviour he mumbled apologies. 'God, what an idiot, I'm so sorry Jason, bet you weren't expecting to spend your evening with a snotty, blubbering wreck!'

Laughing, Jason said, 'Well it wasn't quite the reaction I expected. Are you OK?'

Wiping his face and blowing his nose Peter nodded. 'Just embarrassed at making such a fool of myself.'

'Don't be.' Jason took Peter's face between his hands and kissed him. Just one tender kiss, but in that moment Peter knew this was forever. 'OK?' Peter just nodded, not trusting his voice. 'Good. Then take me home, lets both take some time to get our heads straight, though hopefully not too straight,' Jason grinned, 'and then we'll talk properly.'

Letting out a long breath, Peter said, 'All I've been doing since I first saw you is try to get my head straight. It probably sounds stupid, but even though I wasn't interested in girls, it had never occurred to me that I was gay.'

Jason's eyes widened. 'Well that explains your reaction tonight,' he laughed, 'I've known for as long as I can remember, but I've never done anything about it 'cos my Dad is stuck in the dark ages, and will kill me. I suggest we take it slowly and make sure we are really sure before we say anything.'

32

Peter agreed, gave Jason a hug, and drove them home, the conversation turning to safer topics. After agreeing to meet the following evening, Jason got out of the car and Peter continued on his journey. He was grateful his parents had gone to bed and a quiet 'goodnight' as he passed their room was all that was needed, as his mother would have immediately known that something had happened.

He went for a shower, letting the hot water pulse over him as he thought back over the day. His feelings were jumbled. Part of him was scared about the path he had embarked on, but another part of him couldn't keep the grin off his face. Jason felt the same way, it wasn't just him, and the memory of that kiss would live in his dreams forever. Coming out and facing everyone's reaction was a problem for another day, and he and Jason would face that together. As he climbed into bed, still smiling, he wondered how Paul's evening had gone. Probably not as well as his, but he hoped things weren't too bad.

As Peter fell asleep, across town, Paul was already fast asleep, having had a difficult but seemingly productive evening. After Peter had dropped him at home that afternoon, Paul had taken a deep breath and steeled himself to face the music. He had made some decisions over the last few hours and was determined to put them into action. The house seemed remarkably quiet and he wondered if Felicity had gone out.

When he walked into the sitting room, Paul didn't notice her at first, so it came as a surprise as he sat down to see her curled up asleep in the armchair. He watched her for a while, and sighed deeply. She looked so vulnerable curled like that, her hand near her hair, which she had obviously been twiddling the way she did when she was nervous. He went over and knelt by her chair.

33

'Fliss,' he called gently touching her arm. Felicity woke with a start, and uncharacteristically threw herself into his arms. 'Whoa, what's up?'

'I thought you'd left me! I was all alone in this house last night. I didn't know where you were. I called the office, but they just kept telling me you weren't there. They wouldn't let me speak to you.'

'I wasn't there Fliss, I spent the day with Pete.'

'Why? Why didn't you come home?'

'Because it doesn't feel like home to be honest. We need to do some serious and honest talking Felicity.' Felicity just nodded, looking at him with wide, frightened eyes. Paul led her over to the settee and they sat together holding hands.

For the next two hours Paul and Felicity talked, as they had never done before. They were more honest than they had ever been and managed to do it without raising their voices or falling out. By the end of the second hour they were both pretty exhausted. Paul went to make a cup of tea for them both.

'Paul, I don't want to go and talk to a counsellor,' Felicity said as he came back into the room.

'OK, but then you have to talk with me. We can't leave this now, not if we want our marriage to work. Are you hungry?' She shook her head. 'OK, why don't we just drink this tea and go to bed? We're both shattered, and if I promise not to make any moves on you, maybe we could just cuddle up together eh?' This time Felicity nodded.

They drank their tea slowly, watching each other guardedly. Then Paul took her hand and led her upstairs, Felicity resisting the urge to say she needed to wash the mugs and tidy up. For the first time in their married life, the couple lay together in the bed instead of at opposite edges and both quickly fell into a deep and restful sleep.

Paul woke first and for a few moments was totally disorientated. Then he remembered the events of the night before. He looked at Felicity, still sleeping with her head on his shoulder. He hoped when she woke up she would still be in a friendly mood. They had covered a lot of ground yesterday.

He now better understood her need for the perfect house, to her a sign of the perfect housewife. He understood that pleasing her parents by being perfectly dressed, polite to visitors, achieving good marks at school had brought material rewards and so when she wanted something material, she offered him the thing she thought he wanted most. He understood that affection in her family was shown by material things not physical closeness.

Paul hoped she now understood that he didn't want her to treat him like that. How, if anything, it had the opposite effect on him. That he wanted them to be friends, and hopefully lovers, but he understood that that would take a lot more time and talking to sort out. He knew that if they could just be as close as they had been last night he could cope with being patient with her. It may never be as strong and solid a marriage as his parents had, but it could be better than it was, it could be manageable. Hopefully they could work something out that would make them both, if not blissfully happy, at least content.

Felicity began to stir, and Paul felt his stomach tighten as he waited to see her response. She looked momentarily confused, then smiled shyly at him.

'Morning,' she whispered.

'Morning gorgeous,' he replied. Felicity giggled, then moved as if to get out of bed.

'Don't move yet, lets just enjoy a few more minutes.'

'You'll be late for work. I'll go and make breakfast.'

Paul sighed as she left the room. Well, he thought, Rome wasn't built in a day. At least she had smiled and not looked horrified. He swung his legs out of bed and made his way to their en-suite shower and brought his thoughts onto business. Within minutes he was showered, dressed in a grey suit and, tying his tie with a full Windsor knot, as always, was totally in business mode.

Chapter 6

The following two days seemed to pass quietly. Peter spent some time with Jason, but also had to study for an exam, so had to drag himself away, albeit reluctantly. Paul and Felicity began to settle into a new routine, which was peaceful and friendly, although they both avoided any more discussions, needing time to come to terms with things that had already been said.

Naomi had the feeling that the crisis had passed for both boys, but still wondered what had been troubling them. Bernard reminded her that they were adults who could solve their own problems and had obviously done so. Smiling, he told her that they must have done a fantastic job to raise such well adjusted adults, and then suggested that maybe a few days away would do her good after all the worrying she had been doing.

Sunday had brought a family gathering for Bernard's father's birthday. Everyone had gathered at Jennifer's house, where she had made a buffet tea with a beautiful cake. Even Felicity had entered into the family atmosphere, although she was always better when she was with Paul's cousin Rachel, her childhood friend, who was responsible for the two of them meeting.

Peter had wished Jason could be there too, but knew it was too soon for that to happen. He glossed over the questions about any girls on the scene, claiming his studies and acting took all his time. Paul smiled at him, and commented on how dedicated his brother was, wishing they had had time for a good long chat for him to find out how things were going, although he guessed things must be ok because Peter looked a lot less tense now.

Now it was Monday morning, and Naomi had made Peter sit down to a proper breakfast before his exam. He usually took exams in his stride, being naturally talented at studying and medicine, so he wasn't too nervous. He knew however, that Naomi would worry all day, and him eating a full English breakfast helped her to cope. Both he and Paul had had to eat huge breakfasts before every exam they had ever taken.

Bernard gave him a pat on the shoulder before he left for work and wished him well. Peter thanked him, gathered what he needed and left, promising to call his mother as soon as the exam was finished. He had also promised to phone Jason at lunchtime, as he too was worrying for him. It was a strange feeling to have someone other than family caring so much, but Peter liked it. They were planning to spend some time together tonight after rehearsal. Peter just hoped the rehearsal went well so they could get away quickly, and without attracting too much attention, as they were not ready to share their new found happiness with the world just yet.

After another night of being closer than they had been in the past, Paul started his day feeling happy. He was hoping for word on the new contract today. If it came his way he was planning to surprise Felicity with a holiday. Maybe it would even turn into a second honeymoon, although he wasn't going to spoil things by pressurising her. They could go in a couple of weeks, as he had some work things that needed sorting first and he didn't want to miss Peter's play. If things continued as they were Felicity might even go with him to see it. He found himself singing along to the radio in the car, and smiled at the difference a few days could make.

Naomi washed up the breakfast things by hand, as though by doing that she was helping Peter to do well. She always worried so much when either of her sons were taking exams, although as they both did well every time she had no need to.

She watched the cats chasing butterflies in the garden, and thought what a pleasant day it was. She had a few bits to get from the shops and then she was meeting Jen for lunch. Usually they met on Tuesdays or Wednesdays, but, as Jen was going off to spend a few days with Eve from this evening, they had arranged to meet today. She decided she would go out soon, so that she had time to buy some baby things for Jen to take across for her.

What a pleasure it was to be buying things for the next generation. She hoped one day soon it would be her own grandchild she would be buying for. She knew Felicity would be very fussy about the things she wanted, as she was for everything else, but it would still be a pleasure, and Paul would make sure that she and Bernard got some good quality time with any grandchildren that they had.

Bernard sat in his office, supposedly getting some paperwork done before his clinic. He was glad that Naomi had stopped seeming so worried about the lads. He had started to worry himself, she was so concerned. He knew Paul was not the happy-go-lucky person he had once been, but he wouldn't pry. He had offered him a listening ear, and made sure he knew he was there for him, but he was an adult, running a successful business and his father had to trust him to make his own decisions.

Peter was another kettle of fish. There was something Bernard couldn't put his finger on. He didn't think the boy was worried about his studying, that came easily to him. Perhaps he was bothered that most of his friends were paired off these days, though it had never bothered him before. Bernard thought that he would talk him into a game of golf next weekend to give them a chance to have a chat. He shook his head to clear his thoughts and turned to the day in hand.

He had a heavy clinic this morning and was on call this evening so it was going to be a long day, and his patients deserved his full attention. He buzzed his secretary and had her bring through his list, along with a coffee and one of the homemade biscuits she always had for him. Spoiled, that's what he was, he knew, totally spoiled, by his wife at home, and by his secretary here. It was a good life, and Bernard sent up a thank you prayer for the blessings that were his each day.

By lunchtime, shopping done, Naomi was settling to a leisurely lunch with Jennifer. She had bought some lovely baby things which they sat and cooed over. Suddenly they were both laughing at themselves, acknowledging that they were terribly sentimental at the thought of the first member of the next generation arriving. Jennifer was looking forward to spending some time with her eldest child, just wishing Eve would be well enough to enjoy the time too. Her doctor had signed her off work for a couple of weeks to rest. Hopefully by that time the worst of the morning sickness would have passed and she would begin to feel better and be able to enjoy her pregnancy.

It was while they were eating desert, a sweet but light raspberry pavlova, that Naomi's phone rang. With a worried look at Jennifer she answered it.

'Hello? Oh hi honey, how did it go? That's good. Well do you want me to save you some tea? Ok then, we'll see you when you get home tonight. Bye.'

She turned to Jennifer with a smile. 'It went well, and he's out celebrating, so won't be home for tea!'

Jennifer smiled, 'Did you expect any different?'

Having phoned his mum, and left a quick message with his Dad's secretary, Peter rang Jason. He still felt his stomach lurch every time they spoke. Jason answered on the second ring and sounded relieved to hear from Peter. They arranged to meet in town, and then go together to the rehearsal that evening. Gradually they were becoming more and more relaxed with each other.

Although their relationship was not yet very physical, it was becoming a strong emotional connection already. They were happy just to spend time together. So it was with a light step that both of them made their way into town.

Time passed more quickly than either would have liked and, before they knew it, it was time to get to rehearsals. Usually rehearsal was on a Tuesday but tonight was the full technical run through, and had been brought forward because the lighting guy couldn't make it tomorrow.

Jason was going even though the scenery was finished. Thursday would be the dress rehearsal, and then the performances were the following week. Jason was dreading it coming to an end, as he was unsure what would happen then. How would they meet up? How much time would they get together?

The rehearsal went well, and the two of them went for a drive as was becoming their routine. Peter noticed that Jason seemed a bit quiet. 'What's up?'

'Just thinking about what will happen after the play ends next week.'

'Usually a very good party,' laughed Peter. 'I seem to remember not getting home 'til lunchtime the next day after the last one!'

Grinning Jason said 'That wasn't what I meant, though that does worry me. What if people realise, at the party, how close we are? But afterwards, how often will we be able to meet up? How long will it be before we have to say something?'

'Nothing wrong with a lad's night out once or twice a week! We will have to be careful at the party, though most people will be too drunk to notice much I expect. And as for coming out, we can decide when that happens, and whilst I know my family will be surprised, I'm not expecting any great dramas really. Are you?'

'I've told you about my dad, it will be awful.' Jason paled just at the thought of it. Peter caught hold of his hand. Jason looked at him and said, 'I'm ready to tell the world about you, everyone except my father.'

'I'd like to tell my family soon, then I can bring you home and we don't have to sit in the car for hours on end, but I'll wait until you are ready,' Peter reassured him. They spent some more time talking about the way forward, and then Peter decided it was time to lighten the mood, and turned the conversation to events at the rehearsal that evening.

At about the same time, Paul was sitting in his lounge with his feet up after a lovely evening meal. Felicity came through having finished tidying up in the kitchen. Paul smiled at her, and patted the settee next to him. She came and sat down, although she left a space. Paul tried not to react and asked how her day had been.

After listening to a long tale about nothing in particular, he commented, 'I had a good day. I got the contract your dad passed my way. Its worth quite a bit, so I was thinking, maybe we should plan a holiday. I can't be out of the office for a couple of weeks yet, but we could look and book something this weekend if you want. Or we could look on the teletext now and see what we can find.'

Felicity looked a bit wary. He could sense she was wondering what ulterior motives he had. He was quick to reassure her. 'No pressure, just a holiday, time to enjoy each other's company. You must admit the last few days have been better, and I thought a week or two away might do us good. But if you think it's too soon, we can wait.'

Felicity relaxed and said, 'No, a holiday sounds good. As long as it's not an attempt to push me faster than I want to go, I would like that. Can we afford somewhere hot?'

Paul was taken aback by the question. Usually Felicity just expected the best, not considering whether they could afford it. 'Yeah, we can't stretch to a world cruise, but a nice apartment in the sun is within reach.' Felicity smiled and offered to pick up some brochures the next day.

Naomi and Bernard were also discussing a few days away. Naomi wasn't interested in going anywhere hot. A few days in a country hotel were her idea of quality time with Bernard. She wasn't bothered where, it was enough for her that Bernard had thought about it, and that they would enjoy it, wherever they went.

She went to make supper, with the cats at her feet expecting their supper as soon as she was in the kitchen. She fed them, and then carried the tray through to the lounge. As they were finishing the cheese and crackers, the front door opened and Peter arrived home. He came into the room, flung himself into the chair and threw his legs over the arm. 'What a day!' was his only comment. Bernard laughed and offered to get him mug of tea.

As they all fell asleep that night, all of them feeling contented, only Jason had any misgivings about what the next few weeks would bring. And not even he could have any idea of how their lives were all about to change.

Chapter 7

The play was a sell-out every night. Peter was in his element, enjoying the praise from everyone. Even Felicity managed to say nice things to him. She was overheard, boasting to someone who had commented on his performance, 'He's my brother-in-law. We are all so proud of him, and he's training to be a doctor as well. Poor boy has so little free time, yet he still manages to give his all to his acting.'

Peter smiled. 'That's the first time I've heard her say anything nice about me! Bet she won't when she finds out the rest though eh?'

Paul grinned back at him. 'I take it things are going well?'

'Very well. Want to meet us for a drink sometime soon? I really want you to get to know him. I am hoping to tell mum and dad soon as well. It's just that it won't be as easy for Jay. His dad isn't like ours, though I have to admit it's not going to be the easiest conversation of my life either.'

'Sure, but we are going away the day after next so it will have to be when I get back. I'll be with you when you talk to mum and dad if you want moral support.'

'No. Thanks for the offer, but I need to do it myself. I'm glad you understand though, it makes it easier.

Paul patted him on the shoulder, and the two brothers went to join everyone else. Peter introduced a few people to his parents, including Jason, who they greeted like any other friend. Peter was pleased that they had the chance to meet, and the fact that his parents seemed to like him. He thought it was the perfect end to a brilliant week. Part of him was glad that the next few weeks were not going to be as busy, for as much as he loved the drama, and studying to be a doctor, he had hardly had a free moment lately.

The family left Peter going off to the cast party and went home. Paul and Felicity went with Naomi and Bernard for supper. It was a rare event for Felicity to go to their house, and she even offered to help Naomi in the kitchen. Over supper the four of them talked about the holiday Felicity had chosen in the Algarve. Bernard raised his eyebrows when he heard it had been her choice, as it wasn't the usual destination she would want.

Paul put his finger to his lips hoping his dad wouldn't say anything. Naomi chatted about happy holidays they had had there over the years, enjoying this new, more open approach her daughter-in-law seemed to be showing.

The pair had managed to get a last minute bargain and were leaving in a couple of days. Paul had had to juggle things to be able to go away so soon, but had been so surprised when Felicity had rang him from the travel agents to say there was a bargain if they could go sooner, that he would have moved heaven and earth to achieve it. Bargain was not a word his wife was usually interested in.

As they got ready to leave, Paul's parents wished them a happy holiday, Naomi hugged her son and asked him to let her know he had got there safely. He promised he would and the two of them got into the car to drive home.

They were having dinner with Felicity's parents the following evening, something Paul never looked forward to, but he was determined to try as hard there as she just had with his parents. He was really beginning to think that his marriage had a chance of working at last, and he wouldn't do anything to jeopardise that.

Peter finally got home at eleven the next morning, having had a good time at the party. He and Jason had survived a couple of comments about how they always seemed to be together these days, but had decided that they would speak to their parents that day. Both of them knew they couldn't keep it a secret any longer, what they felt was too strong.

Peter had worked out, in his own mind, that he would talk to his dad in the greenhouse in general terms and then sit his parents down together to tell them how he felt about Jason. He was nervous, even though he was secure in the love his parents had for him. But the nerves he had for himself were nothing compared to those he felt for Jason.

Although he had never met Jason's family, the way he spoke of his father chilled Peter. He couldn't imagine living in a family ruled by such a horrible man. He felt sorry for Jason's mum, who sounded as though she was in a living hell with that man. He also felt sorry for Jason and was worried that coming out might not be such a good idea. Maybe they should have decided that he would tell his parents, but Jason should wait.

Naomi and Bernard were still at church when Peter got in. He went for a shower, made himself some breakfast, and tried to rehearse what he was going to say. As he was loading his dish into the dishwasher he heard his parents come in. His stomach lurched, but he determined to go through with it. He put the kettle on, and asked if they wanted tea or coffee. Once it was made he looked at his dad and said, 'How are the plants coming on in the greenhouse these days?'

Bernard knew this was a hint that he wanted to talk, so he invited him to bring his tea down with him and have a look. The pair left Naomi starting on the lunch and walked down the garden.

Peter spent a few minutes looking at the plants and making conversation about them. Bernard let him, knowing it must be something important if he needed that time to compose himself. Eventually Peter looked at him, and cleared his throat.

'Dad, you know how people have a kind of idea of how life is going to pan out?' He paused, and Bernard waited patiently, picking off a couple of loose leaves. 'Well, suppose it doesn't work out like that? Suppose what you were expecting doesn't happen and what you weren't expecting does happen?'

Bernard looked thoughtful. 'Well, things don't always go to plan Pete, you know that. Are we just talking in general terms or it is something specific that's worrying you?'

'Well, what if...... you know that you can't help it, but you are probably going to hurt the people you love most? Should you be honest? Or should you try to keep things as they have always been?' The words were coming out in a rush and it wasn't going the way Peter had hoped it would. He was beginning to think this wasn't such a good idea.

Bernard hated to see his son so worked up over something and pulled him into a hug. 'Son, there is nothing that can be so bad that you can't come to your mum and me. There is nothing that will stop us loving you, you know that. Whatever it is we will help you deal with it.'

Peter clung to his dad as he hadn't since he was a young child and murmured, 'I hope so Dad. I don't want you and Mum to be disappointed or ashamed of me. Can we go in so I can talk to you both together?' Bernard hugged him, and reassured him again that it didn't matter what it was, he was loved and always would be.

The minute they walked in the door Naomi could sense that something was wrong. Bernard was very solemn and Peter looked as though he was going to cry. 'Come and sit down with us love,' Bernard said, leading her into the lounge and sitting with her on the settee. Peter sat across from them and sighed deeply.

'I want you both to know how much I love you,' he started. Naomi started to panic. Thoughts of him telling her he was leaving the country were rushing through her head. 'You know a few weeks back you thought something was wrong, well it was. I couldn't tell you then, 'cos I didn't really have my own head round it. I don't want to hurt you but I have to be honest. I hate you not knowing how I really am.'

Naomi went to speak and he stopped her. 'Mum please just let me get this out before I chicken it. I have met someone. Someone who means a lot to me. In fact, I'm in love for the first time in my life. But it's not what you are going to be expecting 'cos it's not a girl. Its Jason, the guy I introduced you to the other night.' Suddenly it was all out in a rush.

There was a long silence as his parents both sat processing the news. Peter watched their faces intently. 'Please say something,' he whispered.

Bernard opened and closed his mouth a couple of times without anything coming out. Eventually he managed to say, 'Well that's the last thing I was expecting! It doesn't change how much I love you, but you will have to give me time to get used to the idea.'

Naomi started to cry. 'You're not leaving home then? I thought you were going to say you were emigrating or something.' Both the men looked at her in disbelief. Somehow she seemed to be having a different conversation to them. 'Don't look at me like that. I did hear what he said, but I had convinced myself when he started that he was going to tell me he was going away, and I couldn't bear that.' She crossed the room and threw her arms around her son. 'It doesn't matter to me that you are gay, if that's what you are, you are my son and I love you and nothing will change that.'

The two of them sat hugging and crying, neither noticing that Bernard had left the room. He went to his study and sat at his desk. He was ashamed of the fact that he had not been as quick as his wife to reassure Peter, when he obviously needed to know that it made no difference to them.

It wasn't that Bernard was homophobic, just that it was the last thing he was expecting his son to say to him, and he needed time to get his head around the idea. He was even more ashamed of himself as he realised that the thought of telling everyone else bothered him. He continued to sit there looking out of the window but not really seeing anything.

Naomi and Peter sat together for a long time. As they both calmed down, Naomi began to ask him to tell her about how he felt and about Jason. It didn't take long for her to realise how much he meant to Peter.

His eyes lit up as he spoke of him, and his smile was the brightest she had ever seen. Whilst there was a part of her brain grieving for the grandchildren she would never have, she was happy to see her son so happy, and knew already that she would defend him to any length. The lioness was ready to protect her young.

Eventually she went to finish lunch, and Peter sank back into the seat relieved it had gone so well. It was then he realised that his dad hadn't said much and had left the room. He tried not to worry, but it was hard not to. He hoped things were going as well for Jason. They had agreed that Peter would not ring him, but would wait for Jason to call once he had spoken to his parents. They both knew that Peter would have the easier ride.

Lunch was a quiet meal. The conversation was kept light and about anything other than the subject hanging over them. It was a late meal, after all that had happened. Towards the end of it Bernard cleared his throat.

'Peter, I'm sorry. I should have been more supportive earlier. I am not proud of the way I dealt with the news, but I needed time to process it really.'

'Dad its fine. I knew it was going to be a bombshell, I wasn't expecting you to hang the flags out. I'm just glad you are still speaking to me and I'm still welcome here.'

'Did you really think we would have reacted so badly as to throw you out? You will always be my son. I might not know how to handle this yet, might not be sure what I will say to family and friends when they ask how I feel about it, but it doesn't alter the fact that I love you and I always will. Why don't we go for a drink? You will still go for a drink with your dad I presume?'

Peter laughed. 'Of course I will. I'm just hoping Jason will ring soon. He won't have had it as easy as me, and he too was telling his parents today. I hope you will get to know him and like him.'

'I'm not sure I'm ready to take you both for a drink just yet, but let's go out and if you need to go when he rings I will understand.'

Naomi happily saw her men folk off to the pub. She knew Bernard was finding it harder than her, she felt for him, and she loved him for making the effort to be with Peter tonight. She settled down to watch a bit of telly with her beloved cats at her side.

Chapter 8

Naomi was engrossed in the middle of a good murder mystery when the phone rang. She lifted Basil off of her knee and put him next to his brother on the settee, then walked over to the telephone and picked it up.

'Hello?'

'Mrs Smedley? Is Pete there?' said a voice she didn't recognise. Whoever it was sounded strange and Naomi wasn't sure how to react.

'I'm sorry, he's out. Can I tell him who called?'

'It's Jason, I'm sorry to bother you. Do you know when he will be back?' He winced as he said it and Naomi sensed that something was wrong.

'Jason, are you all right? What's happened?' The sound of crying came down the phone to her. 'Where are you?'

'The phone box on Church Street. I've lost my mobile so I couldn't call him on his. I got your number from directory enquiries, but I didn't mean to bother you. I'll call him later.'

'Stay there! I'm coming to get you.' Naomi put the phone down, kicked off her slippers and grabbed her car keys whilst trying to get her shoes on. She was out of the door in less than a minute, and hadn't even stopped to turn the TV off. Somehow she sensed that something was very wrong. Within five minutes she was on Church street, and as she pulled up at the phone box the sight that met her eyes took her breath away.

Jason was sheltering in the box, but even before he turned round Naomi could tell he had been beaten. She was out of the car and with him in seconds. Without a word she helped Jason into the car, and drove away from the group of people watching with interest. All the way home

Jason apologised for being such a nuisance and Naomi kept assuring him that he was not any such thing.

Once home she helped him into the lounge and sat him down. She then phoned Bernard and told him she needed him home, without wasting time explaining. She got Jason a glass of water, and told him to sip it slowly, which was all he could do through his swollen lips. His eye was rapidly closing, and every breath sounded painful.

Naomi wanted to hug him, but was scared of hurting him. She hoped Bernard wouldn't be long, this boy needed a doctor, probably hospital, and she wanted Bernard's strength there to support them all. She gently held his hand, which was also bruised and made soothing noises as they waited.

When Naomi heard Bernard's key in the door she went to meet him. She didn't want Peter to walk in and see Jason like that without warning. One look at her ashen face and Bernard knew something was really wrong. She took hold of Peter's hands and gently told him that Jason was there, but that he had been in some sort of accident.

Without waiting for more Peter was past her and in the room. As he saw Jason sitting there he cried out and rushed to him. Bernard followed him in and was shocked by what he saw. He was even more shocked by Jason's reaction to him.

'I'm sorry, I didn't mean to be a nuisance, I'll go,' the lad stammered, trying to get up and cowering slightly, his eyes showing his immense fear that Bernard would not want him there.

'You are going nowhere until we get you sorted,' Bernard said. 'Peter move away and let me look at him. How did this happen? Or should I say who did this to you? We need to get you to hospital, you'll need x-rays, and we should call the police as well.'

Jason began to cry and begged Bernard not to involve the police. He also claimed that he didn't need hospital treatment. 'I'm the doctor, so I'll decide that!' Bernard told him gently. 'Naomi fetch me some hot water, towels, and my bag please. Peter move away, you are not helping!'

Peter tried to protest, but one look from his dad told him it was pointless. He felt helpless, and also felt guilty. He could guess what had happened. He wished he hadn't suggested they came out to their parents, or at least that Jason hadn't told his.

With tears in his eyes he moved away so that his dad could assess the situation. After carefully washing the worst of the blood away, and checking him over carefully Bernard insisted that they went to the hospital for x-rays.

Jason cried and pleaded not too, but Bernard insisted, saying that he would stay with him and take care of everything. Peter insisted on coming with them, as did Naomi, whose gentle heart was moved with compassion for this poor young man.

It was hours later that they got home. The only reason Jason had been allowed to come home with them was because Bernard was able to guarantee he would stay at their house, and that he would oversee his care. He had four broken ribs, numerous bruises, one eye was now closed, and the other bruised. His nose was broken, and he had stitches in a couple of the cuts. He was also going to need some dental work. He had taken a major battering and Bernard was angry that the man responsible was not in police custody. Naomi quickly made up the bed in the spare room and they got him into it. She sat with him until he was asleep.

Downstairs, Bernard poured a brandy for himself and Peter. He was too angry to be able to speak, but the hug he gave his son spoke volumes. Peter was in shock, and alternated between tears and anger. Neither of them felt they would be able to sleep yet, and so they sat, in silence, supporting each other. Eventually Naomi came down to join them.

'He's asleep,' she said, 'and he will be staying here even after he is well again. I won't have any arguments on that. He needs us and we will not turn him away.' She sat next to Peter, who at his mother's words finally gave into the wave of sorrow inside him and wept in her arms. She comforted him as she always had as a child, and looked across at Bernard with tears in her own eyes.

'You will get no argument from me,' he answered the question he knew was hanging in the air. 'I may not have been thrilled with the news today, but how any man can call himself a father and do that is beyond me. I hope when he wakes tomorrow Jason will see sense and let us call the police.'

'Dad, please don't pressure him, I shouldn't have let him tell his dad. He warned me what he was like. He knew he wouldn't understand.'

'That doesn't excuse his behaviour. Even if he couldn't accept how his son is, even if he told him to leave, beating him is unforgivable and needs to be punished. But we will concentrate on getting him well again. Don't worry; I won't push him at all. I don't want him to be scared of me the way he was when we met tonight. I want him to concentrate on healing, both physically and mentally.

Be prepared for him to look even worse tomorrow as more of the bruising comes out. It is going to take weeks, Peter, not days and you need to be strong for him. When you need to let off steam, come to me and just let him speak as and when he is ready.'

The family sat in a solemn silence for a while longer, and saw the dawn break through the window. Naomi suggested the three of them tried to sleep, and checking on Jason once more and finding him still sleeping from the sedative Bernard had given him, they went to their rooms. Peter to cry himself to sleep, and Naomi to do the same in Bernard's arms.

After just two hours, Bernard quietly got up and got ready for work. He intended to do what he had to and then leave his staff to it and return home to care for his family, including its newest member.

When he returned, just before lunch, he found Naomi in the kitchen, cleaning as though her life depended on it. He knew it was her way of dealing with all the emotions she was feeling. He walked across, took the cloth out of her hand, and pulled her into his arms.

For a while they just stood there, both needing the comfort that came from the familiarity of knowing each other so well. Naomi reported that both boys were still sleeping the last time she had been up. As Bernard looked over her shoulder, he saw a pan of chicken soup on the hob and smiled.

'He won't have any choice but to get well will he? Not with you about to feed him up and mother him. I love you Mrs Smedley, and one of the myriad of reasons is that you would never let me behave badly towards our children. You are the perfect mother!'

'With good reason to try so hard as you well know. And don't go thinking badly of Jason's mother, the poor woman may be beside herself for all we know.'

Bernard nodded, and left the room. He went upstairs and after checking on Peter, who was still asleep, he went into Jason. He tried to sit up as Bernard walked in, and he gently told him not to try and move. He checked him over and then sat on the edge of the bed and asked if he was ready to talk about any of it yet.

The story that Jason told him was worse than any Bernard had ever heard. He, like Peter, had returned home from the cast party ready to tell his parents about his relationship. He was nervous, he knew it wouldn't go well, but even he had never expected such a reaction as the one he got. He had waited until after their Sunday roast, when his mum had cleaned up, as she always did, and they were all sitting down to watch sport, his dad's choice, on the TV.

Eventually he had summoned the courage to open up and begin to tell them. His dad had started to scoff before he had got further than saying he had met someone. He jeered that he bet he hadn't told her about the 'poofter' design course he was on, although if she was interested in him, she obviously wasn't looking for a real man. And so it continued. Jason was hardly able to get a word in, whilst his dad continued his tirade about what a disappointment his son was to him.

Eventually, Jason just blurted out that the person he had met wasn't a girl. For a minute of two there was silence. His mother seemed to guess what was going to happen before he did. She tried to catch hold of her husband's arm as he rose from the chair. For her daring she had received a black eye. Jason had no time to move before he was lifted from the seat and the beating began.

He sobbed as he told Bernard how his father had cussed him, and beat him, until he could hardly move. He then grabbed him up and threw him out of the house, telling him never to darken his door again. As he fell, his mobile had dropped from his pocket, and his father had stamped on it.

Jason explained that that was the reason he had had to phone the house last night, as he no longer had Peter's mobile number. He apologised for bringing all this to their door, and said he would go as soon as he was able.

Bernard raised his eyes at this. 'Peter hasn't told you about his mother then?' he asked. 'If you really think you will leave here any time soon you are most mistaken.

Naomi is already making you chicken soup to aid your recovery. She will mother you to death Jason, and she has already told us that you are staying. Get used to the idea. This is your new bedroom. All I ask is that you and Peter give me time to get used to you being a couple before you become too open about it in the house. I may not have reacted as your dad did, but I am not proud of the way I took the news either. I will come to terms with it, but I need time.'

Jason promised him that they would be very circumspect around him and respect his views. He also thanked him repeatedly for his help, both last night and for listening now. Bernard gently asked if he had changed his mind about involving the police, but he hadn't.

He said his only worry was that his father would have trashed his room and all his design work. He was in his final year, and needed his portfolio. He would never be able to replace it all in time for his finals.

Bernard asked for his address and said he would go and collect his things for him that evening. He intended to have stern words with Jason's father, but he didn't tell Jason that. He asked for his home phone number as well, and went to phone his mother to ask that she got the things ready for him to collect. He kept the call brief and told her he would be there at seven that evening. She asked him to come earlier, before her husband got home, but he would not be swayed by her pleas.

'I intend to have words with him,' he told her, 'and if he gives me any grief at all I will bring in the police, whether or not Jason wants me to. I suggest you just get Jason's things ready and don't warn your husband I will call.'

She must have taken his advice, for when Jason's father opened the door he seemed surprised to see Bernard standing there. Bernard introduced himself as Dr

Smedley, the doctor who had dealt with his son at casualty the night before. He then said he had come to remove Jason's belongings for him, and that if he was not able to do that he would call the police and give them the medical reports that would see him behind bars.

The man was unable to string a sentence together at all. He stammered and stuttered, going red in the face. He was a man unused to being outwitted and he knew he had met his match here. Bernard loaded the things into the car, receiving no help at all, which came as no surprise. As a final warning he said, 'I will also be checking that your wife has no more injuries sir, and believe me these are not idle threats. Men like you are a disgrace.'

As he walked to the car, Jason's mother came out to him. 'Thank you,' she said, teary eyed, 'tell Jason I'm sorry, and that I love him.' Bernard squeezed her arm and assured her he would.

He felt so sorry for her, and wanted to tell her to leave that waste of space inside, but he knew it was not his place to do so. Maybe in time Naomi would be able to invite her to their house and befriend her; she certainly looked as though she needed a friend.

Chapter 9

On Tuesday morning Peter went in to see Jason before leaving for med school. He sat and held his hand for a while and asked how he was feeling. He hated the idea of leaving him there, but knew he couldn't afford to miss lectures, and that he was in the best hands with Naomi to look after him.

After Peter had gone, Naomi came up with a breakfast tray for Jason. He apologised again that she was having to do all this running round after him, but she would hear none of it. She sat and chatted to him whilst he ate. She asked if he would mind if she looked at some of his design work, and within minutes they were deep in a discussion about his ideas.

Naomi suggested that once he felt well enough he should redecorate his room, which brought tears to his eyes again. She also claimed to need some ideas of what to do with her dining room, as it needed a revamp. Jason had seen how beautifully her house was decorated and arranged and knew she needed no help at all, but he appreciated her involving him in the family like this and went along with her.

Naomi was supposed to be out for lunch, and she was hesitating as to whether she should go or not. She could always ask Jen to come here instead, but she didn't want to make Jason feel uncomfortable. She pondered over what to do as she washed up. Then she smiled as she realised that, yet again, she had forgotten to use the dishwasher. In the end she went to ask Jason if he would manage if she went out for a while. He assured her he would, so, having left him with a flask of tea and a sandwich to try and eat, she went out as usual.

Jennifer was a little late arriving, as she was still staying with Eve, and hadn't left her that morning until she had stopped being sick. She was beginning to look a little better each day, and the sickness was at a more manageable level now so Jennifer had driven back into town with her case in the car to return home after lunch.

Over lunch they filled each other in on the events of the last week. For Naomi this took quite a while. She slowly told Jennifer all that had happened, and she was shocked to hear how his own father had beaten Jason. She assured Naomi that Peter being gay would not alter how his family felt about him. They arranged for Jennifer and Bill to come over for supper the following evening.

Suddenly they were both laughing. Usually their lunches were light affairs with lots of girly chat, but today they had both unburdened themselves and they felt better for it.

'Not often we have such deep discussions in here is it?' said Jennifer. José had somehow sensed that his two favourite ladies were in a deep discussion and had left them alone. Now he walked over, bringing another pot of tea.

'You look very serious today,' he said. 'I hope everything is ok. I have brought you a pot of tea on the house' He kissed both of them on the hand, clicked his heels and left them.

'He is such a smoothy, you can't help but love him can you?' said Naomi. 'He certainly knows how to keep customers coming back.'

They both drank their tea in silence, thinking about all that had happened. Then, with a last mouthful, Naomi said she should leave. She didn't want to leave Jason alone for too long. They both gathered their things, settled the bill and left. They came to Naomi's car first. Jen pulled her into a big hug, 'Try not to worry,' she said, 'it will all settle down soon, and with you and Bernard supporting them, they will get through this, you'll see.'

When Naomi got home, she hung up her coat, changed into her slippers and then went to check on Jason. He was asleep, and she went to start preparing the dinner so that once he awoke she could spend some time with him. She decided to cook something soft in the hope that he would manage at least a little. Boiled fish, mashed potato and peas, with a trifle for desert.

Once dinner was organised, Naomi made a pot of tea and took a tray upstairs. Jason was just waking when she went into the room, and he smiled at her, and then winced with the pain it caused.

'Sorry, I guess my smile must look awful at the moment.'

'You must stop apologising all the time dear. I've brought you up a cup of tea, and some company if you want it.' Over the tea, and a few biscuits they chatted about nothing in particular. Then Jason asked if Naomi would mind if he had a bath. She was surprised by the question.

'Let's get one thing straight right now,' she said, attempting to sound stern, 'this is now your home, and I want you to make yourself at home. Washing in the basket, help yourself from the fridge, put the kettle on when you want a drink kind of at home.'

Jason smiled at her again. 'Why are you being so kind to me?' he asked, his eyes filling with tears once more.

Naomi patted his hand and rose to leave saying, 'We'll talk about that another time, it's a long story. Now if you feel up to coming downstairs for a while after your bath do, but if not I'll bring you up a tray when dinner is ready.' She left him wondering what story Naomi had to tell. Peter was right in what he had told him about her, she was a wonderful and special person.

Dinner that night was a jovial affair. Jason had managed to come downstairs, and although he was still very uncomfortable sitting, it made everyone feel better to see a slight improvement. Bernard chatted about his day at work, Peter about the really boring lecturer and how no-one was paying attention by the end. Bernard tried to look stern and say that wouldn't help him qualify, but failed as he could remember similar lectures when he was at med school. Soon they were all laughing, though Jason didn't quite manage it.

After dinner, Jason offered to wash up, but the look on Naomi's face had him backing away with his hands up in defeat. He and Peter went into the lounge and sat watching some TV. Bernard helped carry things through to the kitchen, and then went off into his study to do some reading.

Naomi hummed to herself as she loaded the dishwasher. A noise at the window made her look up to see her two cats sitting there. They often waited for her to open the door for them rather than use the cat flap, and Naomi indulged them by doing so. She even put a few cat treats down for them, before going to join the boys watching TV.

Bill was also relaxing after a lovely evening meal. He would never tell his wife that the house hadn't been right while she was away, or make her feel guilty for going, but he was glad she was back. He was also glad that his eldest daughter was beginning to get over the worst of her sickness. He was happily snuggled with his wife, not caring that she was watching soaps on the telly; she was there next to him where she belonged.

Jennifer had waited until they were settled, and Rebekah had gone out for the evening with her latest boyfriend before she told Bill of the events of the day. Like her, he was surprised at the news, and shocked that any man could behave like that to his own son.

'Our family are strong, Jen, we will pull together through the tough times like we always do. We should be thankful that we have such good relationships with our children. Even Rachel who is far from being easy, has always known that we love her unconditionally, which is perhaps why she takes such liberties, but we are still there for her and always will be. We have so much to be grateful for, and Jason will be welcomed in as part of the family. That in itself will bring healing.'

The two sat in comfortable silence for quite a while, Bill gently stroking Jennifer's hair. They were still there when Rebekah got home.

'Look at you two, all loved up!" laughed Rebekah. "Is it OK if Adam comes in for a coffee?"

'Of course it is,' said Bill, 'I'll go and put the kettle on.' He stretched as he moved away from Jennifer and stood up ready to go into the kitchen. Adam walked into the room and smiled shyly at Rebekah's parents. 'Tea or coffee?' asked Bill walking into the kitchen.

'Coffee please Mr Fletcher,' Adam called.

Bill poked his head back around the door with a smile. 'It's Bill, I don't answer to Mr Fletcher in my own house, and if you are going to be a regular visitor its best you get used to calling us Bill and Jennifer.'

Adam blushed and continued to stand until Rebekah pulled him down onto the couch next to her. Over coffee and biscuits the four of them chatted about nothing in particular. Adam gradually relaxed and Rebekah was pleased to see him and her parents getting along so well. She had a feeling that he was different to the other boyfriends she had had, and it was important to her that her parents liked him.

Eventually, Bill hinted that it was time for Adam to go. Rebekah went with him to the door. "Don't be too long," said Bill with a wink. Both Rebekah and Adam blushed as they left the room. At the door she hugged him close, and the kiss he gave her left her wanting more. She closed the door behind him and lent against it hugging herself and sighing deeply. This was it she was sure, she was head over heels in love with him.

She walked back into the lounge smiling and raised her eyebrows at her parents. 'Well?'

'Seems a nice young man,' said Bill with a nod. 'Yes, very nice. I take it we will be seeing a lot of him then?' Rebekah never brought a lad home unless she was getting serious about him, but Bill sensed this one was very special judging by the look on his youngest daughter's face.

'I hope you will,' said Rebekah shyly. She went over to her dad, sat beside him and snuggled in for a hug. 'How do you know when it's the real thing?' she whispered.

'Ooh,' said Bill, 'With your mum I just knew. She was different to every other girl I had been out with. It was the way I felt when I was with her, still feel comes to that. It was how I felt when I wasn't with her, like a part of me was missing.'

'It's early days dear,' said her mum, 'just enjoy it, and in time you will be sure. He seems very fond of you, and I like him. But right now you should be getting to bed, you have work tomorrow.'

Kissing both her parents goodnight, Rebekah went up the stairs still smiling. They liked him, and she was in love with him, and what's more, earlier that evening, he had whispered that he loved her as they cuddled in the pictures. She fell asleep still smiling.

'What a day!' said Jennifer.

Laughing Bill replied, 'It's certainly not boring in this family. I'd better buy a lottery ticket, looks like we might be saving for a fourth wedding. Thank goodness this will be the last one!'

'I'm not ready for our baby to be so serious about a lad,' Jennifer moved into Bill's open arms. He held her tight, feeling her pain and sharing it too.

'We are moving on to the next stage of life my dear. We have a grandchild on the way. And, like you said to Rebekah, it's early days yet. Just because she is hinting she is in love with this one, doesn't mean a quick wedding, and anyway, the last few weddings I've been to, I have quite fancied the bride's mother.

Jennifer shook her head at him, smiling. 'You are always able to make me feel better about things.'

'Well let's get upstairs and you can make me feel better! I've missed you this last week.' Giggling and teasing they went upstairs to bed, glad to be together, thankful for all the happiness they had.

Chapter 10

'Oh, can I come? It's ages since I had a good chat with Pete. I've got loads to tell him, and I didn't get the chance to tell him how good the play was last week.' Rebekah was bubbling this morning and hardly noticed the look that passed between her parents as she spoke. She had always been close to her cousin, both of them being the youngest. As neither of her parents answered, she lifted her head from her cereal bowl and looked at them. Her eyebrows raised in question and she waited for an answer.

'I'm sure they wouldn't mind you coming with us dear,' said Jennifer. 'I'll check with Naomi later.'

Rebekah now looked totally confused. 'OK what gives? First you don't reply when I ask if I can come, then when I do get an answer, you say you'll have to check with Aunty Naomi!'

Jennifer sighed. She wasn't sure how to explain things to Rebekah, without going into details that she wasn't sure Peter would want sharing. But the girl would have to know in the end, so she explained as simply as she could what had happened. 'I'm not sure that he wants everyone to know yet though,' she finished.

Rebekah pulled a face, 'Mum! Get a grip! It's nothing to be ashamed of these days you know. Pete is still Pete; being gay doesn't change who he is you know.'

'I didn't mean that love,' Jennifer explained patiently, 'I meant what happened to Jason. He might not be ready for lots of visitors yet, he is still badly bruised and in pain.'

Tears filled Rebekah's eyes. 'Poor Jason! And poor Pete! I can't imagine anyone being so bigoted in this day and age. I'll phone Pete in my break this morning and see if he minds me coming.' With a quick kiss on her mum's

66

cheek she bounced out of the room to go and finish getting ready for work.

Bill laughed at the look of amazement on Jennifer's face. 'Oh the confidence of youth!' he stated. 'Not for a minute does she doubt her place in the family, or how life should be. And we are obviously so old we need her to explain to us how it works these days.'

Peter was studying at home for the day. Well that was the theory. In truth he was sitting with Jason in the lounge. Jason was moving a little easier today, but was still in pain. Peter kept looking over to him, then asking if he could get him anything. Jason tried to smile back at him, but it was still lopsided. 'You are supposed to be studying, not fussing over me.'

'Can't help it,' Peter grinned back at him. 'I feel really guilty about it all still, and I want to make it better.'

'Pete, even in pain this is better than what I am used to. No one has belittled me, made snide comments at me, made me feel inadequate or treated me as worthless since I arrived. Your mum loves my design work, and is spoiling me rotten, your dad is kind and caring, even though I have turned his world upside down, and you are with me. What more could I want?' Peter reached over and hugged him gently.

'I'll always be here for you. You have given up so much for me and I will never let you down. Are you ok with my aunt and uncle coming round tonight? We could always go out if you aren't ready to meet them.'

Jason laughed at the very idea. 'Oh yes, 'cos no-one would stare at me if we went out would they? Pete, be realistic, it's going to be a while until I can go out, though I have to get some college work sorted, and I need to get a new mobile and try to remember some numbers. I think I'll just tell people I was mugged and my phone taken. I know it's not really true, but it's easier than trying to explain the truth. As for meeting more of your family, I have the feeling that if they weren't going to be supportive your mum wouldn't be letting them through the door.'

They were still laughing at the thought of Naomi taking on the world for them, when Peter's phone rang. 'Hello? Oh hi Bekka, how are you? ..... Yeah sure you can come over tonight....... well I hadn't told anyone, except Paul........ yes I know I can trust you. Look, come tonight and we'll have a good chat.' Eventually he managed to get off the phone and turned to Jason. 'That was my very exuberant cousin Rebekah, Bekka to me, and she is coming over with her mum and dad tonight. You'll probably need extra painkillers for the headache you will get,' Peter laughed, 'She is a bit loud to put it mildly, and she can't believe I hadn't told her about you, and she also has a new boyfriend that she can't wait to tell me about.' They both laughed, and then Jason stood up.

'I'm going to go and have a rest, so you can get some work done. That way, at least when Naomi gets back from the shops she will find you with a book open!' Peter gave him another hug and let him go. He would sooner have been with him than studying, but knew Jason didn't want Naomi to catch him skiving in case she saw him as a bad influence. He knew that his mum knew how often he skived when he was home, supposedly studying, and wouldn't have blamed Jason, but also understood that Jason didn't want to rock the boat.

When Naomi came home she was surprised to see Peter with his nose in a book. 'I thought you would be with Jason, is he sleeping?' Peter got up to help her with the shopping bags explaining that Jason had gone to rest so that he would work, and also that Rebekah had phoned and was coming round later. He then went to put the kettle on and made a pot of tea.

Bernard had not long been home when Bill, Jennifer and Rebekah arrived. He had had to deal with a patient who had deteriorated quickly and needed to be admitted. It had been a sad time for the husband and children of his patient, and he knew the outcome was not likely to be good. He was tired, and part of him wished they were not having company tonight, although he knew it would help him lift his mood. He heard them arrive and quickly finished dressing after his shower and made his way downstairs.

He noticed that Jason was sitting looking nervous, and went over to join him on the settee. He smiled at him, giving his arm a squeeze. 'OK?' he whispered. Jason nodded.

'So, Rebekah, I hear there is a new man on the scene?' He looked questioningly at his niece. She blushed, and smiled.

'He still won't take the place of my favourite uncle,' she teased, coming over and sitting next to him, snuggling in for a cuddle. That set the tone for the evening. There was much laughter and teasing, an easy atmosphere, and Jason soon found himself relaxing and joining in. By the time Naomi called them through for supper both he and Bernard were feeling better.

After the meal, Bernard, Naomi, Jennifer and Bill went back into the lounge. The youngsters had offered to clear up and for once Naomi agreed. They could hear a lot of laughter coming from the kitchen as they settled down and caught up with news of the other members of the family.

Naomi and Bernard had received a call from Paul and Felicity that morning, saying they were having a good time. Bill and Jennifer's daughters were all well. Besides Rebekah who was happy in her new relationship, Leah, and her husband Greg, were settling into married life well and she was enjoying setting up her own home.

Rachel was happily bossing husband Nigel around, and now that her best friend, Felicity, was on holiday, was nagging about a week away for them, and Eve was over the worst of the morning sickness and beginning to be able to enjoy the thought of motherhood.

As the three younger members of the group continued to clear away the supper things Rebekah suddenly flicked Peter with the teatowel. 'I am so cross with you! How comes you didn't tell me anything? Why am I the last to know?' Her indignation caused both Peter and Jason to laugh at her, although Jason's laugh still caused him to grimace.

'You are far from the last to know! Mum and Dad have only known since the weekend and Paul a little longer. I have yet to face the wrath of my darling sister-in-law or her dear friend, your sister, Rachel!'

Seeing the worried look on Jason's face, Rebekah was quick to reassure him. 'Jason, don't worry about them two! No-one takes any notice of them, and in fact the very fact that they will be appalled will just endear you to the rest of us.'

She pulled him into a hug. 'I am so glad you're here, I can see how happy Pete is, and I can't wait to drag you shopping. Imagine having a design expert in the family!'

Her enthusiasm was catching, and both boys joined in the laughter. Letting Jason go Rebekah moved over to the work surface, jumped up, crossed her legs, placed her hands on them and coyly said, 'Anyway, you are so full of your own news Pete Smedley, you've not even asked me about mine.'

Laughing Peter said, 'I take it that means you want to tell me something?'

A wide smile appeared on Rebekah's face. 'Oh yes......... I too am in love Cousin Dearest.' Peter had heard this statement from Rebekah a number of times, so he just raised his eyebrows. 'No, this time it's different, honestly it is.'

She spent the next ten minutes gushing about the wonders of Adam, how it felt to be with him, how he kissed better than any man she had ever met. How his hands were strong, yet gentle, how just being with him made her feel really alive for the first time.

When she finally paused for breath Jason said, 'yep, she's in love!'

The following morning, as she brought him a cup of tea, Naomi found Jason staring into the mirror in his room. She put the cup down, walked over to him and put her arm around his shoulders. 'The bruises will soon fade. By next week you could get back to college. You'll see, it will soon pass Jason.'

A tear slipped down his cheek, 'I'm not vain, really I'm not, it doesn't bother me what I look like. But what am I going to say? I told Pete I would say I was mugged, but I'm not sure I can. How can I admit to people that my own father did this? Why? I don't understand it myself so how will I answer the questions people will ask? I need dental work, but what will I say to the dentist?' Suddenly the dam broke and Jason was sobbing. Naomi led him to the bed, sat him down and held him while he sobbed.

As the sobs subsided he began to apologise and Naomi hushed him. 'Don't you apologise for having feelings, for letting your emotions show. That is nothing to be ashamed of. Let's start with the practicalities. If you want a cover story we can create one, or we can rehearse some simple answers.

As for the dentist, our Leah is married to one, I am sure he will see you and Jen can make him aware of the situation to avoid awkward questions. And for the rest of it, you have the right to feel angry, the right to feel let down and the right to question why. Sometimes the people we love, the people who should love us back, with an unconditional love, are just unable to do it. We may never know why, may never know what it was in their own life that caused them to be so cold, so ungiving, but with love from others we can be strong, can survive and can, in time, overcome the hurt they have caused us.'

As Naomi stopped speaking, Jason realized that she had been speaking as much to herself as him. 'You aren't just speaking about my father are you?'

With a gentle smile and a hand on his cheek, Naomi answered in a quiet voice, 'No, I too have been where you are Jason. The other day you asked me why I was showing you so much kindness. Well, it's because I too was shown kindness at a time of great need.

Now, I'll leave you to have your tea, shower and dress. Then come down and I'll tell you my story, not to make you feel sorry for me, but to encourage you that with the love of a good man, you too will become strong.'

After she had left the room, Jason just sat for a moment, wondering what had happened to Naomi in her past, and how, if she had suffered as he had, she was such a wonderful, sweet and strong woman now. He wasn't sure he could ever get over what his father had done, and he certainly would never forget.

He wanted to be with Peter, more than anything he had ever wanted, but it hurt to be here. Seeing the love, feeling it engrained into the very fibre of the house, only served to make his own pain more real. He shook his head to clear his thoughts, drained his cup and went off to shower.

Chapter 11

When Jason entered the lounge he found Naomi sitting looking thoughtful. 'You don't have to tell me anything, if it makes you uncomfortable.'

Naomi smiled and sighed, 'Eventually you will relax with us enough to stop all this apologising for existing, but it reminds me of myself so long ago. I think telling you my story will help you Jason, and it will remind me once again what a very lucky woman I am, and how much I have, both to give and in what I receive.'

She patted the seat next to her, 'so, come, sit, make yourself comfortable, and I will tell you about my past.' The story Naomi told was hard to believe, and yet he knew every word was true, without exaggeration.

Naomi's childhood had been very different to the life she lived now. She was the only daughter born to a strict orthodox Jewish couple. They had three sons who all towed the line and did as their parents expected. As soon as she was old enough to understand, Naomi followed the example of her brothers.

She tried hard at everything she did, yet received little praise. The best she could hope for was to receive little criticism. There was no outward show of love, no cuddles, kisses or even an occasional pat on the head that she saw other children at the synagogue getting. She never doubted, however, that her parents loved her. She just saw them as being strict. She showed her love for them by being a good, hardworking, obedient child.

It was when she was seven that Naomi had unwittingly committed what was, in her parents' eyes, her first terrible crime. Her Father, having done well in business, bought a new house in a better area. It was still at the edge of the Jewish area of town, but meant the children changing schools.

At her new school, Naomi was made to sit next to a girl called Jennifer. Very soon the two girls became firm friends. Naomi knew that she was not allowed to bring friends home. It had never been said, but even at such a young age she knew better than to ask. However, she came home from school one day very excited, for she had been invited to Jennifer's house for tea the next day.

Her mother stared at her as though in disbelief, but that was nothing compared to her father's reaction. Naomi had never seen him so mad. She was bringing disgrace on her family. Yes, he knew there were gentiles as well as Jews at that school, but he never for a moment expected his daughter to mix with them.

How could she defile herself? How could she even consider being friends with Goyem, let alone going to a house where nothing would be Kosher? They would feed her pig, would cook meat and milk in the same pans, they would not say the blessings or keep the Sabbath. How could his daughter want to mix with gentiles when, not so long ago, those very gentiles were trying to exterminate her own people?

Naomi was sent to bed without tea. Although she had not been physically beaten, the verbal attack from her father left her shaking. How could he think Jennifer was bad? She was just a little girl like Naomi, a girl who was friends with her when others would not even speak to her but called her names as she passed them.

The little girl sat on her bed hugging her knees, rocking gently. She tried to make sense of it, but failed. Not one of her brothers came to her room to offer her comfort. In fact all three of them ignored her for days afterwards.

It was with a very heavy heart that Naomi went to school the next day. She didn't know what she was going to say to Jennifer but she was sure that she would lose her friendship. Her enjoyment of school was based largely around the fact that she shared it with Jennifer. She was keen to learn, but day after day without a friendly word, or a playmate would be hard.

Briefly in the playground, with head bowed, Naomi explained that she was not allowed to go to Jennifer's house, that her parents did not want her to mix with gentiles.

'It's ok,' said Jennifer, 'Mummy said you might not be able to come because we aren't Jewish. But we can still be friends in school.' Naomi had looked at her with wide eyes. She had been so sure her friend would hate her. A tear slid down her cheek.

Jennifer had hugged her and told her not to be silly and then had pulled her over to the hopscotch. Their friendship had been sealed that day, and although Naomi never once mentioned Jennifer at home, she defiantly kept her as her very, very best friend. A friend she would do anything for.

Both girls were bright enough to get into Grammar school. And it was this that helped them develop a little social life as teenagers. Naomi became adept at telling her parents she was off to the library to study. She would, of course, go the library for a short while, but then she and Jennifer would bag up their books and go to the local milk bar, which had a juke box! There they would sit singing along to all the latest tunes, discuss the latest fashions and which boy was top their list at the moment.

Even then, though, Naomi knew in her heart there was only one boy she wanted to be with – Jennifer's older brother Bernard. He would often leave his friends for a few minutes to come over and speak to his sister.

Naomi watched the way that he smiled, laughed and joked with his sister, so unlike her own brothers. She loved

75

the way they were so close and the way he kept an eye on Jennifer but without being overpowering. At night, in her bed, Naomi would imagine what it would be like to be held in his arms dancing, to hold hands as he walked her home, and then to be kissed. She knew it would never happen, partly because she would never be allowed and partly because he never even seemed to notice her.

Looking back, Naomi often wondered how she was never caught, but even to this day she was thankful that she hadn't been. Her biggest challenge had come when Jennifer begged her to come to her eighteenth birthday party.

'Oh Jen, how can I, you know how it is at home.'

But Jennifer had pleaded and begged, and helped her plan. Somehow she had managed to convince her parents that a group of girls from school were getting together to work on a history project, and as it was after the Sabbath had ended, she really wanted to go and not miss out.

Only because it was schoolwork was she allowed to go, and her father would not be moved on the issue of her staying over. She was to be home by 10pm at the latest.

At the time she had been disappointed not to be sleeping over at Jennifer's house. Her disappointment turned to delight however, when Jen had told her that her brother had offered to see she got home safely.

It was at that party that Bernard had first asked her to dance. She had thought he was just being kind, but as they danced he had told her how beautiful her eyes were and how he had been waiting for a chance to be with her without his sister monopolising her.

As they walked home, Naomi having changed back out of the dress Jen had lent her and removed every trace of makeup, Bernard caught her hand and asked to see her again. She had explained how impossible that would be, but Bernard hushed her, and as his fingers left her lips he dropped his head and kissed her. In that moment Naomi knew that, whatever it took, and whatever it cost she would spend the rest of her life with this man.

Somehow they had managed to meet, though not as often as either would have liked. Things became easier once Naomi left home to start a teacher training course.

She wasn't sure she wanted to be a teacher, all she dreamed of was being a perfect housewife and mother, but going to college was a way of leaving home and gaining more freedom.

It had worked for two months. For the first time in their relationship Naomi and Bernard could see each other whenever their studies allowed. Then one night they went to the pictures. As they were strolling back towards Naomi's halls of residence hand in hand, her father confronted them. Naomi would never forget the way he spoke to her that night.

'So, the rumours are true! You have disgraced not only yourself but your whole family. Sir, let go of my daughter this instance. Naomi you are coming home with me. No more college, no more choosing for yourself. You will hang your head in shame and stay home until the dust settles. Your poor mother is home weeping at the disgrace you have brought on us.'

Bernard had interrupted this tirade. 'It is not a disgrace to fall in love. I love your daughter with all my heart, I respect her, and I will not allow you to speak to her this way.'

'You will not allow? Not allow? She is nothing to you sir, nothing. She is my daughter and I will deal with her as I see fit. Now, Naomi, come with me.' He had caught hold of her arm and began to drag her away. 'We will collect your things in the morning. I will explain to the college that your mother needs you at home. And that is where you will stay, for no decent Jewish boy would touch you now you have defiled yourself.'

Naomi was weeping quietly and looking at Bernard, trying to seal the image of his face in her mind. Bernard was fuming. He was not about to let this man steal away his soul mate. 'Naomi, don't go. Stay here with me.'

Her father stopped in his tracks. 'I cannot believe your audacity,' he bellowed. 'Very well then, we will see just what kind of hold you have over Naomi; but you will be sorely disappointed. Despite your leading her astray she is still my daughter, and I have taught her right from wrong.' He let go of Naomi's arm and turned her to face him, lifting her head so that she was looking straight into his eyes.

'My child, it seems you must choose. Come home with me and in time this will pass. Things will be as they have always been. But if you continue to disobey you father, your people, you will end up with nothing, with no one. I will not support you as you study, you will never see your mother or your brothers again.'

'Papa, that's unfair,' Naomi sobbed, 'You cannot make me choose. I love you all.'

'Choose you must, and quickly now, it is getting late and we must get home. Say goodbye to your.......... friend and come.'

Naomi looked at Bernard. His eyes were bright with tears. He spoke no words, but his soul called to her. Somehow they both knew what the other was thinking. 'Where will I go? What will I do?' It was a whisper from a heart that was breaking.

'Papa, I'm sorry, I cannot come with you now. Please, please give me time.'

'There is no time. It seems you have made your choice.' He turned his back and began to walk away. Over his shoulder he called, 'You are welcome to your tainted whore. She is no daughter of mine.'

Naomi collapsed to the floor and wept. Bernard pulled her up and held her tight. He stroked her hair, and muttered soothing words, but Naomi was broken and could not stop weeping or shaking. Her father never looked back.

Eventually, Bernard managed to get Naomi to walk a little further along the road to a phone box. There he dialled his parents' number and asked his father to collect them. He offered no explanation, as he didn't want Naomi to be put through having to hear it again. He just said Naomi had had a shock and needed his mother's help.

In the fifteen minutes it took his dad to arrive they stayed in the phone box. There was, fortunately, no-one else around. And all the time Naomi sobbed. She didn't utter a single work, her whole body shook, and she sobbed.

Bernard sat in the back of the car with Naomi and held her. He didn't know what else to do. He wanted to tell her how much he loved her, how much it meant to him that she had chosen him, but he knew her wounds were too raw to hear it now.

He hated her father, and couldn't believe that any parent could treat a child that way. Even after all Naomi had told him, even though he knew their path would not be a smooth one, he had never thought it would come to this.

Chapter 12

When they had arrived at home, his mother had gently prised Naomi from Bernard's arms. This had caused another bout of weeping and screaming. Naomi was sure they were taking Bernard from her and she would have no one just as her father had predicted. Taking hold of her hand, Bernard was quick to reassure her, 'I am going nowhere, but darling we have to get you into bed.'

His father was already on the phone to the doctor. Naomi would have to be given a shot of some sort to calm her. Slowly and patiently they led her up the stairs.

Elizabeth managed to get her into one of Jennifer's nighties and tucked her into bed. Bernard then entered the room and sat on the edge of the bed holding her close.

His parents still had no idea what had happened. It was not until after the doctor had left and the medication had made Naomi sleep that Bernard went downstairs to tell them.

He had remained strong for Naomi's sake, but now he too sobbed. His mother held him as he had held Naomi. They were shocked at the story he told. Elizabeth insisted that he too needed to sleep. 'We can sort things in the morning. You cannot possibly try to deal with this now. We will talk in the morning and between us we will sort things out.'

In fact all the decisions had been made by the time Naomi recovered. The doctor had come again the next morning and suggested she must be kept quiet for a few days. He left more medication for her to be given if needed. It was four days before she spoke a word. Each night she screamed out from the nightmare going on in her head, and each time Bernard would go into her and reassure her that he was there.

Elizabeth had contacted Naomi's college and told them she was ill. She had asked them to get a message to Jennifer asking her to come home that evening. She had also called Bernard's school of medicine and told them that he was unwell. Thomas had set off early for work, giving himself time to call on Naomi's parents. He tried to reason with them. He invited them to visit their daughter but was met with the reply of, 'We have no daughter.'

'Then you are the poorer. In fact I pity you. You have lost a wonderful girl and all through your own stupidity and stubbornness.' He turned on his heel and walked away.

On the fifth morning as Elizabeth brought in a breakfast tray, Naomi looked at her with almost blank eyes and muttered, 'What am I going to do?'

'Do? Well first you are going to try and eat a little of this breakfast, then I suggest a nice warm bath, get dressed – you can borrow something from Jen's bulging wardrobe – then come downstairs. After that, we can talk and I'll tell you what we've arranged. It's Friday so Jen will be home again tonight. Dad is going to collect her and she is bringing some of your things.'

Moving on some kind of autopilot, Naomi did as Elizabeth suggested. Once downstairs she stood in the lounge, not sure what to do next. Elizabeth bustled in and exclaimed, 'My dear child, don't just stand there, come and sit down. You are going to be staying here; at least Bernard is hoping you will agree to that, so make yourself at home.'

Gradually over the next few weeks, Naomi settled into a new routine. She couldn't face going back to college, but everyone told her that didn't matter. She should take her time and wait until the New Year before she even thought about what she wanted to do. She was still grieving for home, even though everything about her new surroundings was far better, especially the atmosphere. As Hanukah drew near, Bernard sensed something was wrong.

81

He asked Jennifer if Naomi had said anything. 'No, but its Hanukah soon and it's an important time for her, so it could be that.'

From somewhere Thomas managed to acquire a Hanukah candlestick and, as a family, they celebrated in a small way, with Naomi saying the familiar blessings. She loved them all for doing this for her, even though each night as the candles were lit she cried.

Then she was introduced to her first Christmas, and Bernard laughed at her child like wonder. She could hardly believe the piles of presents that appeared under the tree, and was amazed that some had her name on. She had bought a small gift each for the others, but hadn't known to place them under the tree. 'Didn't you send them for Father Christmas to deliver?' Bernard teased her. He had told her all about the Christmas traditions, but for her it really seemed that Father Christmas had come!

It was Christmas that finally made Naomi feel she was a part of the Smedley family, and it remained her favourite time of year. Christmas was also the first time she went into a Church. She felt peaceful there, as though the God she had grown up with was also here. Yet even He seemed somehow more loving to her, perhaps because instead of being told repeatedly of his rules and punishments for breaking his laws, they talked about his love. She knew that many of her Jewish friends had grown up with an understanding of a loving God, but in her home he had been portrayed as a harsh judge of everything she did. Now she began to see things differently.

Over the next few months Naomi adjusted to her new life. She still missed her mother dreadfully, and felt the pain of it on a daily basis. Her eldest brother's wedding came and went. Bernard took her out to the coast for the day to keep her occupied, but she still shed a few tears. She started to work in the corner shop, and loved every minute of it. She got to know the regular customers and often came home with bits of gossip to share with Elizabeth, whom she grew ever closer to.

Suddenly, Naomi was brought back to the present by the gentle thud of paws onto her lap and a head nudging her hand. Basil had decided that these two had ignored him long enough and it was his turn for attention. Jason laughed and said, 'I think he wants your attention.'

'Well, fortunately I had told you most of the important bits,' laughed Naomi, 'so he has saved you from me rambling on with the rest of my life story, but I also think he knows when his mummy needs a cuddle, and he's right, whenever I think back to all that I need a cuddle at the end of it!'

'I'm sorry, you shouldn't have told me if it was painful. Though I know what you mean about Basil knowing when you need him, he keeps creeping into my room in the mornings and sitting on the bed with me.'

Naomi smiled. 'He is just one of those animals that senses when you need him, and that is the first time you have referred to it as your room, which proves I was right to share my story with you.'

Jason blushed and took hold of her hand, 'You have made me so welcome it hard not to start thinking of this as home. And now I know what makes you such a wonderful and complete person, and what makes Pete the way he is. He somehow has your perceptive caring nature mixed with Bernard's strength, all of which makes me very lucky.'

Naomi patted his hand and unceremoniously plonked Basil onto his lap. 'I'll go and make us both a cup of tea; I think we could do with it.'

They spent the rest of the morning quietly. Jason worked on a design for his portfolio and Naomi pottered around the house doing jobs. They had soup for lunch and Jason then offered to cook the evening meal, laughingly telling Naomi that it would have to be spaghetti Bolognese because that was all he could cook. For once Naomi agreed to let someone else into her beloved kitchen, knowing that Jason needed to feel that he was playing his part in the family.

As it happened though, Naomi was very involved in cooking tea. Jason started, but then came in to say he couldn't find a jar of Bolognese sauce in the cupboard. Laughing Naomi went into the kitchen and quickly it became a cookery lesson. The only time packets and jars were ever in Naomi's cupboards were if she and Bernard were away and the boys had to look after themselves. Everything in Jason's home had come out of packets and jars and he openly admitted to Naomi that he didn't even realise you could make your own Bolognese sauce. He really enjoyed working with Naomi, and it was a house full of laughter that greeted Bernard when he got home. He then joined in and all three of them were suddenly surprised to find Peter at the kitchen door watching them, smiling.

The meal was a great success with the three Smedley's pretending to believe Jason's story that he had cooked it all himself, and only let Naomi in because he didn't want her to think he was taking over her kitchen. When they finished eating Naomi suggested the boys went out for a drive. While Jason was feeling so bright she wanted to get him over the hurdle of leaving the house. Peter thought it was a great idea, and although Jason's face showed he wasn't sure, he agreed and they were soon out.

Bernard helped load the dishwasher, and then sat down and patted the seat next to him. 'So what happened today then? You seem to have worked your usual magic somehow?' His raised eyebrows made Naomi giggle.

'Well, let's just say we had a long chat about things, including my past, and I think he is beginning to realise that life will go on and it is likely to get better.' Bernard hugged her close, and they spent the rest of the evening like that, watching rubbish on the TV but both contented to do so, just happy to be together and both thinking back to how difficult it had been for them at the start.

Peter and Jason drove to their usual spot. It seemed strange to be there, so much had happened since the last time. 'Its ages since we've been alone, or it feels like it anyway,' Peter said, 'I seem to be with you less now we live in the same house than I did before.'

The anxious look that had been there so often in the last few days returned to Jason's face. 'We have to respect your parents' wishes in their house. I mean, they have been so good about it all, so good to me, and I would hate to upset them.'

Peter held his hand tightly. He looked deeply into his eyes and reassured him once more. 'I know we have to be careful, but we also need to get out like this sometimes and have some 'us' time.' They spent the rest of the evening just chatting about nothing important. After the last few days, it was important for both of them to get back to some kind of normal conversation, and gradually their old ease with each other came back.

Towards the end of the evening Peter pulled Jason into a hug, careful not to hurt him. For a while they just sat like that, Jason relaxing as he began to feel safe once more. Eventually Peter pulled back, gently kissed Jason on the forehead and they drove home.

Naomi could tell the moment they came in that her instincts to talk to Jason, and then to send them out had been right. Now they could begin to move on. She made a light supper, after which they all went up to bed. She smiled as she saw Basil creep into Jason's room. He, like her, would help him through this. She had known when she chose him from the litter that he was a special cat. Alfred was different. He too had something special that had drawn her to him, the runt of the litter, but he would sleep happily in his basket at the side of her bed, being near her all he needed to feel secure.

As she fell asleep that night, Naomi was contented. Peter was sorted, Jason was well on his way to recovery and even Paul had seemed happier before he left for his holiday. She only hoped the holiday would do them both good, then all in her world would be fine. This was the easiest she had felt for a long time. She gave thanks for her husband, her children, her in-laws, and for life itself.

Chapter 13

Over the next few weeks life fell into a happy routine. Bernard and Naomi were thinking once more of having a few days away somewhere, Peter was on hospital duty and loving every minute of it, Jason had returned to college and was spending every spare moment working on his portfolio. He had also started applying for jobs, as he was due to graduate this summer, the same time as Peter would qualify as a doctor.

Paul and Felicity had returned from their holiday looking tanned and relaxed. He had been surprised to find Jason living at his parents' home, and shocked to hear the reasons why. Felicity had yet to realise the true reason he was there, simply presuming that Naomi was playing mother hen to a friend of Peter, who had fallen out with his parents, and everyone felt it best to leave her believing that.

Jennifer and Bill were beginning to feel the excitement rising at the thought of becoming grandparents, and Jen was knitting at furious rates daily, completing item after item. Eve was feeling better every day and was really blossoming. Rachel was nagging Nigel that they too should be having a holiday, and he had compromised when she suggested that she and Felicity could go away for a couple of days at a spa in the meantime. Leah and Greg were still in honeymoon mode, and although she was feeling quite broody now that her sister was expecting, they had agreed to wait a while before trying for a baby themselves. Rebekah was still head over heels in love with Adam, and her parents were seeing less and less of her as she was out almost every evening now.

Naomi hummed along to the radio as she started to prepare the evening meal. As Felicity was away, Paul was coming over to join them for the evening, and Naomi was very much looking forward to an evening with all her men folk around her. She had spent the morning looking through some brochures and had chosen a small family run hotel about an hour's drive away. She was waiting for Bernard to look at it before she booked it, but smiled, knowing that he would agree to anything she had chosen.

Jason arrived home, calling 'hi' as he walked in. Naomi smiled even more. It pleased her so much that he now thought of this as home, and let himself in with the key they had given him, instead of knocking as he had for the first couple of weeks of having it. Then wiping her hands on her apron, she picked up a letter that had arrived for him that morning and waved it at him. He opened it tentatively, not sure he wanted to know what it said inside. It was from one of the companies he had applied to for a job – Hamilton Fields – and a slow smile spread across his face as he read it. He had been offered an interview, one week from today.

Naomi hugged him, 'You deserve it,' she said, 'and when they see the quality of your work, they would be foolish not to offer you the job!'

'I don't think so, they are one of the biggest design companies in this part of the country, and take on one or two young designers each year. If I got a job with them it would make me one of the top graduates this year, and I can't see that happening!'

'Not *if* but *When!* Think positively Jay, you are a very talented designer, and we have a week to convince you of it, so that you walk in there letting them know they are lucky you are considering them!' Jason laughed at the forceful way she spoke.

'I do believe you would actually march in there and tell them if I let you.' He gave her a hug, which she returned. Naomi was growing fonder of him every day. She could see what had captured her son's heart and was pleased that he had someone so special to be with. She returned to the cooking, with Jason sneaking a peek into the pots to see what was in them. She gave him a piece of carrot and shooed him away. 'Go on, or it will never be ready.' He dropped a kiss on her forehead and left the kitchen.

He sank into a chair in the lounge and sent Peter a quick text telling him he had an interview. His phone rang almost immediately, and Peter, like Naomi, was really confident that he would get the job. Jason's view was that even getting an interview with Hamilton Fields was a feather in his cap, and anything above that would be a bonus. He just hoped he managed to get a job somewhere so he could pay his way. He still felt guilty that Bernard and Naomi were letting him live in their house for nothing, since he lost his part time job due to having so much time off after his father's attack. They had encouraged him to concentrate on his studies rather than look for work, as he was so near to graduating.

Jason's news turned the evening meal into a celebration. Everyone was really pleased for him, and Jason again felt the wonder of belonging to this close family. He sat back and listened to them teasing and laughing with each other, something his own family had never done. He wished he could phone his mum and let her know about his interview, but knew it would only cause trouble. That was the only thing casting a shadow on his horizon.

Paul told them more about his holiday, and Felicity's need to be at a spa so soon afterwards. She had claimed it was for Rachel's benefit, but Paul knew from Abe that Rachel has claimed it was for Felicity. 'Both played their husbands well then,' Bernard commented.

Paul smiled, 'Yeah, but I knew what she was doing, and it gives me a few days peace, and wins brownie points so I don't mind at all. Not sure Nigel is so aware, but that's not my problem. He came over today to pick up some accounts, and he is such a pain, if he wasn't family I would take my business elsewhere'

'You need to do what is best for you, never mind family loyalty,' Bernard commented. 'It may upset Rachel, but business is business.'

'Well, he knows his stuff, and gets the accounts done; he is just such a pain. He whines on and on, and has so little personality. I'm sure he is getting worse – must be the Rachel effect!' Everyone laughed, knowing how controlling she could be. They finished their meal and enjoyed a pleasant evening together. Even the cats came and sat in the lounge with them, and Naomi was at her most content. She showed them all the hotel she had chosen and Bernard told her to book it as soon as possible.

Finally, Paul decided he had better make tracks and go home. Naomi invited him to join them again the following evening, but he had a business meeting and had to decline. He thought it was a shame, he had so enjoyed the evening with them – just like old times. Jason fitted in so well, if only Felicity could do the same life would be almost perfect.

The following day Jason went to college with a big grin on his face. He couldn't wait to tell everyone about the interview. His tutor was pleased for him, and also felt that he had a good chance of getting the job if he showed them his real worth in the interview. He offered to give him some tips and interview techniques in a tutorial the following day, which Jason gratefully accepted. He spent the afternoon sorting through his portfolio, choosing which pieces to take with him. They wanted to see four contrasting designs and would also be giving him a task on the day, which he would have no prior notice of, but he would have use of their resources to complete it. Jason asked three friends to give him design requests so he could practise.

Before he had realised it the whole afternoon had passed and the caretaker was throwing him out so that he could lock up. Jason made his way home, head still full of ideas. After dinner he excused himself and went off to his room to continue working. After a while Peter came in to see how he was doing. He brought a coffee with him and insisted Jason stopped for a while. He looked through the designs scattered across the bed and was genuinely impressed. Even allowing for his bias, he knew what he was looking at was really good.

He hugged Jason tightly. 'I'm so proud of you. You deserve to get that job. Then we can start to look for our own place somewhere and you can design the interior and use it as a show case to get commissions. I reckon you could have your own business up and running in no time.'

Jason laughed. 'Nice dream doctor, nice dream. I suppose you want to be a kept man?'

'Well not necessarily. I was thinking more along the lines of making my dear cousin and sister-in-law really, really jealous.' They both laughed, knowing how true that could be. 'Though how Felicity will deal with the dichotomy of wanting the best designer redoing her whole house with the fact that he is her brother-in-law's partner would be fascinating to watch.'

Jason worked hard over the next few days, hardly stopping to eat. He was determined to give it his best shot. If he didn't get the job, he at least wanted to know that he had done his best. When he woke on the day of the interview he felt sick. He lay staring at the ceiling taking deep breaths to try and calm himself. There was a knock at the door, and Naomi came in with a cup of tea and some toast. One look at Jason and she put the breakfast tray down on the bedside cabinet, sat on the edge of the bed and gripped his hand. 'You'll be fine!' She patted his hand

91

and left the room. Going to Peter's room she knocked and walked in. He was still asleep, his rumpled hair on the pillow reminding her of the little boy he used to be. She gently woke him. 'Go in to Jason, he's feeling really nervous and needs some moral support.'

Peter was out of bed in seconds. He went in to Jason, and shared his toast, making light conversation. They went down together to face the cooked breakfast Naomi insisted he ate. Peter then helped him to choose the tie to go with his new suit, and went to get ready himself, as he was driving him to the interview.

Naomi waved them off, feeling nervous herself. She was meeting Jen later that morning, but would be thinking of Jason and waiting for him to call. They arrived with time to spare and sat holding hands in the car park. Peter hugged him and wished him luck and then spent the longest couple of hours waiting for him to come back to the car.

Jason sat in the office set aside for interview candidates. He eyed up the competition. One was looking as nervous as he was, the other was scary. She looked as though she already knew the job was hers, and actually considered herself to be doing Hamilton Fields a favour by turning up. High heeled shoes, a stern looking suit, hair, nails and make-up perfect, she seemed indifferent to the others in the room.

Jason was the first one to be called in. With a deep breath he stood and followed the secretary down the corridor and into the MD's office. There were three people on the panel and each asked questions in turn. They made the interview quite relaxed and Jason felt he answered the questions knowledgeably. Then they gave him the design task, and showed him into a small office to work on it. He had one hour to come up with ideas and prepare a theme board. It was quite similar to one of the themes he had worked on during the week so Jason felt at ease and soon had ideas flowing.

Meanwhile, Peter tried to occupy himself as he waited. This was worse than going for an interview himself, which he would be doing in a few days, but hadn't yet told anyone. He hadn't wanted anything to distract from Jason's day. He sat reading through a couple of medical books; swotting up on things he might be asked. He found it hard to concentrate though as his thoughts were constantly turning to Jason.

Naomi had pottered around the house, and then went to meet Jen. At their usual table they sat chatting about anything and everything, the way they always did. Jen smiled, knowing that Naomi was only half listening to anything she said. 'So I put Humpty Dumpty in the same room as Jack and Jill,' Naomi nodded as though this was normal conversation. Jen roared with laughter. 'You really aren't here today are you? He will be fine, you know he will.'

'I am sorry,' Naomi sighed, 'I just worry about him. He has been through so much these last few months, and it would do him good to have something go right.'

'Finding Pete and coming under your wing may have not been an easy path, but it's right, you can see how happy he is and how his confidence is growing day by day. And I don't doubt that he will get a good job, if not this one, then the next. Then you will be worrying that he and Pete will be leaving home.' The look of horror on Naomi's face made Jen laugh all the more. 'They will never be far from you, don't worry. Although I am beginning to think it won't be long before I am having empty nest pangs. Our Bekky seems set on Adam, we hardly ever see her these days.'

'Do you think he's the one then?' Jen nodded and was about to answer when Naomi's phone rang. She looked at it, pulled a face and answered. It was Peter, updating her that Jason had been asked to wait, but seemed to think it had gone well.

The wait seemed to be forever. Eventually Jason was called back in. He could feel his heart beating, and it seemed so loud he was sure everyone else could hear it too. The MD, Cedric Hamilton, smiled. 'Don't look so scared Jason, take a seat. We have to say we are all really impressed with your work, both the pieces you brought with you and the theme board you did for us. In fact we would like you to do some more work on that, it can be your first job, that's if you are still interested in coming to work for us here.'

Jason could hardly find the words to accept. He could hardly believe that they were really offering him the job. He knew it was going to be hard work, but would look fantastic on his CV, and impress people when he told them who he worked for. He shook hands with each of them and left the office. As he got outside of the building he threw a punch in the air, and Peter, who was watching from the car knew it was good news and rushed to meet him.

Chapter 14

The celebrations went on late into the night. Bernard took them all out for a meal, and then Jen and Bill joined them for drinks, along with Eve, Abe, Rebekah and Adam. Paul had rung and offered his congratulations, but since she got back from the spa Felicity hadn't been feeling so well and he didn't want to leave her.

Jason couldn't believe his luck, the job of his dreams and the family he had always longed for. Again his thoughts went to his mum. She would be so proud of him, and he planned to pop in and see her, or arrange to meet her somewhere in the next few days. Peter seemed to sense his pensive mood and put a hand on his arm. 'You ok?' Jason smiled. How could he not be ok when everything was turning out so well? A few months ago he would never have dreamed of finding Peter, being accepted for who he was, and landing such a prestigious job. In fact, had it not been for Peter and his family, he would never have even had the guts to apply to Hamilton Fields at all.

'I was just thinking about my mum. I wish she could be here to join in the celebrations.' Naomi heard him and came across. She felt sorry for him, but also for his mother. She could not imagine not being there for every important moment of her sons' lives. Or even the not so important ones. She needed contact with them daily. She decided there and then that she was going to do something about the situation. She knew not to mention it to Bernard because he wouldn't want her going anywhere near that family after his encounter with them. No, she wouldn't tell anyone, wouldn't get Jason's hopes up in case it didn't work out, but she would try and do something before they went away next week.

Peter then decided to announce that he too had an interview, which was cause enough for another round of drinks. Jason was cross with him for not saying sooner, which took his mind off of his family, exactly as Peter had intended it to do. Bernard knew the consultant that Peter would be working under if he got the job. He had a good reputation and was a good man. He knew Peter wouldn't want him to say anything, but he intended to phone him tomorrow and put a word in for his son.

Eventually they all made their way home, tired but content. All lost in their own thoughts. Naomi planning to call on Jason's mum, Bernard thinking of the phone call he intended to make, Peter and Jason both thinking alternately about Jason's job and Peter's interview. It took each of them a while to fall asleep, which was unusual. The cats must have sensed that Naomi was restless, both jumping up to snuggle in for cuddles on the bed. Bernard snorted at them, 'Typical, any excuse and they are here. You could have cuddled me if you couldn't sleep.'

'You didn't make the move though, they did,' laughed Naomi, but she put her arm across Bernard and rested her head on his shoulder. The cats resettled themselves on the pillows above her and they all gradually fell asleep.

Meanwhile, over at Paul's things were less calm. Felicity had flown into a rage earlier, over nothing at all, and the row was still going on. Paul had had enough of the tantrums she had been having lately, ever since she came back from the spa. She seemed to have picked up some kind of bug whilst she was there, but refused to see the doctor. She had been peaky for a day or two and since then had been having terrible mood swings.

So much for a restful stay at a spa. Paul made a mental note not to agree to pay for such events next time. Now though he needed some sleep and decided the spare room was probably his best bet. Felicity realised what he was doing, and started to cry. 'What now?' Paul's tone was impatient. 'You want me to stay so we can argue some more?' She shook her head. 'Then what?'

'I don't know,' she sobbed, 'You can't begin to understand how bad I feel.'

'Then see the doctor. If you have picked up a bug or a virus or something he can give you something to make you feel better.' He put his arm around her, but she pulled back.

'I'll be alright, you just need to stop pressurising me.'

'Pressurising you? And how exactly am I doing that? I haven't been near you since we came back from Portugal, and I didn't put pressure on you there either. Make sense woman! Either you don't want me near you, in which case don't make such a fuss about me going to the spare room, or you want me here, in which case stop throwing a hissy fit over the slightest little thing.'

Felicity sank back against the pillows. 'Suit yourself; I am too tired to bother.' Paul climbed into bed beside her and they lay with their backs to each other. Paul was at a loss as to what to do with her. Perhaps it was her hormones he thought with a bitter laugh.

Naomi woke first the next morning. She went down to the kitchen and set about her usual routine. Basil and Alfred were at her feet, waiting for breakfast. After she fed them, she took tea up for Bernard and herself, and snuggled in next to him. Her cold feet woke him with a jump, and she laughed at his indignation. They shared some precious moments together before he got up to shower. Naomi then went down and started on breakfast for everyone. The boys arrived one after the other and both devoured a full English without any hesitation at all.

'You know, Mum, I may not bother to even think about getting my own place once I start work. The service here is too good,' Peter joked. Naomi, didn't take it as a joke though, she looked devastated.

'I didn't think you would be moving out,' she said in dismay. The boys both laughed at the look on her face.

'Well, eventually we will want our own space,' Peter said gently. 'But don't worry it won't be for a while yet.'

'It needn't be for a long time yet, you could stay here while you save up a decent deposit. I will speak to your father about you being together here.'

'Please don't upset him,' Jason urged, 'we are fine as we are. Pete is just teasing. You're right, it will take time to save up a decent deposit and we don't want some grubby bedsit in the meantime. If you are happy to have us here we won't be going anywhere.'

'Of course we are happy to have you here, surely you know that. I am not ready for an empty nest.'

'Ok, we will stay here, and when we do eventually move into our own place you can come over and cook and clean for us so you don't have time to worry about your empty nest,' Pete grinned at his mum. She swatted him with the tea towel just as Bernard entered the kitchen. He pretended to cower by the door and tentatively asked if it was safe to enter.

'As long as you don't even joke about ever leaving home you'll be safe,' Peter laughed and left the room to go and get ready for his day. Jason was left to explain the earlier conversation.

Bernard laughed. 'Even if the two of you stay here for another ten years she will never be ready for you to leave. I know you will want your own space soon, but we will all have to work on Naomi, so that she gets used to the idea. Just make sure it's not too far away, and that you visit regularly, and phone her at least three times a day.' Jason laughed with him and then went to get ready for college to share his good news.

Once they were all out of her way Naomi rushed through her housework, and then sat with a coffee trying to decide her best course of action. She decided to start with a phone call, that way if Jason's dad answered she could say it was a wrong number. She remembered to dial 141 first so that her number wouldn't be displayed. The phone was answered after a few rings and a woman's voice gave the number. 'Oh hello,' Naomi said, 'I'm hoping to speak to Jason's mum.' The woman confirmed that she was his mum and Naomi explained who she was, and asked if it would be possible for them to meet. She suggested her usual café in a town and they agreed a time.

She went to get ready, and had the forethought to put some photos of the Jason and Peter that had been taken the other week into her bag. Then she set off into town. It was a bright sunny day, and Naomi hoped that was a good omen. She parked the car and walked into the café. José was surprised to see her, having only seen her the previous day, but greeted her warmly. She sat at a table in the window and waited. A small, tired looking woman walked in and looked around. Naomi smiled at her and she walked over.

She nervously asked if she was at the right table, and then urgently checked that Jason was ok. Naomi felt sorry for her and reassured her that he was fine. 'I don't want to steal his thunder and tell you all his news,' she said, 'I just wanted to meet with you to see if somehow you would agree to see him. I know he misses you a great deal.'

'I miss him too. I worry about him everyday, but I don't see how I can see him. His father won't even have his name mentioned and I daren't defy him. You've seen what can happen when someone crosses him.' She hung her head in shame and Naomi's heart melted.

'I don't want to interfere, and it's not my place to do so, but there are options open to you, and I am sure I could help if you wanted to get out.'

'I have thought about it so many times, but he would find me, and my daughter, Debbie, has married a similar man, heaven only knows why, and I would lose her and my grandchildren. So you see I can't win. I am glad Jason is free from him, and I would love to hear how he is, and hope he understands and can forgive me for being so weak.

Naomi reached out and took hold of her hand. 'Only you can make the decisions about your life. Jason is fine. He doesn't know I was planning to speak to you today. I didn't want to get his hopes up.' Tears filled his mum's eyes and she looked at Naomi with an almost hopeless expression.

'Please tell him I think of him, but the only way I could see him is like this, during the day when his dad is at work, and even that is risky.'

'I wish I could make things easier for you, I really do. Take my number and if you want us to help you at any time you only have to ring.' The coffee arrived then and they both sat deep in thought as they drank. 'Oh I almost forgot, I brought some photos with me that we took the other week, if you would like to see them.'

She did and almost fell on them. It was as though she want to make the images permanently imprint on her brain. Naomi offered to let her have them, but she declined for fear that her husband would find them. Eventually the two women left the bistro and went their separate ways. Naomi was not sure if she had made things better or worse for her really and was saddened by the encounter. She knew she wouldn't mention it to Jason, as it would be sure to upset him.

She made her way home with a heavy heart, and set about cooking a family favourite for the evening meal. She shed a few tears as she worked, and was glad to have an onion to blame it on in case anyone should question her red eyes.

Bernard was on the phone at that very moment. He had not had time earlier in the day, but was determined to phone before he left for home. The surgeon on the other end of the phone was not surprised in the least to hear from Bernard. 'Bernie, was wondering if I would be hearing from you. This wouldn't be about some interviews I am holding on Friday would it?'

Bernard laughed. 'He only told us last night that he had an interview, or I might have phoned you sooner.'

'Well I can't be seen to show favouritism, but tell me, is he a chip off the old block?'

'Depends whether you think the old block is a good thing or not,' Bernard replied. 'He is a good, hardworking lad, and everything I hear from people is good, but they may just be telling his old dad what he wants to hear.'

'Well I've heard good things too. Between you and me, on paper he is the best candidate, so as long as he doesn't make any dreadful mistakes in his answers in the interview it should go his way. I am quite looking forward to working with him. But don't you go telling him that!' They both laughed and then chatted for a while more about work and their respective families. They had known each other since med school but rarely got to meet, as the man split his time between two hospitals now.

Bernard decided he wouldn't mention the call to Naomi, not knowing that she too had made the decision not to tell him about her day. It was unusual for either of them to keep secrets, and neither would suspect the other of doing so. He made his way home, looking forward to an evening with his wife. He knew the lads were going out for their own celebration this evening, which would give him and Naomi some much needed time to themselves. Unlike her he looked forward to the days when they had they house to themselves. He loved his children dearly, but he was ready for the youngest to spread his wings and fly.

He pulled into the drive, got out of the car and went into the house with his usual 'honey I'm home' call to Naomi. He found her in the kitchen and noticed the red eyes. He presumed she was still upset from the morning teasing over the soon to be empty nest and pulled her close. 'They will be here for a while yet, my darling. And you know that part of bringing them up is to prepare them to set out on their own. Think yourself fortunate that you have done such a wonderful job that they will never be far from you, and that you are not a different species, 'cos its only humans that keep their young about them for so long.'

Naomi shooed him away, telling him it was the onion, and Bernard nodded in a way that told her he didn't believe her, but would accept her excuse. She felt bad not telling him the real reason for her tears, but knew he would be cross with her for making that call so didn't say a word.

Jason was home before Peter that evening and was full of everyone's comments on his job. There had been one or two bitchy remarks from some jealous girls, one of whom knew the girl that had been there for an interview too. She had also been offered a job and her friend told Jason that she would show him up in no time. She was sure to be their top designer within a matter of months. Most people however, had been really pleased for him. A couple of his friends had also found work, ready for when they graduated, but most were still looking. It wasn't an easy time to be going into design and Jason knew he was being given the chance of a lifetime.

Peter eventually made it home, just as Naomi was dishing up the meal, having decided it would wait no longer. They sat and enjoyed a pleasant meal, after which the youngsters went and changed to go out. Peter was looking forward to some time to themselves which, considering they lived in the same house, they seemed to get very little of.

Bernard settled with Naomi on the settee, after helping her to load the dishwasher, having found her filling the sink to do the dishes by hand yet again. 'It's like a mood barometer that sink,' he teased. 'I can always tell when something has upset you, because you ignore the dishwasher! It won't be all bad once we have the house to ourselves you know.' He pulled her closer. 'It will be like when we were first married again.' He started to drop little kisses on her neck and Naomi laughed at him and pushed him away.

'Behave yourself! I have knitting to do. I promised Jen I would do some, and so far I have only managed to finish one cardigan.' However, not much knitting got done that night. The two of them needed each other, neither knowing what the other was thinking, but finding in each other everything they needed. Naomi was so grateful for having such a loving husband.

By the time the boys returned home the living room was in darkness. Peter suggested they had coffee, and so they then sat and snuggled on the same settee that had accommodated his parents earlier. Jason was worried that Bernard or Naomi might come in, but Peter reassured him and they sat drawing strength and comfort from each other for well over an hour before going to their separate rooms. Peter sighed as he got into bed. He wanted them to get their own place as soon as possible. He didn't want to upset his parents, but he wanted to be with Jason, wanted to say goodnight and still have him there.

Soon everyone was asleep and peacefully dreaming, although Peter's dream drifted into a nightmare where during his interview he was asked to perform life saving operations on three people at once. He woke in a cold sweat and lay there panting. He got up and went down for a drink. As he stood by the sink he heard footsteps and Naomi walked in. 'Sorry mum, I tried to be quiet.'

'I always hear you, I'm your mum, it's what we do,' she laughed. Peter opened his arms and she came and hugged him. 'Interview nerves?' she asked. Peter told her about his dream and laughed.

'I didn't realise I was nervous about it, but obviously I am,' he commented.

Naomi decided to tell him about her day. He listened in surprise that she had done it. They discussed the options and came to the agreement that she should tell Jason. Although he was likely to be upset that she still wouldn't do anything about her situation, it would be good for him to know she still cared. Maybe they could arrange to meet at some point.

Peter hugged his mum tightly. 'Thank you Mum, you are so brilliant, and I am so lucky to have you and I know I don't tell you often enough.' She kissed his cheek, then shooed him off back to bed. She stood for a while longer herself, giving thanks that her children were safe and well and turning into good men. She rinsed Peter's glass and left it to drain.

Chapter 15

The following morning, which had come much sooner than Peter had wanted it to, Naomi was busy ironing when the phone rang. She put the iron down and went to answer it, not recognising the voice at the other end. 'Hello, is that Naomi? Its Brenda, Jason's mum.' Naomi was surprised, but pleased, to hear from her. 'I haven't been able to sleep thinking about yesterday. I've come out to a phone box so that your number doesn't show up on the bill. I just wondered if you had spoken to Jason yet and what he said.'

'I haven't had the chance to speak to him yet, but he's here, revising for his exams. I'll call him and you can speak to him, or better still why don't you come over here for lunch?' After some persuasion Brenda agreed to come. Naomi decided not to tell Jason but to let him open the door. She quickly put the ironing board away and went to prepare a simple lunch. She decided on sandwiches so that they could have as much time together as possible, and she intended to make herself scarce.

She called Jason down ready for lunch just before his mum was due. She chatted easily about his studies, and he sounded confident that he knew the things that were likely to come up in the exam. He had got a first for his coursework and was hoping to do just as well in the exams.

As they were chatting the doorbell rang and Naomi asked Jason if he would get it. He went and she heard the surprise in his voice when he saw who was there. Both of them just stood there looking at each other, both with tears pouring down their faces. Eventually Naomi went and brought them into the lounge. She made a pot of tea, and put it and the sandwiches on the coffee table, then left the room.

Brenda explained how Naomi had phoned her the previous day and how grateful she was. They sat holding hands and Jason began to tell her all his news. She was so proud to hear that he had got a job and relieved to see that he had no permanent scars outwardly from what his father had done to him. She knew that there were scars that ran deep, she knew because she carried them too. But her son was here, safe and well, loved and cared for.

She told Jason about his sister and her children. She was careful what she said and what she left unsaid, and Jason knew there were things she was leaving out. Eventually he said, 'Once I am working I will help you find somewhere else to live so that you can get away from him Mum.' She shook her head, but he refused to listen to her protests. 'Yes I will, I'll find somewhere where you and I can live, and then once Pete and I buy a place you can stay there and I will help you pay the rent. Mum you have to get away. I know there is a lot you aren't telling me, and we both know you won't be able to say where you have been today for fear of a beating. I've hated it all these years, and now I am nearly in a position to do something about it. I want to know you are safe.

I've loved being here with Pete and his family, but seeing how they are with each other has just reinforced how damaged our family is. You are a good woman, and you don't deserve to spend your days in fear of him, so let me help you. I wish you could stay long enough to meet Pete, but he won't be home 'til later. Perhaps next time. Look I'll give you my new mobile number, hide it under another name so at least you will be able to contact me.'

Time passed quicker than either of them wanted. Brenda held him close for a long time, and it was a hug that spoke the words that neither of them had been able to speak. She also hugged Naomi, and thanked her again, both for caring for her son and for contacting her and giving her the opportunity to see him again. She left looking back time and again before she turned the corner.

Jason slowly closed the door and stood with his back to it, tears again streaming down his face. Finally he walked back into the lounge and Naomi opened her arms. He fell into them sobbing, trying to thank her for what she had done but unable to speak. Naomi just held him and let the hurt come out. 'Hush now, hush, that's the hard part done. You know now that she still wants you, and somehow we will make it possible. Hopefully she will gain the strength she needs to make the break herself, and I'll help in any way I can.

Bernard and Peter were amazed to hear the events of the day when they got home. Bernard scolded Naomi for making the call, asking what she would have done if Jason's father had answered. She explained that she had thought about that and had her answers ready. Both men were pleased for Jason, and Bernard added his hope to Naomi's that Brenda would find the strength to leave her brute of a husband.

Peter spent most of the evening with Bernard in his study going over possible questions and answers. Bernard was impressed with his knowledge and thought he should do well. He advised an early night, which Peter decided to have and this time he slept well.

The following morning it was his turn to be woken with tea and toast in his room. Naomi gave him a big hug and he knew she was nervous for him, but she told him she was sure he would do well. She intended to keep herself busy cleaning the windows, with the phone at her side ready for his call.

Jason went with him, though Peter had to drive himself. He commented that they must get Jason driving soon. They parked in the hospital car park and sat holding hands, as they had before Jason's interview. He was going to wait for Peter there. He had a couple of text books to look at, though he knew he would find it hard to concentrate on anything.

Naomi was up on a step ladder cleaning the same bit of window over and over again. She jumped when the phone rang and slipped off the ladder. She called out as a pain shot through her ankle. The pain was unbearable and she felt faint. She just managed to answer the phone, and heard Peter's excited voice before she passed out. He was surprised at the lack of response and called her name. Realising something was terribly wrong he ran the rest of the way to the car.

Seeing the look on his face Jason thought the interview must have gone badly. Peter quickly told him he had the job and then explained what had happened. 'My phone is still connected to home, can I use yours?'

'Better still, I'll use it to phone your dad and you start driving, but be careful.' Peter whipped the car into reverse and raced out of the car park. Jason managed to get hold of Bernard and explained that although the phone had answered Naomi hadn't spoken. They were still calling her name and hoping for a response. Bernard said he would meet them there.

Suddenly, as Jason called her name once more, Naomi answered. Her voice was weak but she managed to say hello. They managed to understand that she had fallen, and so Jason again used his phone, this time to phone for an ambulance. Then he phoned Paul. He answered expecting it to be news of Peter's interview and was shocked to hear the news. He too said he would meet them at the house.

Peter and Jason got there just ahead of the ambulance and let the paramedics in. Naomi was still on the floor, and green in colour. Her ankle was at a strange angle, and it took only seconds for the paramedics to realise it was dislocated. Peter held her hand, whilst one of the paramedics went to get the Entonox. Bernard arrived and rushed to be at his wife's side. Only then did she begin to cry, and was cross with herself for doing so. She began to scold them all for making so much fuss and tried to convince them that she really didn't need to go to hospital. With two doctors looking over her, as well as the paramedics, she wasn't going to win that argument.

Paul arrived just as they were putting her into the ambulance. Naomi was cross that he too had rushed out of work, and told him to go back at once. He laughed at her indignant tone, asking her what she expected and what she would have done if the roles had been reversed.

Bernard went in the ambulance with her and told the boys to stay at home. He promised to call them as soon as they knew whether there was a break as well as the dislocation. Secretly he was hoping not, as he knew only too well how hard that would be on Naomi, and the long lasting problems it could bring.

As they went back into the house, having assured the neighbours that all was ok, Jason went and put the kettle on. 'I got the job by the way,' Peter said, just to make conversation. Paul congratulated him, but guessed the celebrations would have to wait.

It seemed like an age later that the phone rang and Bernard gave them the good news that there was no break and the ankle had been put back into its proper place by the orthopod, a close friend of the family, who had rushed down when Bernard called him.

Naomi came home, and leaning heavily on Bernard's arm, came into the house. She was soon settled on the settee, with four men fussing round her. Bernard needed to go back to work, but was satisfied that Jason and

Peter would not let her move. Paul too apologised but said he really should get back to work.

The phone rang just after they had left. It was Jen enquiring how Peter had got on. He told her both his good news, and his Mum's less wonderful news. Jen was distressed to hear about the fall, and offered to come over. Naomi was insistent that she shouldn't come, but no-one seemed to listen to her today. 'It seems dislocating your ankle stops your voice from being audible,' she said with a sigh. Peter and Jason just laughed at her and continued to fuss. Jen arrived with grapes and magazines. She insisted on putting a casserole in the oven for them to eat later. She also offered to sit with Naomi for a while so the boys could go out. They went reluctantly.

Realising they had had no lunch, they made for a burger bar. Jason felt bad that, after such celebrations for his interview success, Peter wouldn't be getting the same due to Naomi's accident. He said as much and Peter shook his head. 'I've had plenty of other celebrations, and you know what they say about the mountain and Mohammad – we'll collect the champagne and take it home with us. We'll have the party around the invalid on the sofa.' Jason laughed at his easy response. They devoured the burgers and went off in search of goodies for the evening celebrations.

They returned home with champagne, flowers, chocolates and some groceries. Naomi was touched by the gifts, but still felt silly that such a simple accident was creating so much fuss. She was used to being the one fussing around her brood, not lying on the sofa being on the receiving end.

Then Bernard arrived home with yet more flowers. 'This house is beginning to look like a florist,' Naomi murmured. Jen put them in a vase, then gathered her things and got ready to go. She kissed Naomi and encouraged her

110

to make the most of the rest and to let them all run around after her for a while. She hugged Bernard, congratulated Peter once more and then left.

Bernard began to fuss around Naomi. He plumped the cushions, offered her more pain killers, made her another cup of tea, and then settled on the chair next to her and held her hand. She kept trying to say there was no need for all the fuss, but it fell on deaf ears. Jason and Peter were also hovering, waiting for any chance to make themselves useful.

Naomi felt very loved, having them all around her, but mostly she felt an enormous ache in her ankle, and annoyed with herself for having the accident. She was grateful that the pain had eased the moment the ankle was put back in place, but was feeling slightly weepy from all that had happened. She knew if she gave into the tears that were so close they would all go into overdrive, and she really couldn't cope with that, so she had to keep control of herself.

Just as she was struggling with this the door bell rang. Peter went to the door, and walked back in followed by Paul and Felicity and the biggest bouquet of flowers yet. Felicity had had them arranged by the florist into a beautiful crystal vase, so all Bernard had to do was to find somewhere to put them. She then took his place at Naomi's side and holding her hand asked, 'Does it hurt terribly?' Naomi assured her that it wasn't so bad now that it had been repositioned correctly. 'You are so brave, I can't imagine how I would cope if something so terrible happened to me.'

As she said this she glared around at the men in the room, as though they were to blame for Naomi's misfortune. They were all left speechless at this scene, which Peter later referred to as something out of the twilight zone. Felicity continued to fuss around Naomi, insisting on

111

more pillows, a fresh pot of tea, a blanket and even a cold compress for her head.

Naomi too was speechless. Felicity was acting out of character and actually became quite weepy when Paul dared to suggest that his Mum looked fine and maybe didn't want people fussing round her. She ran from the room and locked herself in the bathroom for the next twenty minutes. Paul apologised for her behaviour. 'She's been like this since she came back from the spa – I don't really know what's going on in her head at the moment.'

Naomi thought it looked and sounded hormonal, but kept her thoughts to herself, simply saying, 'Well viruses can make you feel out of sorts for a while. Is Rachel alright? It's not something they ate is it?'

'Magic mushrooms?' replied Peter with an overly innocent look on his face. Naomi rolled her eyes at him, and then settled herself back on the pillows. All the excitement of the day was beginning to take its toll.

When Felicity returned Bernard suggested it was time for a toast. They all made a fuss of Peter for landing such a good post. The consultant he was to train under was highly regarded, and it was a great start to his career. Paul then added another toast to Jason and Peter, both having done so well.

Felicity looked a little confused as to the way in which Paul was speaking of them, almost as though he was praising the happy couple. She would have to tell him later, he would be embarrassing them if he went on saying things like that, but she would wait until they were home so as not to draw more attention to his faux pas.

Eventually Paul said they should leave, and he and Felicity made their goodbyes. After they had gone the three men all sank onto chairs quite worn out by the performance. 'I know it's not my place to say, but how does Paul cope with her day after day?' Jason asked.

'That was very out of character. I have never seen her like that before, anyone looking at that would have thought you were her favourite mother-in-law dear,' Bernard remarked.

'I think its her hormones,' Naomi mused with quite a wistful look. The three men looked at her in amazement, but were too lost for words to comment.

Chapter 16

For the next few days Naomi rested. No-one in the house would let her lift a finger, and the cats rarely left her side. Whilst Bernard was at work, the boys took shifts in being there, ready to stop her if she made any attempt to try and do anything. Naomi, however, had little inclination to do anything. She couldn't believe how tired she felt. She was also quite weepy, which she was trying to hide from everyone in case they thought there was something really wrong.

Her in-laws came over on the second day and they shared a pleasant morning together. Elizabeth seemed to sense how Naomi was feeling, and sent her husband and Jason off to the shop for a few errands. While they were gone she got Naomi to open up a bit. 'Well the shock is enough to knock you off side for a few days dear. You should just take it easy. It's a good thing you and Bernard are going away at the weekend. I should suggest to him that he extends the stay and keeps you away until you are back to yourself.'

'I just feel guilty; everyone is making such a fuss.'

'Well let them! You spend enough time fussing over your family. And the truth is, none of them see it as a bind, they all love the chance to spoil you a little.'

Naomi then told her about Felicity's odd behaviour. Elizabeth also thought it sounded very hormonal behaviour and the two women exchanged glances, neither wanting to voice their thoughts. They did, however, move on to talk about Eve and how well she was looking.

'She looks more and more like Jen doesn't she?' Naomi said. 'It's so lovely to see, and so exciting to think we are starting on the next generation of the family. Leah will probably be next, as I can't quite see Rachel in the maternal role can you?'

'She is so different to the rest of the family, I sometimes wonder where she came from,' Elizabeth remarked. It was rare for her to say anything less than complimentary about anyone, but Naomi knew exactly what she meant. She wished Rachel had been more like her sisters, then she may not have had Felicity as a friend, and then she may not have set her sights on Paul. But it was no use thinking like this. Felicity was her daughter-in-law and she needed to get used to the fact.

Before Elizabeth left Naomi asked her to help her pack. 'I know Bernard would do it, but who knows what I would end up with, and how screwed up it would be by the time we got there. Elizabeth had laughed and after helping Naomi up the stairs had made her sit on the bed whilst she packed. Seeing the case packed Naomi had begun to get excited about their time away. She wouldn't be up to walking that far, but the hotel grounds were beautiful and if the weather held they wouldn't need to go far. She had put aside a couple of books to take with her, but decided to ask Jason to pick up a couple more for her. He was more likely to make a good choice than either Bernard or Peter.

On the Friday both boys had an exam, and Naomi was almost beside herself not being allowed into the kitchen to make them a good breakfast before they went. It was almost as if she felt sure they wouldn't do well without her input, and that she would be responsible for them failing.

'We will do fine. You have seen how much study we have both been doing and you should have faith in us.' Peter was quite impatient with her.

'We know you would have if you could have, and the support is still there and will still get us through,' Jason reasoned with her more gently. She touched his cheek, and then gave them both huge hugs and kisses before she let them leave the house. She was able to get around as long as she was careful and she was looking forward to having the house to herself, albeit under strict instructions not to do any housework.

No sooner had they gone than she had the duster out, but after a few minutes she needed to sit down. She decided to phone and see if she could get an appointment with her GP. She didn't want to worry Bernard, but she was concerned that she still felt so lifeless.

As she wasn't driving, she had to order a taxi to get there. She then waited nervously until she was called in. She explained to the doctor, who was also a family friend, about the fall and how she was feeling so tired and weepy ever since. He looked at her ankle which was healing nicely. He then checked her over and asked a few questions. 'A fall like that can take it out of you Naomi,' he said, 'and you are so used to being active it will have come as a shock to your system. It's most probably nothing more than that, but I would like you to have a few blood tests just to be on the safe side.'

Naomi must have looked really scared, as he then said, 'Don't worry, I just want to check your hormone levels. It could be that you are heading towards the dreaded menopause. That does make some women tired, and clumsy! I don't for one minute think it is anything more than that. Were you feeling ill at all before the fall? No? Well then we are most probably dealing with nothing more than shock. Maybe your body is just telling you to take it easy for a while. Let everyone else run around you for a change, make more time for yourself.'

Naomi was reassured by his confidence, and returned home to find Bernard just pulling into the drive. 'Where have you been? I called and got no answer and thought maybe you had fallen again.' Naomi laughed at the concern in his face. She explained that she hadn't wanted to worry him, but had been to check out her own concerns,

116

forgetting to take her mobile with her. He agreed with the doctor's diagnosis.

They went inside and shared a coffee before he returned to work. They were to leave for the hotel once he got home that evening. Naomi had purposely booked them to leave after the last exams, as she wouldn't have coped with being away before then. She had also thought that Peter and Jason would appreciate having the house to themselves for a few days, without lectures and work and study getting in the way. It would be the first time they would have the chance to just enjoy being together, and Naomi hoped it would be wonderful.

Both boys were there to wave them off that evening. Jason had planned a romantic evening for them. He had sorted the meal with help from Naomi, and had bought a DVD they had both wanted to see. It was wonderful just having time to themselves. Both had turned down parties tonight, preferring just to be together. They spent the evening snuggled up on the sofa, simply enjoying each other's company. Peter then suggested they went up to bed. Jason looked worried at the suggestion and Peter laughed at him. 'I'm not planning on forcing you into anything, I just thought it would be nice for once to be able to fall asleep in each other's arms and wake with you there.'

'I would love that, it just seems wrong to go against your dad's wishes.'

'I know, but look at it this way, he just asked us not to flaunt it in front of him, and we aren't because he isn't here. When he gets back, we go back to being in our own rooms and he is none the wiser. Mum knows, she even as much as suggested to me that we made the most of our time alone, which is strange 'cos she wouldn't have let Paul have Felicity over before they were married. I guess she just accepts that it's different for us. We would be planning a wedding were we allowed to do so, but we can't, so we just have to be as we are. I love you, and want to spend the rest of my life being with you. How we work that out I don't know for sure, I guess we just go with the flow as it were, but I want you with me and tonight, for once, that is possible so please say yes.'

Jason knew that Peter didn't find it easy to open his heart, at least not to put it into words. His eyes glistened as he took hold of Pete's hands and pulled him into a hug. 'Of course I want to be with you. Nothing could be better than just being together, and you are right, whilst your parents are away we have the chance to be together. As long as you are sure it's ok I'll happily sleep with you.'

They both slept peacefully that night, secure in the love they shared. It was quite late when Peter woke the next morning. He felt Jason at the side of him and smiled. This was exactly as life should be. He felt complete. He had finished med school and, banking on passing his finals, was a qualified doctor at last. They both had jobs waiting for them and life was about to start for real.

As much as he loved being home with his parents, he intended to talk Jason into looking for their own place as soon as possible. He was ready to set up home with the love of his life. He looked at Jason sleeping so peacefully and his heart filled with love. He had had the easier path. Jason had given up everything for him, and he intended to spend a lifetime making sure he never regretted it.

He got up quietly, trying not to wake Jason. He went downstairs, made a pot of tea and some toast and walked back up to his bedroom. Jason was just stirring as he walked in the room. 'Room service,' Peter sang and plonked himself back on the bed. They enjoyed a leisurely breakfast, and made their plans for the day. The weather was beautiful, so they decided on a day at the coast. It would have been nice to stay over, but they were on cat sitting duties so would have to be back at a reasonable time. Having decided that making a picnic would waste precious time, they were soon showered dressed and out of the door. The poor cats had been unceremoniously ushered out of the back door. They were really missing the pampering that came with being so loved by their mistress.

'I think I should change this car once I am working,' Peter mused.

'Why? There's nothing wrong with it.'

'Yeah but we could have matching convertibles.'

Jason laughed at the idea. 'You seem to think we are going to have no end of money, and we don't need two convertibles. You have one if you must, a little run around will do for me. Just something to get me to work and back.'

'You need to dream big Jason. You need a car that says "I've made it" to all your clients. Let them know you are successful. That way you can start to build up a private client list.'

'I'm not sure HF would like that,' Jason smiled at Peter and ran his hand over his hair. He loved being with him like this. Carefree, no-one to answer to but themselves, and on the brink of everything life had to offer them. Sometimes he still had to pinch himself to believe this was all real and not just a dream.

They had a wonderful day, and came home tired but happy. They brought in a take away rather than cook, ate, fed the cats, and went off to bed, watching TV for a while before falling asleep.

Paul had spent his day stuck in his office. He had come home tired but pleased. He had landed another big contract. He was becoming very successful considering his age. He had a head for business and everything he did seemed to strike gold. Felicity seemed pleased to hear his news, and was more like her normal self which was a relief.

119

They shared a salad on the patio and then went for a drive to a country pub before coming home.

They were both asleep quickly and dreaming pleasant dreams. Paul was suddenly aware of a bell ringing, and couldn't quite work out where it was coming from. He stirred in his sleep and eventually realised the phone was ringing. He picked it up, still groggy with sleep. 'Ello?'

The voice on the other end was breaking up, trying to speak between sobs. Paul sat up, suddenly fully awake. 'Abe? Is that you? What's up?'

Between sobs Abe managed to tell Paul he was at the hospital. It was hard to make sense of what he was saying, and it didn't help that Felicity had woken and was indignant that anyone should phone them in the middle of the night. Paul silenced her with a move of his arm. He listened carefully, trying to put together what had happened. 'I'm on my way. Just stay calm. Have you rung Bill? OK I'll ring them, you just stay calm. I'll be there as soon as I can.'

Even as he explained to Felicity what was happening, Paul was pulling clothes on. He then rang his uncle and carefully broke the news to them that Abe and Eve had been in a car accident. They said they would meet him at the hospital. Paul's face was ashen as he left the house. He carefully pulled the car off the drive and started for the hospital. He was praying all the way there. He drove, almost on autopilot, glad that there was little traffic about. He just hoped Abe could hold it together until they got there, and that things weren't as bad as he had suggested on the phone.

Chapter 17

Paul pulled up at the hospital just seconds before his aunt and uncle. He saw them driving in as he was rushing towards the doors. Normally he would have stopped and waited for them, but Abe needed him. He rushed on, knowing they would join him. Abe was sitting, looking deathly pale. He was just staring into space, and it took Paul a couple of minutes to get his attention. He had a cut on his forehead, but apart from that looked unharmed. For an instant Paul was relieved. Then he realised that Eve was nowhere to be seen.

Abe looked up at him. Tears were streaming down his face. 'She's hurt bad. I've hurt my beautiful Eve. Paul help me.' He couldn't say more, and all Paul could do was hold him as he sobbed. Jen arrived at his side and took Abe from Paul. She held him close, but he struggled from her arms. 'Don't. I've hurt your beautiful daughter, don't be nice to me. You told me to look after her, and I promised you on our wedding day that I would never let any harm come to her.' He began to sob again. Jen was crying too.

Bill walked over to join them looking white. He had been to speak to the doctors to find out what was happening. 'She's going into surgery now.' He caught Jen as her knees buckled. She was sobbing and he pulled her close and held her tight. Abe watched them and felt for the chair behind him. He sat down and dropped his head into his hands. He didn't understand how all this had happened. Paul sat down next to him and put a hand on his shoulder. None of them yet knew the details, so it was hard to make sense of it. Eventually Bill sat Jen down next to Paul. He saw a policeman walk in and speak to the nurse in charge so he walked over to him.

Paul watched the conversation and knew from Bill's body language that it wasn't good. He waited, trying to give comfort to the people either side of him. He felt cold and tried to find some inner strength to help them all get through this.

Bill walked back over to join them. He crouched down in front of Abe. 'Look at me,' he said quietly, but firmly. 'Look at me Abe. I've spoken to the policeman. The accident was not your fault. You need to stop blaming yourself for what has happened. You haven't broken your promise to me. You risked your life pulling Eve from that car. You have to stay strong for her now. She is going to need you when she comes out of surgery. We must pray for her now, pray that she makes it through the surgery,' his voice broke as he spoke.

His words seemed to penetrate Abe's brain. He looked at Bill and tried to speak, but no words came out. Bill stood and straightened up. He took a deep breath and then spoke to them all. 'Come on, let's go and wait near the theatre so we get news as soon as possible.' They all followed him, though the nurse tried to convince Abe to stay there so they could keep a check on him. In the end Paul said they would watch him, and at the first sign of anything they would bring him back down to the emergency department.

It seemed to take forever to get to the waiting area, and all the time both Jen and Abe were crying quietly. Paul wished he knew what to say. He had a feeling that maybe he should comfort his aunt, as Abe seemed to respond better to Bill. It was as if he needed Bill to forgive him for being involved in an accident that wasn't his fault. So Paul took his aunt by the arm and led her to a seat.

She looked towards him, but didn't really seem to see him. No-one had yet told them what the surgery involved and Paul was too scared to ask. Any surgery was risky for a pregnant woman. It was two lives the surgeons were fighting to keep and that thought brought a lump to

122

his throat. He couldn't imagine how any of them would survive if the surgery wasn't successful. He pushed the thought away as soon as it arrived.

Bill was having similar thoughts. He had never felt so helpless in his life. His little girl. His beautiful, beautiful daughter. So young, with so much of life ahead of her. This was unfair. Abe and Eve were good people. He was a curate for goodness sake, surely that should have protected them. He could feel himself getting angry at God. He knew he should be praying, asking for God to guide the hands of the surgeon, but at the moment he felt like he wanted to fight the angel of death. He was not prepared to let go of his little girl. He wanted to scream, but he knew that Abe was in no state to cope on his own, and Jen was sinking into despair as the moments passed.

Abe sat staring into space. He kept rerunning the accident, and wondering what he could have done differently. They had gone for a drive and had tea out. It was just an ordinary outing. They were just like many other couples who had made the most of the weather and been out that day. They were driving home, chatting and laughing. They were listing silly name ideas for the baby, a competition to see who could come up with the weirdest suggestion.

Had his concentration wavered? He felt he would never know for sure. He was a safe driver, he kept to the speed limits, and he paid attention to the road. So why hadn't he seen that car coming round the bend on the wrong side of the road in time to swerve? Eve, his gorgeous, kind, funny wife. His very reason for being. How was he going to cope with knowing that he had been driving when she had been injured?

He didn't know what had happened to the kids in the other car. He knew they were young, but wasn't even sure if there had been two or three people. He had

123

managed to climb out through the broken windscreen. He could smell petrol and knew he had to get Eve out. She wasn't conscious and there seemed to be blood everywhere.

He knew you weren't supposed to move people, but he also knew that the car could go up in flames at any moment. Other cars were beginning to stop, and someone was at his side trying to pull him away. But he needed to get Eve. He climbed back into the car, and managed to get her seatbelt undone. He still wasn't sure how he had managed it, but he had lifted her from the car. A man took her from him as they got onto the bonnet. Someone else helped him down and away from the car. A minute or so later it burst into flames.

Now she was in surgery and he was here, sitting helplessly, wanting to tell people it wasn't his fault, yet knowing he was the only one who they could blame. A sob caught in his throat, and Bill placed a calming hand on his shoulder.

Jen was sitting a couple of seats away. Every fibre of her being was urging her daughter to make it through the surgery. If she could have gone in there and breathed life into her she would have. Scenes from Eve's life flashed through her mind. The first day of school nerves, the first lost tooth, the tears and triumphs that had made her the good woman she was today. 'She deserves to live,' Jen told God, 'Her and the baby deserve to live.' She repeated those lines over and over in her head as though if she said them often enough God would hear and make it so.

They all sat there lost in their own thoughts. Each willing Eve to do her part and fight. Each wishing they could do something constructive, yet knowing they were helpless onlookers. Paul wondered who was operating; maybe it was someone his dad knew. Maybe somehow they should get a message to him that this was Bernard Smedley's niece. Paul knew that would make no difference, the surgeon would do his or her best regardless, but he wanted to tell them all the same.

It was hours before the surgeon, a middle aged woman Paul recognised, came out of the theatre and walked towards them. Her face was grim, and Jen gasped and started to sob uncontrollably. She quickly put her arm on Jen's shoulder. 'She is alive.' All of them let out a breath they hadn't even realised they were holding. 'It was touch and go for a while. She had severe abdominal trauma, a broken pelvis. We managed to stop the blood loss and fix the pelvis, but there were some complications we were unable to sort. I am so sorry, but she has lost the baby.'

Abe stood up and screamed at her, 'NO! no, no, no.' Bill grabbed him and pulled him close. He was devastated for his own loss, and knew Abe must be feeling it even more. Jen gripped Paul's hand, tearing streaming down her face once more. Her poor baby girl robbed of her own child.

The doctor continued to speak, needing to give them all the details before she left to check on Eve once more. 'The baby was already dead before she got to theatre. It was a little girl, and you will be able to see her if you wish.' She took a breath and then continued, 'We were unable to stop the bleeding and had no alternative but to do a full hysterectomy. I'm so sorry. Eve has been taken into recovery and will then be taken to intensive care. You will be able to see her there, but we will be keeping her under sedation for the next few hours.'

She stopped speaking and stood for a moment, waiting in case they wanted to ask anything, but knowing that the news she had just given them meant they would be too stunned to ask much, if anything. She hated her job on nights like this. She hated losing the battle in the theatre. She had been lucky to save the girl's life but she knew that the loss they were suffering would take some getting over.

She just hoped they were strong enough as a family to make it through. Heaven knew that girl was going to need them to be strong for her.

Paul realised that no-one was managing to react, and so he stepped forward and thanked the doctor. He said he was sure he recognised her and mentioned his father. She at once responded with a smile, and they passed a few pleasantries. She then took her leave of them.

Bill was now crying with his wife, the two of them grieving for their loss. Abe had slid down the wall and was sitting on the floor his head in his hands once more. How he wished they had stayed home that night. He wished he had cooked instead of taking Eve out so that she didn't have to cook. He hated himself for that innocent decision, one he would regret for the rest of his life.

Paul squatted down beside him, and reached out to him. He didn't know what to say to him, but wanted to reach him somehow. He slowly helped him to his feet, and together they all made their way to the intensive care. As they arrived at the door Paul's phone rang. He looked at it in surprise. None of them had realised but while they had been waiting morning had arrived.

It was Felicity on the phone, surprised to have woken and found the bed empty next to her. Paul quickly filled her in with what had happened and she asked him to give Abe a hug from her. Paul didn't even bother to pass on the message as he knew at that moment in time it was worthless. The call did, however, make him realise there were other calls that needed to be made. He offered to phone people but Jen spoke up, 'No Paul, thank you but I have to tell the girls myself. You can phone others but please let me break the news to them.'

Paul started with a call to Abe's parents, who rushed to be with him straight away. He then rang Peter, and discussed with him whether he should tell their parents or

126

wait for them to return. In the end they agreed that they needed to phone them, Naomi was sure to want to be there. He found that call the hardest to make, and was glad that his dad picked up the phone in the hotel room.

He was surprised to hear Paul's voice, and then devastated to hear the news. He said they would return at once and would meet them at the hospital. He gently broke the news to Naomi, who cried when he told her the extent of the damage. They quickly dressed, packed and checked out of the hotel, promising themselves they would come back and have the longed for break as soon as possible.

Abe was the first to go in and see Eve, although he couldn't really see much through his tears. He sat by her side, held her hand and told her that he was there and that he loved her. He hoped she could hear him. Part of him actually envied her being sedated. She didn't yet know how great the loss was, or perhaps she did, perhaps somewhere deep within she knew that their baby had gone. Part of him was sure she would know. Eve had been so in touch with the baby. She was ready to be such a good mother and it was cruel beyond belief that she had been robbed of that chance.

After a while he was aware that Jen was standing beside him. She too was lost for words. How do you begin to express the depth of emotion you are feeling? Bill tried to get Abe to come away and get some rest himself, but he refused to move. He stayed by Eve's side until his parents arrived. His dad then forced him to come out of the room. He mum held him and he let go once more. His father joined the huddle and the three of them wept together. They, like Bill and Jen were to have been first time grandparents and had shared the excitement of it all. They were also really fond of their daughter-in-law and worried about how she would cope with all this.

When Naomi and Bernard arrived, he quickly took charge of the situation. He insisted that those who had been there all night should go and rest. He checked Eve's progress and reassured everyone that she would not wake; she was being kept under sedation for that day at least. Abe didn't want to leave her, as though going would put her in danger somehow. His mum and dad offered to stay whilst he went home to rest, and at last convinced him that he would be no use to Eve when she did wake if he had had no rest himself. Paul drove him to his parents' house, and left him in the care of Peter and Jason whilst he went home to try and sleep himself.

Bernard and Jen had decided not to tell their daughters over the phone, but to visit them and break the news face to face, and despite having had little sleep the night before they set off on that sad task.

It was a very sad group of people who walked out of the hospital. Each lost in their own thoughts of how they would help each other through this dreadful event. Each willing Eve to grow stronger, yet dreading the moment she awoke and faced the realisation that her daughter was gone, and with her the chance of any other children.

Chapter 18

Rebekah was still eating her breakfast when her parents walked in. She had wondered where they were, but presumed she had forgotten them telling her they had an early start. She didn't seem to hear much that was said to her these days, except the sweet nothings Adam whispered into her neck as they cuddled. Just the thought of him made her tummy feel funny and she was longing to see him again. She hated saying goodnight to him, just wanted to be with him twenty-four-seven.

Something about the look of her parents brought her back to the present. 'What's wrong?' She had the feeling that something really bad had happened. Her mum was crying, her dad struggling to hold back the tears. Bill walked towards her and pulled her into his arms. Rebekah began to cry, she didn't know what it was, but something big was happening.

'Darling, I have some really bad news to tell you,' her father began. Then as gently as he could he told her about the accident, how a young man driving recklessly had stolen Eve and Abe's baby, and any future babies they may have wanted. He tried to reassure her that Eve would be fine, but Rebekah was beyond hearing that. She hit her fists against her dad's chest time and again, crying and screaming about how unfair it was.

Jen left the room, unable to cope with her daughter's grief. She quietly phoned Rebekah's work and explained that she wouldn't be in that day due to a family loss. She then phoned Greg. She caught him just leaving the house. She refused to give him details, but asked him to keep Leah there until they arrived. He promised to do that and went back into the house, sat his wife down and together they waited for her parents to come.

Rebekah refused to be left home alone, and Bill felt happier taking her with them anyway. So, together, the three of them set off for Leah's house. They were silent in the car, the two women still crying silently. Once they arrived at Leah's house Bill once more took the lead as he had with Rebekah.

Greg stood with his hand on his wife's shoulder as they heard the sad story of the night before. Leah began to cry and Greg turned his face away, trying to imagine how he would have felt in Abe's shoes. Leah turned and clung to him, sobbing. He smoothed her hair and cooed to her to offer some sort of comfort. He drew her from the kitchen stool into the living room and onto the sofa. There he sat on one side of her and Jen on the other, both trying to comfort her. Bill stood across the room, Rebekah in his arms. It was a sad scene, nothing being said and yet support for each other filling the room.

Eventually Bill said they needed to go. They still had Rachel to tell. He asked Greg if he would care for Rebekah for them until they returned. He assured him that he would, and asked if there was anything else anyone could do at the moment. Bill shook his head sadly. 'All we have now is time. Time, to wait until she awakes, and then time to help her heal. We are a strong family, and we will come through this together. Just take care of my girls for me, we'll get back as quickly as we can.'

Bill and Jen drove on to Rachel's house. Bill was hoping that Paul had had the forethought to stop Felicity from ringing Rachel. He had, and she was surprised to find her serious looking parents on her doorstep. 'What are you two doing here? And why the long faces?'

Bill ushered her back into the house. He sat her on the sofa and gently told her the news. She was solemn as she listened and then tears filled her eyes. 'Poor poor Eve, she was so looking forward to being a mother.'

Jen looked at her daughter in disbelief. Was that it? Was that the total reaction she was going to have? Everyone else was so devastated and yet she was hardly moved. Anger began to rise in her. She tried to control it, knowing it was just a sign of how much emotion she was feeling, but it took every ounce of self control she had not to get hold of Rachel and shake her.

Bill sensed that his wife wasn't coping and decided to get her away as soon as possible. 'Do you want me to call Nigel for you?' he asked his daughter.

'Oh, no it's ok, I'll phone him. You get back to the hospital. But do keep us updated. Let me know when she is up to having visitors.'

Bill quickly caught hold of his wife's arm and with a quick kiss on Rachel's cheek they left. He had no sooner driven out of her drive when Jen started. 'Is she inhuman? What is wrong with her?' Her voice rose on every word. Bill tried to soothe her, but was pretty angry himself. 'I mean she reacted as though we had told her Eve had appendicitis, not that she has just lost a baby, been in a terrible accident and had her whole life shattered.' Jen continued to fume all the way back to Leah's.

Greg let them in, and they found Rebekah and Leah cuddled together still crying. Jen began to tell them about Rachel's reaction, and they joined her in being angry. Bill and Greg left them to their ranting and went into the kitchen. Greg automatically put the kettle on.

'How are you coping?' he asked gently.

'I'm not really. I guess we will all take time to come to terms with it, but I am dreading the moment Eve awakes. I think Abe is holding it together to a certain extent until then. I think the two of them will break together, and somehow we have to catch all the parts, and help put them back together again.'

131

'If any family can do that, this one can. I don't know of a stronger family Bill, well with the obvious one exception in Rachel, but even that is giving the girls something to focus their anger on which may not be a bad thing.' Bill nodded and accepted the cup of tea Greg offered him. He was suddenly very tired, and he felt old.

They walked back into the lounge and offered tea to the others. Each took a cup, for the comfort of having something to hold more than for the drink. For a while they sat in silence. Then Bill said they should go home and try to sleep for a while before going back to the hospital. Jen tried to resist, but was so weary she had no fight left in her. Rebekah asked Leah if she could stay there, and was grateful that she agreed.

Meanwhile, Bernard had dropped Naomi at home, where she was glad to find that Abe had fallen into a deep sleep. She decided to stay there ready for when he awoke. Bernard went off to break the news to his parents. Naomi was happy to find the breakfast pots waiting, and set about washing them, despite the protests from the boys. She fussed over the cats and put some extra biscuits down for them. Then she sat on the sofa and Peter held her hand as she bowed her head and prayed for her family.

Peter and Jason just sat, quietly, both lost in their own thoughts. It was so hard to come to terms with. They had been out the evening before. Peter almost wished it had been them in the accident, at least that way the baby would still be here.

Paul was sitting in his lounge wondering what he could do to be proactive. Eve, and hopefully Abe, were asleep, so he couldn't be with them. In the end he decided to go to the scene of the accident. What he found there horrified him. How either of them had got out alive was nothing short of a miracle. The car was a wreck, a burnt out wreck. Accident investigators were there at the time. Paul introduced himself and tried to get them tell him what they thought, but they were tight lipped.

He made his way from there to the police station. There he managed to speak to the officer in charge of the case. He told him how lucky he thought his friends were, though he had been sorry to hear about the baby. Two of the youngsters in the other car had walked away, but the front seat passenger had died. The driver was to be charged with reckless and dangerous driving. That was no comfort to Paul at that moment, but at least he could use that information to reassure Abe that he wasn't to blame.

Abe had been so sure that it was his fault the night before. Paul determined to get his best friend through that. He wasn't going to let him punish himself with guilt that he didn't deserve. He returned from there to the hospital. Abe's parents were still there, sitting outside of Eve's room, watching her through the glass.

Paul got coffees for them all, which were gratefully received. They took turns of going in to spend a few minutes with Eve, speaking softly, assuring her that they were there. It seemed useless, but people said that patients could still hear you, even when unconscious, so they tried. It was hard to think of things to say. Paul recalled some of the funny things that had happened to them over the years.

They were sweet memories for him, but brought tears to his eyes, as he looked at Eve looking so small and helpless there. He wondered how he would feel if it was Felicity in that situation, but somehow he couldn't imagine it. Losing a baby must be one of the hardest things to face. He tried to imagine what it might be like to be an expectant father and then having that snatched from you.

He decided to leave Abe's parents there and go to his parents' house to be with Abe. He arrived to find Abe was still asleep and Naomi intended to leave him there for as long as possible. In sleep he didn't need to deal with the realities he was facing. Paul updated everyone on what he had managed to find out. Bernard had returned home and was sitting quietly in his study. He had phoned the surgeon who had operated on Eve, and learned a lot more of the details. He didn't go into all the ins and outs of it, but told everyone how lucky they were to still have Eve with them.

He knew that there would be times when she was coming to terms with her loss when she might wish she hadn't survived, but eventually she would be able to recognise what a lucky, lucky girl she was. He hugged Naomi, which all of them seemed to be doing in turn. She returned each hug, and gave thanks for a family that pulled together when they had to.

The whole family found themselves going through the motions that day. In each house, someone would boil the kettle, or make some sandwiches, but everyone was really on autopilot. There was nothing to be done until Eve awoke. Then they would all rally round. Then they would all have things to do. But for now they just had to wait.

Abe awoke mid afternoon. For a few seconds he wasn't sure where he was. Then reality hit him. It was like a ton weight being dropped on him. It winded him, and left him struggling for breath. In an instant he remembered. Eve was in hospital, sedated, and he was going to have to tell her that their precious baby girl had died. He pulled himself out of the bed and walked down the stairs. Naomi was there immediately and fussed around him.

He wanted to push her away, but knew it would be unkind. He forced himself to eat the food on offer, and then had a quick shower, borrowed some clothes and asked Paul to take him back to the hospital. He wanted to be there. He wanted answers from the doctors. They drove in silence, neither needing words. As they drove into the hospital car park Abe began to tense. Paul stopped the car,

134

and then put his hand on his friend's arm. 'You ok?' Abe nodded and together they walked into the hospital.

They arrived at the intensive care unit and Abe's mum rose to hug him. He held her tightly, drawing strength from her. Then he entered Eve's room and sat beside her. 'Hey baby, I'm back. I love you so much Eve, please come back to me soon. I need you here with me.' Tears slid down his face and he brushed them away impatiently.

After a while he went back outside. He wanted to ask the people there for some advice. He wasn't sure whether he should go and see the baby, or whether he should wait to do that with Eve. Part of him felt it would be disloyal to go on his own, that it should be something they did together, but the other part of him didn't want his baby girl there by herself. He wanted to go and tell her how much they loved her, and how sorry they were that she couldn't stay with them.

In the end he decided that Eve would want someone to have been there with their baby. His mum offered to go and buy some prem baby clothes for them to dress the baby in. Abe smiled at her and whispered, 'Thank you.' Then he went with Paul to arrange to see the baby. A very kind nurse came and took them to a small room where the baby was lying in a crib. She was tiny, but perfect. Abe's heart broke as he saw her. He touched her tiny face with one finger and wished he could somehow breathe life into her. She looked as though she were just sleeping. Paul stood at the side of him with tear filled eyes. Together they just looked at her, and then Paul left the room, giving Abe some time alone with his daughter.

'Hello, precious one. It's Daddy. Mummy has to sleep at the moment, but she will come to see you soon. We love you so much. I'm so sorry you couldn't stay here with us, but you make sure you are ready to meet us when we come to join you. I'm sure God has a special angel there to look after you for us. Just know that you are going with every ounce of love we have. We will never forget you.'

Abe was present a few hours later when they took Eve off of the sedation. He asked everyone else to leave. He wanted to deal with this alone and they all respected his wishes. He never told anyone what was said between him and Eve. Somehow he told her that their baby had died. Somehow he broke the news that there wouldn't be any more babies. It was hard, it was painful, but they grieved together, and their love was strong enough to bring them through.

Chapter 19

'It needs to be a bit higher on the right hand side.' Adam rolled his eyes at Greg, who smiled back. The two of them were busy putting up the welcome home banners ready for Eve's return. Leah and Rebekah had been fussing all morning, wanting everything to be perfect. The two men were just following orders, and trying to be patient.

Over the last six weeks the house had been transformed. At Abe's request the four parents had packed all the baby things away. The mother's had lovingly folded all the baby clothes and placed them in a box in the loft, in case Eve wanted to look at them. The furniture had been dismantled and placed there also. The nursery had then been redecorated by the two dads. It was in neutral shades, with a bed settee, a bookcase, and little else in it.

Abe had asked them to do it because he couldn't face it, and it needed doing before Eve came home. He wasn't going to let her face that. She was doing well, but still had times when she would cry uncontrollably. The two of them were having counselling, arranged by Abe's boss, and it was helping, but it was a long road.

Just recovering from the physical damage was going to take enough time. Eve was walking again, but still needed a lot of physio. She would be off work for a few months yet, and Abe was hoping to convince her not to go back. If he could he would have her wrapped in cotton wool and kept her safe forevermore. He fussed over her continuously.

Occasionally Eve got cross with him, but most of the time she felt comforted having him there. In the same way that he felt guilty for the accident because he was the driver, she felt guilty for having been unable to save their baby. Sometimes in the dark of night when she was alone, Eve worried that Abe would leave her and go off to be with someone who could give him children. Those were her darkest moments. Her parents had other children who could give them grandchildren, but Abe was to be left childless because of her.

Right now though, Eve was fighting another battle. She was putting off leaving the security of her hospital room for as long as possible. She hadn't told anyone how scared she was of getting into a car again. Abe was chivvying her along, trying to get her organised and she was becoming short tempered with him. 'Just leave me be. I'll do it at my own speed and it that isn't quick enough for you go on without me.'

She sat on the bed, tearing streaming down her face. Megan, the ward sister, came and sat next to her. She shooed Abe away to get coffees. 'Now then, come on Eve, what's really bothering you?' She patted her hand softly. Eve knew her hands were shaking and guessed that Megan could feel that too. She couldn't bring herself to actually say the words. Megan however, had seen patients recovering from serious car accidents many times before. 'Is it the thought of going in the car?' Eve just nodded.

'OK, that's not uncommon with people who have been through what you've been through. And I'll say to you what I always say to them – think of all the times you have been in the car and nothing bad has happened, and weigh that against the one time something bad did happen. Then find that rational part of your brain and tell yourself it's not likely to happen again.'

Abe arrived back with two coffees. 'None for me then,' Megan teased. 'Abe, is there anyone else who could come to pick you up? Could you leave your car here and come back for it later?'

'Well I could ring my Dad, why?'

'Eve is nervous of being in a car again. For you it was easier, you had to be back in one the following day. Eve's had six weeks of the fear building to an irrational level. And, before you even think it, it isn't your driving. I just think it would help if you were in the back with her, holding her hand.'

Abe nodded and went to call his Dad. He said he would come straight away. Abe turned back to Eve, 'Why didn't you say something?' She just shrugged her shoulders. He pulled her into a hug and dropped small kisses on the top of her head. 'I want to help you through this Eve, but you have to talk to me, I can't help you if you don't.'

The journey home was uneventful. Abe's dad drove very carefully, so as to make no sudden braking movements. Eve found it hard to breathe, but gradually began to relax with the two men making light conversation all the way. As they pulled onto their drive Eve was surprised to see the door open and people come flooding out of the house. Her eyes filled with tears as she realised all the people who meant most to her were there.

It was Paul who opened the car door and bowed deeply. 'Welcome home milady.' She laughed and gave him her hand to help her out of the car. Then Rebekah and Leah were there hugging her, her parents and Abe's mum standing just behind them. Naomi and Bernard, Peter and Jason were also there. Eve was moved to tears, not that that was rare at the moment.

'Alright, let the girl get in the door,' Bill chided his younger daughters, and drawing his eldest from them he hugged her whispering, 'Welcome home darling.'

The party atmosphere in the house was rousing. It was impossible for anyone to feel down with so much love and laughter surrounding them. Abe felt as though he couldn't get near Eve at all, so many people wanted to assure her that they were there for her. He was glad they were there, but was also ready for them to go and leave them alone for a while. Jen seemed to sense his need, and began to move people towards finishing drinks and saying their goodbyes.

Abe went with Paul to pick up his car and by the time he got back just the parents were left with Eve. Their mothers hugged them both, and so did their fathers. 'All you need to do is lift the phone. Anything you need, anytime day or night,' Bill was choking on the words. She may be a married woman, with a husband to look after her, but Eve was still his little girl. He would have given anything to take this pain away from them.

Abe shook his hand once more, 'We know, and thank you, all of you. We couldn't have got through this without you, but there are bits we need to do on our own, and getting used to being home is one of those. We'll see you soon.' He showed them to the door, and then came back in and sat next to Eve.

'At last,' she said with a sigh. 'It was so lovely of them all to come, but I was beginning to think they would never leave. We are blessed to have such good people surrounding us, but all I want right now is to go to bed, and cuddle my husband. Do you think that's possible?'

Abe didn't need asking twice. He stood and held out his hand. He knew, because he had already checked, that the door to the room which would have been the nursery was closed. It was safe to take Eve up to their room, where they could shut the world away and just be themselves.

Abe had been given some compassionate leave from work, which was starting now that Eve was home. They could take their time, grieve and heal as they needed to. They had held a memorial service for their daughter, Eva Marie, in the hospital chapel, attended by family and friends. It had been important to them to have that. As had the photograph the hospital had arranged. It was in a silver frame at Eve's side of the bed.

She looked at it now as she lay there. Her beautiful baby girl. 'Abe, we have to make sense of this,' she said quietly. 'There has to be a reason, we have to make something good come out of it somehow. I won't survive if we don't.'

'I know,' he replied, 'but we don't have to do it today, or even this week, or month. In time we will see the way forward. For now we just have to concentrate on getting strong. I love you, and if anything I love you even more now than I did before. Those hours when I thought I was going to lose you were the longest, loneliest of my life.' He cuddled up behind her and that is how the two of them fell asleep and stayed there until the morning broke.

Paul had gone home from the welcome home party and decided to catch up on some paperwork. He was glad Eve was home, but was still feeling sad for his friends. It was a great loss to overcome, and whilst he knew their love was strong enough to make it, it was still going to be a painful walk. He took a pile of post that was sitting on his desk waiting to be filed. He had hardly done anything with post since the accident. He pulled out his credit cards bills, and was just about to file them without close inspection when something caught his eye.

It was an item from a Women's clinic. The amount made him take a closer look. What on earth had Felicity had done now. He checked the date. It was while she was at the spa, so there must be some mistake. All the treatments there had been included in the price, and he should know he had baulked at the amount she had claimed it cost.

There was a sudden cold knot in the pit of his stomach. Part of his brain was telling him to file it and enquire no further. Another part was making him determined to get to the bottom of it. He dialled directory enquiries and got the phone number for the clinic. Then before he could think twice about it he phoned them. It took a while to get through to someone who would speak to him, and even then they wouldn't give any details, but Paul gleaned enough to realise what Felicity had done.

He sat with the phone still in his hand for a long time after the call ended. He couldn't think straight. He wanted to tell himself that there was some mistake, that this wasn't happening. Time passed and still he sat. The phone ringing brought him back to the present. It was Naomi inviting them over to dinner the following evening. Paul made excuses, hating fobbing his mum off but unable to do anything else. Felicity and he wouldn't even be speaking by the following evening, though he didn't tell Naomi that.

Felicity entered the room. 'Who was on the phone?' she asked. Paul looked at her in disbelief. Was she really speaking to him as though there was nothing wrong? Yet actually she had been doing that for weeks, how was she to know he had just found out what she had done?

A part of him, desperate to be wrong, wondered if maybe he had made a mistake. Maybe it wasn't what he suspected. Maybe he should ask her. But he was scared to ask. Somehow he managed to control himself enough to say it was his mum, nothing important and that he was busy so could she leave me to get his work finished. If she noticed anything strange in his tone Felicity said nothing, but Paul doubted she would have noticed. Too wrapped up in herself for that. Both she and Rachel had been missing from the homecoming earlier, both claiming that it would be better for Eve not to have too many people round her.

Felicity hadn't gone with him once to the hospital. 'You know I'm not good around sick people,' she had whined when he had asked for the umpteenth time. He suddenly saw what a pathetic excuse for a human being his wife was. Paul tried to control the anger rising within him.

He couldn't think of another time when he had felt like this.

His next call was to the spa. He said he was checking his accounts and could they clarify for him to total bill and itemise it for his wife's recent stay. The receptionist, falling for Paul's charm over the phone was very helpful. She checked on the computer, and then double checked. 'I'm so sorry sir, I can't seem to find a booking for Mrs Smedley,' she told him politely. Paul thanked her and rang off.

No, Mrs Smedley hadn't been at the spa, he should have known that. He wondered whether Nigel knew anything. He doubted it. He would have been an innocent in all of this. But Rachel knew. Rachel, his cousin. Without thinking, Paul grabbed his keys. He went out without a word, got into the car and drove to his cousin's house.

Nigel was still at work, which made it easier for Paul. He intended to get answers from Rachel, and at this moment in time he wasn't bothered how he got them. He rang the door bell, the irony of that polite gesture suddenly striking him as funny. So it was a smiling face that greeted Rachel as she opened the door. Surprised to see Paul there she invited him in. He followed her into the lounge and closed the door.

Suddenly the friendly appearance was gone. 'Care to tell me where you and my wife really went recently?' Paul's voice was cold and hard and Rachel was taken aback.

'Don't you dare come in here speaking to me like that,' she shouted.

Paul was in the mood for shouting too, and his voice was so powerful that it left Rachel in tears. 'I will speak to you however I damn well want. Now I want to know where the two of you actually went. And bear in mind that I must have a fair idea that I have been lied to, to be here asking.'

Rachel sank onto the sofa and went white. 'This is nothing to do with me. If you want answers you need to go and ask your wife. But, think on this Paul, if you had been more reasonable in your demands on her, she wouldn't have been pushed this far.'

'More what? Reasonable? You have got to be joking Rachel. Do you fall for every line she feeds you? .... Oh what's the point? You won't believe a word I tell you anyway.' With that he slammed out of the room, got back into his car and drove home. Felicity obviously hadn't missed him as she seemed surprised to see him coming through the door. The phone was ringing. 'That will probably be your dearest friend telling you I am on the warpath, and you'd better believe her and get her off the phone. We need to talk,' he spat at her as he pushed past.

Chapter 20

Felicity answered the phone, but soon put it down again. She walked into the lounge where Paul was waiting for her. 'What have you done to Rachel, she sounds traumatised?' she began obviously trying to get Paul on the defensive, but it didn't work. Paul was not as successful in business as he was to be easily swayed from his argument.

'You have one, just one chance to tell me the truth, and don't try me on it Felicity, because you will regret it. So tell me, and think carefully before you answer, where exactly did you and Rachel go a few weeks back?'

Felicity went white and plopped onto the sofa. She opened and closed her mouth a few times, but no words were coming out. Paul continued to stare at her and raised his eyebrows. 'You obviously know or you wouldn't be asking,' she finally managed to say.

'I want you to say it,' he screamed.

'We went to stay at a hotel.'

'And?'

She began to cry. 'I went to a clinic and had an abortion.' It was the smallest of whispers, and actually hearing the words he had feared completely winded Paul. He dropped onto the other sofa, head in hands and cried. For a few moments Felicity seemed at a loss to know what to do.

Then she crossed the room and tried to comfort him. His next words left her in no doubt that she was not going to win him round easily. 'Get away from me, bitch. I never want you anywhere near me again.' Felicity felt as though he had slapped her. Never had anyone spoken to her like that, least of all her adoring husband.

'Please Paul, you have to understand........'

145

'Oh I understand perfectly. You decided to murder my child, taking it that it was mine?' The question caught her off guard.

'How can you even ask me that?' she sobbed.

'Quite easily! I obviously don't know you at all, and to be honest I don't want to. I'm going out. Don't wait up.' He stood and left the room. He got in the car and drove away, and then realised he didn't know where he was going. This was the kind of occasion that he would have gone to Abe. Abe and Eve, how on earth would he face them? This wasn't something that he was going to be able to keep quiet. He didn't really want to go to his parents, but where else could he go?

He pulled up outside the house and slowly eased himself out of the car. Every muscle ached. He knocked on the door, praying that his dad would answer it. He did. Paul looked at him, and his eyes filled with tears. 'How's the greenhouse?' His voice was barely audible but Bernard understood his meaning immediately.

'Doing fine son. Why don't you come and take a look.' Realising that his son wouldn't want any questions asked just at the moment, Bernard led him around the outside of the house. Once there, Bernard began to potter as he always did when either of the boys came here. He always gave them time to collect their thoughts, never rushing them. Paul sat on the stool and began to sob. Bernard waited a few minutes and then moved over to his son. He pulled his face to his chest and held him.

'Nothing can be this bad son,' he commented.

Paul gave a bitter laugh. 'Can't it? I've just found out that my wife went and had an abortion a few weeks ago. Is that bad enough?'

Bernard was stunned by his words and sat on the other stool. 'Are you sure?'

'Yes. She admitted it.' Paul went on to explain what had happened that afternoon.

'What do you want to do?'

'Right now? I want to murder her, which is why I walked out and came here.'

'Good decision,' Bernard quipped. 'You can stay for as long as you need. Be that an hour to calm down, or a few days or longer. We won't be able to keep this from your mother though.'

Paul nodded. 'Can I just go up to my room? I think I just need to be alone for a while. Can you tell mum?' Bernard nodded, and the two of them went round to the front of the house, let themselves in and Paul climbed the stairs to his old room.

He lay on the bed and sobbed quietly into a pillow. A few minutes later there was a gentle tap at the door and his mum walked in. She said nothing, but pulled him to her and rocked him gently. Paul could tell that she was crying and he hated her being hurt like this. He knew she would have loved to have been a grandmother, and would have been a wonderful one.

He couldn't speak, wanted to, but couldn't. Naomi didn't need him too. She just wanted to hold him, comfort him, and like him, right now she would like to murder her daughter-in-law. Hopefully this would bring matters to a head. She wanted her son to be happy, and that woman had done little but make him miserable for the last two years.

Paul spent two days in his room. Naomi took meals up to him, and she and his Dad popped in to spend time with him now and then. She kept Peter and Jason away. Paul needed to clear his own head, needed to make his own decisions, not listen to everyone else's opinion.

On the third morning Bernard answered the door to find Felicity's dad standing there. 'I take it he's hiding here?' he said in an over jovial voice. 'Well time for him to come home and face the music. Rows happen, but he can't leave the girl there on her own without a word.'

Bernard stood to one side and ushered him in. As they entered the lounge he asked Peter and Jason to give them a moment. They both left the room, Jason raising his eyebrows to ask who it was. Peter filled him in and then the two of them went out into the garden.

'So what exactly has Felicity told you they rowed about?' Bernard asked, keeping his voice as light as possible.

'Just some silly row she said, but Bernard, it's not for us to interfere, we must let them sort it themselves.'

'Couldn't agree more, which makes me wonder why you are here?'

The other man blustered, 'Now, now, no need to take that tone with me, your son is clearly in the wrong, and hiding away at mummy and daddy's is not going to solve the issue.'

'If that was what he was doing for one minute I would have sent him back to sort it,' Bernard calmly answered, 'but having found out that your wife has had an abortion is a slightly different matter don't you think.' It was obvious that Felicity's father had no idea this was what the row had been about. He went pale. 'Obviously your daughter was a little precious with the truth, when she rang Daddy to go and sort out the nasty husband. I will encourage Paul to at least be courteous enough to let her know what is happening, but I will do no more than that. This is for them to sort, not us to interfere in. Now, I'll bid you good day.'

With that he showed him the door, and closed it quickly behind him. Naomi met him in the hallway and they exchanged looks. Then together they went up the stairs. Knocking on the door they went into Paul's room. 'Your father-in-law has just been. He now knows more than he did when he came. You don't have to make any knee jerk decision, but you should at least let Felicity know what you are doing for the moment.'

'If you really can't face speaking to her, we could go and collect some of your things,' Naomi added.

Paul sighed. 'No, I have to be man enough to do it myself, but I should probably take a witness with me, she is sure to accuse me of all sorts if I don't.'

'Perhaps you should just talk on the phone then, and we can go and collect anything you need.'

Paul shook his head. He was going to face her, but he was not going to be swayed. She could say what she wanted. The marriage was over, for him at least. He could not forgive her for what she had done. Maybe in time he would come to terms with it, but not at the moment. And even if, or when he did, he wasn't willing to be in a dead marriage any longer.

He went downstairs, out to the car, and drove slowly to Felicity's house. He realised he had thought of it as that without meaning to. It was no longer his house. He knocked on the door.

Felicity opened it, and seemed surprised to see him there. 'Why not use your key?'

'Because I no longer live here, so thought it would be polite to knock.' Paul entered and went straight up to their bedroom. He pulled down a suitcase and began to fill it with his things. 'If you play nicely, I will be generous with the divorce settlement. Be your usual nasty self and I will match you point for point. The choice is yours.'

Felicity was shocked by the coldness in his voice. This wasn't quite the way she had imagined them meeting. He was supposed to come back and apologise for storming out, and then be willing to listen to her carefully planned explanation. She was caught off guard. 'Paul, please, let's

149

just sit down and talk. We are both upset, but that's no reason to throw away our whole future.'

'Like you threw away our baby's future?' Paul didn't stop for one moment. He filled one case and started on the second. 'I'll return the cases, wouldn't want to deprive you of a matching set.' He moved onto the bathroom and packed his personal effects. He then lifted the two cases down the stairs. He went into the lounge, to the CD rack, pulled out a few of his favourites, ones he knew Felicity wouldn't want, and made for the door.

Felicity was becoming desperate. She stood in front of the door to stop him leaving. 'Oh please, don't be stupid about it Felicity. What did you think was going to happen? Was I supposed to say "well done you"? Oh no, I forgot, I wasn't supposed to find out about it was I? Well hard luck. I did, and I hate you for it. My closest friends are grieving the loss of their baby, and the opportunity to have any more. I'm supposed to be comforting them, and instead, if I am to be honest with them, I have to go and admit that my wife just went and got rid of our baby, because it was inconvenient. Just move, or so help me I will move you.'

Felicity was now genuinely scared of the anger in his voice. 'If you would just let me explain my reasons you might be a bit more understanding about it,' she whimpered.

'If you had had genuine, good reasons, you would have discussed it with me, not gone behind my back.' With that Paul pushed her out of the way, opened the door, lifted the cases, and then slammed the door behind him. He put the cases into the boot, slammed that as well, not bothering if the neighbours were looking. They were all upstarts like his wife, all competing to see who had the biggest car, or newest extension and he hated them all. He got into the car and screeched off the drive, knowing it would horrify Felicity and have curtains twitching. It was a cheap shot, but that was how he felt. He wanted to hurt her, even if only in small pathetic ways.

That evening Paul sat downstairs with the family to eat. At the end of the meal he spoke. 'Thanks for just letting me be for the last few days. I know it's hard to have to tiptoe round me. I'm not going to make it public knowledge why I am ending my marriage. If Felicity does then, so be it. I just want to spare others the knowledge of what she's done. I've no intention of going back to her, and will, in time, be seeing a solicitor, but for now I just want to chill a little bit.' He turned to Naomi. 'I am alright to stay here I suppose?'

'You don't have to ask that. You know it's ok. I wouldn't want you anywhere else.' She stopped, noticing the smile on his face. It was the first time he had smiled for days. 'That's unless you take to teasing your poor mum too often. Then I will tell you to pack your bags.'

'That could be difficult. I promised to let her have the suitcases back. They are part of a set, and she would hate not to have them all.' Although he tried to keep his tone light, no-one missed the bitterness in it.

Bernard rose, and patted his son's shoulder as he past. He went into his study. He was beginning to feel old. How could so much happen to one family in such a short space of time? His youngest son had announced he was gay. His niece had almost been killed in a road accident, and now his eldest son was ending his marriage. All that and there was still autumn and winter to go. Heaven only knew what would happen next.

He rubbed his hand over his face. It had been so much easier when they were younger. He laughed at himself. Oh, he wasn't just feeling old, he was sounding it now. If he didn't stop this train of thought, he would be thinking pensions!

Naomi came in with a coffee for him. He pulled her onto his lap and rested his head on her shoulder. 'Darling we have to do something to lift us all out of this. How about we plan a holiday somewhere? Hire a villa in the French countryside, one big enough for everyone to come.' Naomi smiled at him, maybe that was just what they all needed. Peter and Jason had time before they started their new jobs; Paul needed to be away whatever his commitments were. Bill and Jen hadn't planned anything for the summer because they were expecting to be doting grandparents.

'That could be just what the doctor ordered.' She planted a kiss on her husband's lips, which swiftly became increasingly passionate.

'This is what the doctor orders,' Bernard murmured. He stood up and went to lock the study door. Naomi raised her eyebrows. It was years since they had made out in the study, but maybe he was right, maybe some good old fashioned loving was what was needed to put this family back together.

Chapter 21

The holiday was surprisingly easy to book. It took just a couple of days to organise. Bernard found a large villa, which would sleep eighteen, that had ten days available. The only problem was having to book the cats into a cattery, which caused Naomi more stress than she was willing to admit. Bernard paid for the villa himself, and then left everyone to arrange their own ferry crossings.

Paul was travelling with Peter and Jason, the three of them deciding to make a detour for a night in a Paris casino on the way down. Naomi wasn't exactly happy about this, but just asked Peter to keep an eye on his brother and not let him spend too much. He was talking in terms of 'the more I lose the less there is for her to get' which worried Naomi.

Bernard and Naomi were taking his parents with them, as his dad felt the drive was too far for him these days. Jen and Bill were bringing Rebekah and Adam, and Leah and Greg were travelling with Abe and Eve. Rachel had declined the offer to join the family, claiming she couldn't be that disloyal to her best friend. 'Good' had been Paul's only comment to that. If he had thought he was causing a rift in the family he would have been devastated, but he knew Rachel wasn't close to any of her sisters and hadn't been since she came under Felicity's influence. Even before that she had never shared the real closeness of the others.

Those travelling straight down all had good journeys. Eve was very stiff after being in the car for so long, but tried not to make a fuss. They were to be in France on what would have been her due date. She was hoping no-one would say anything, but she planned for her and Abe to find a little church somewhere and have some quiet time to themselves.

153

She also intended to get some time with Paul. She guessed he probably thought her and Abe had enough to deal with at the moment, but she was a little hurt that he hadn't been to see them, hadn't told them what had happened with Felicity.

Rooms were soon sorted, and everyone settled in. Naomi and Jen organised a meal, the men cleared away afterwards and then they all sat in the garden enjoying the evening sun. It was warm, quiet and pleasant, and over a few drinks everyone relaxed and began to relish the idea of the long days ahead. Eve was the first to give in to the tiredness, and Abe went with her.

The other youngsters decided to go for a quick walk into the nearby village. They were soon back, having found nothing open, although they took it in good spirits that they were so far from what they considered to be civilisation. They were a big enough group to make their own fun of an evening. For now they settled for an early night.

Everyone was soon asleep and dreaming peacefully. When he woke the next morning, Abe realised that Eve had slept through and gave thanks, hoping being away but supported by family would do her good. He felt extremely hungry, and wandered through to the kitchen, thinking it was early. He was rather embarrassed to find everyone else there and retreated hurriedly to put on more than his boxers. He returned to find a full English ready for him, and placed a kiss on Naomi's forehead as he took the plate from her. She laughed, 'Nothing changes does it? It may be a while since I had you at my breakfast table but I remember what should be on the plate.'

After breakfast everyone just wanted to be outside in the glorious sunshine. Jen and Naomi wanted to go and get some fresh produce from the village, to go with the supplies they had brought with them. Everyone else intended to sunbathe. Eve was the only one not to show off

154

lots of flesh, conscious as she still was of her scars. Her sisters were both in very skimpy bikinis, being blessed with wonderful figures. There was lots of splashing in the pool, lots of lemonade drunk and generally a good time had by all. Elizabeth helped her daughter and daughter in law to get lunch ready, the three of them then declaring that that was them finished for the day, the clearing up and the evening meal being down to other people.

It was late afternoon by the time that the other three finally arrived. Bernard had watched Naomi checking her watch for the last couple of hours and knew she was fretting. He also knew better than to mention it, but he too was relieved when the car finally pulled onto the drive. The windows were down and the music blaring at ear-splitting levels. 'It was nice and quiet here before you arrived,' he commented as he went to greet them.

'Blame him,' Peter pointed at his brother. Bernard looked at Paul and his face darkened.

'Please tell me he is not drunk!'

'Just good spirits Daddy dearest,' slurred his son. Peter shrugged his shoulders and asked his Dad not to blame him.

'He was on a winning streak last night and it's sort of gone to his head,' he mumbled, hoping not to be questioned any further as he really didn't want to explain the full events of the previous evening and that morning. Naomi arrived at the car and was horrified to see her normally sensible son the worse for wear. Paul, however, was delighted to see her and threw his arms around her, leading her back to the group, who by now were all watching with interest.

'Bring the Champagne Pete,' he called over his shoulder. 'Mummy, I am the man who broke the bank of Monte Paris,' his singing was out of key, but left most of the party giggling, or struggling to control their faces. 'Couldn't

155

lose, didn't matter what I tried, but shhhh,' he put his fingers to his lips, 'don't tell the wicked witch 'cos she isn't having any of it – given it all away!'

'What?' Naomi was horrified.

Jason spoke up, 'He insisted on giving it to me last night, but it's ok, I know he doesn't mean that and its all safe ready to give back to him.' He looked really worried as he said it.

'I did and still do mean it. Told you, use it as a deposit on an apartment for the two of you, 'cos I love you, 'cos you have made my baby brother happy, and he deserves to be happy.'

Naomi sank onto a lounger, at a loss as to what to do. She had never seen her son like this before and was more upset than she was willing to show in front of everybody. Bernard raised his eyebrows at Bill and went to her side to comfort her, and Bill got hold of Paul. 'Come on lad, let's get you to your room for a nice rest,' he carried on leading him despite Paul's protests. He took him to his room, sat him down, pulled off his shoes and then laid him on the bed, pulling the cover over him fully dressed.

'Have a good sleep, because you are definitely going to need it before you face your mother!' Paul giggled at the thought, and shaking his head Bill wandered back outside. He heard Bernard before he saw him and could tell that Peter was getting it in the neck. He saw that his wife was now comforting Naomi, and the other youngsters had made themselves scarce.

Naomi sat with her face in her hands, rocking gently and he could see she was crying. Peter also noticed that, and went over to her. 'Mum, I'm sorry, but honestly we did our best. He would have been worse if we hadn't.' This comment didn't help as much as he had hoped it would. 'He won thousands last night, and they brought him Champagne to celebrate and, well I dunno........ I guess he just let his hair down. After being stifled for so long it's hardly surprising is it, I mean Paul always knew how to have a good time, before she got her claws into him.'

'He never, NEVER, got drunk like that!' Naomi threw her reply at him and Peter closed his eyes in despair. He hated to see his Mum so upset, but the truth was he had known if they had been much longer she would have been worrying, and Paul just wanted to keep on drinking, so in the end he and Jason had decided that the only way to stop him was to arrive and let others take over. Seeing how upset Peter was becoming, Naomi's heart softened. 'I know you aren't responsible for your brother, but it's quite shocking to see him so drunk!'

Pete laughed for the first time since arriving. 'Only you could call it "quite shocking",' he teased. Naomi smiled at him. She was relieved to see the three of them safely arrived. She rose and took him and Jason to see their room. 'You'll have to share a twin room,' she said, as though they would hate the very idea! 'There aren't enough rooms otherwise, unless you and Paul share?'

'We'll manage,' a cheeky grin and a wink brought a smile to Naomi's face.

She swatted him away. 'Don't act too pleased and upset your Dad. Let's try and get through the rest of the holiday without upset.' Peter pulled her into a tight bear hug and dropped a number of kisses onto her head.

'I love you Mum,' he whispered, and all was right once more in Naomi's world. She hated being cross with her boys, although she still intended to have some strong words with her eldest when he awoke.

By the time dinner was ready, cooked by Rebekah and Leah, everyone was back to normal. Bernard had checked on Paul a couple of times and found him snoring deeply. He hoped this was just a one off and not the start of

157

a self destruction process. He had left him sleeping. So they ate without him that night. 'That was some arrival,' Abe commented to Peter, which was the opening for everyone to tease him and Jason mercilessly. Jason explained in wonder how Paul had won repeatedly at the roulette table the night before, drawing quite a crowd around him in the end. It was as if he just couldn't lose. He had placed some quite large bets, even putting money on the number that had just come out, and still he won.

Whilst everyone was listening and laughing and teasing Jason about banking the money quickly, Peter managed to whisper to Abe, 'I need your help. You need to talk to Paul. Gambling wasn't his only vice last night, and he wouldn't listen to me, but he will to you.' Abe raised his eyebrows. 'I don't want my parents to get wind of it, bad enough that he insisted on drinking more on the way down here and arrived drunk.' Abe nodded, hoping his guesses were wrong. He would get Paul on his own the next day and get him talking.

They all sat outside late into the evening, a small breeze being welcome after the heat of the day. Then one by one, they went off to bed, each with their own thoughts on the events of the day. Bernard checked on Paul one last time, and found him still sleeping. It was the middle of the night when he woke, and the munchies sent him in search of the kitchen. His head was hurting, and his eyes didn't like the kitchen light, so he turned if off again and hunted in the dark. Even the light in the fridge was too bright. He grabbed some Brie and closed the door quickly. He took the cheese and a French stick and went to sit outside.

In the coldness of the night he began to think about the night before. He had intended to lose a few hundred pounds, just to make a point of the fact that it was his money and he could do with it exactly as he wanted. Fate had had other ideas. He grunted at the thought of how many people in that Casino wanted to win, some probably desperate to do so, and he had just won time and again. Then his mind went to the rest of the evening. He hoped Peter hadn't said anything, though he was pretty sure his brother wouldn't have let him down. He would probably tell Abe about it, but certainly didn't want anyone else knowing.

She certainly had been worth the money though! Paul had quietly asked at the Casino for an escort to be called for him. She had given him the night of his life, and taught him a thing or two. He had even sent Peter and Jason away this morning to spend more time with her. She had been more than willing, as he had been more than generous in payment. He thought back to those pleasant hours, without regret. He knew it was wrong, knew he would be mortified if his parents ever found out, but he had needed her, and she had sensed his need and met it time and again.

He finished eating and returned to his room. He was asleep again within a couple of minutes, his dreams pleasant and fulfilling. He joined the others for breakfast the next morning, still with a bit of a headache. He offered apologies to all, which were accepted with laughter. Thomas ruffled his hair and told him not to worry; everyone let their hair down now and again. Paul grimaced, 'Thanks Granddad,' he shook his head and winced with pain. Laughing Bernard told him it served him right.

The plan for the day was for the women to go off shopping and the men to play a round of golf, and then pick up the food for a barbeque that night. Eve came over to Paul before they left. 'I've missed you lately you know,' she said gently, 'promise me you'll talk to me over the holiday. I know we've been through the mill, but I still want to be there for you.'

159

Paul's eyes filled with tears. 'Eve, its not that simple. I want to support you and Abe, but if you knew what Felicity had done you wouldn't want me to talk to you now or ever.'

Eve couldn't bear to see him so upset and pulled him into a hug. Whether it was the fact that it was Eve, whether it was that he was still feeling ropey or what Paul didn't know, all he knew was that before he had time to control himself he was sobbing in her arms. Adam was the first to notice and turned to Rebekah, 'Your family are great fun to be on holiday with!' he commented. He was laughing as he said it and she turned to see what he was talking about.

She turned back to him looking confused. 'Normally we are all so normal and boring, goodness only knows what's going on.' She walked over to her parents, aunt and uncle and pointed across to where both Eve and Paul were now sobbing. 'Guess plans are going to alter then?' she asked.

Abe came across then and suggested that the others went off and left them three behind. That way, he was thinking he should be able to get Paul on his own at some point. The others agreed and set off. Abe went into the kitchen, made a pot of coffee and then went outside to Paul and Eve, who were still holding each other and still crying.

'Well this is nice,' Abe said, but got no reply. He waited patiently, and eventually Eve pulled away from Paul and went to sit on a lounger. He followed her across, and Abe poured them all a cup of coffee. 'Drink it while it's hot,' he said and they both obliged. 'So, anyone want to tell me what started all that?'

Paul looked at them both. He didn't know where to start. How could he tell them what Felicity had done? The tears started falling again. 'I love you both so much,' he started.

Chapter 22

Eve took hold of Paul's hand. She couldn't begin to imagine what was upsetting him so much. She was crying quietly as she watched him. Abe pulled her into a hug. 'OK, is this a private pity party or can anyone join in?' He was trying to lighten the mood.

Paul looked at him. 'I am so sorry,' he started. 'I know I haven't been there for you and I know that makes me a bad friend, but I would only make you feel worse about everything.'

'You've been doing that for years and we still put up with you,' Abe joked. 'Look, Paul, you just need to treat us like you always did. Yes it's hard, yes we are hurting, but that's why we need you to be normal with us, that's the only way we will ever get through this.'

'I know that, and I was doing, but then........ Well, things got complicated.'

Eve squeezed his hand. 'Just because we are carrying a heavy burden at the moment doesn't mean we can't help you with yours. We both love you and know that you have been through it with Felicity, well Abe probably knows more than me, but, well, what I'm trying to say is we are not so full of our own woes that we can't help you with yours.'

'Neither of you know the whole story, and if you did I would definitely be the last person you would want anywhere near you.'

'You are a harsh judge, Paul. I thought our friendship was stronger than that.' Abe looked hurt.

Paul looked at them both. He knew the time had come to tell them what Felicity had done. He didn't want to, as he didn't want to cause them any more pain than they were already going through, but if he didn't tell them then someone was going to, and that would be worse. He took

161

several deep breaths, blowing each one out loudly. Eventually he started. He built up the details slowly, putting off the moment when he finally had to say, 'She didn't bother to tell me that I'd hit the jackpot, third time lucky, she just went off and had..... had........,' he couldn't finish the sentence, but they had both guessed what he was going to say.

Abe sat with his mouth open, not knowing what to say. He was angry. Angry that anyone could do that so flippantly, but angrier still that she had done it to Paul. He knew that his best mate would have made a brilliant father, as he had hoped that he would have done. The difference was, Eve had had no choice and was as bereft as he was, whereas Felicity was glad to be rid of an inconvenience.

Paul was staring at the ground not bearing to look at either of them. He wanted to have the strength to walk away and leave them to discuss how they felt, but somehow his legs wouldn't move, and anyway Eve was still gripping his hand, the grip getting tighter by the minute. Suddenly she threw herself at him. Paul found the breath knocked out of him, and then that it was almost impossible to take another breath. Somehow he managed to loosen Eve's grip. As she moved back her eyes held his and he knew that everything was going to be alright. He had so dreaded losing this precious couple, but now he saw how stupid that had been.

Suddenly, she was talking at an alarming speed. 'You poor man, I am so sorry Paul, I can't believe even she would do such a thing. No wonder you have left her, and about time too. She never made you happy. You, like us, have been robbed of the child you longed for and that's wicked. It was a wicked thing to do, wicked. Why didn't you tell us? Why?' She pulled him into another hug, clinging to his neck as though her life depended on it. Paul returned the hug, both of them drawing strength from the other.

162

The moment was broken by Abe. 'Now that my wife has stopped gushing, perhaps I could say a word or two. Paul, I can't believe that you thought for a moment that we would blame you, but I guess emotions have been running high. You are my closest friend. If anything this will only bring us even closer, sharing a loss. At least we could have a service for Eva, you have had nothing. Does everyone else know the real reason you have left Felicity?'

Paul moved away from Eve, standing and turning to face Abe. 'Just my parents, Pete and Jason. Well, Felicity obviously knows, but I doubt whether she will have told her parents, although I think Dad may have told him when he came round. Rachel was with her, when she went for the abortion, so she knows. But of course, she will keep the secret for Felicity, and I am sure by now they have concocted some dreadful tales about me, so that the blame for the marriage failing falls firmly at my feet. So be it, I'll gladly take the blame just to be rid of her. She tricked me into a sham marriage, stopped me from being myself, made my life miserable and now its over. So give us all time to recover from our losses, and then let the good times roll.' He smiled weakly at his friends.

Abe hugged him, the years of friendship passing from one to the other. As they parted Abe quipped, 'Just lets not make too many of the good times like yesterday. I don't think your Mum would cope.' Paul laughed. 'I think you and I should talk about your behaviour since you've been in France. Can't have you going astray now can I?' Paul blushed slightly at the words, guessing that Peter had told Abe what had gone on, if not in detail then in part.

The three of them walked back into the house to find something for lunch. None of them felt like leaving the safety of the villa, and none wanted to deal with other people. Abe found some bread, pate, cheese and fruit and the three of them sat down to a simple meal. The

163

conversation turned to safer topics. They discussed the weather, Rebekah's romance, how happy Leah and Greg seemed to be, and how long they thought it would be before Peter and Jason set up home together. 'It's been a very dramatic year for our family hasn't it?' Eve said at last. 'And this woman needs a rest, so I will leave you two to chat if you don't mind.'

The two men cleared the plates, made a jug of juice and went to sit outside, finding a shady spot where they could enjoy the warmth without burning. For a while they just sat, both quite tired after all the emotion of the morning. Then, knowing he might not get another chance to speak to Paul alone, Abe decided he should broach the subject of Paris. 'So, besides the luck at the roulette wheel what else were you up to in Paris?'

'What makes you think I was up to anything?' Paul kept his tone light, ashamed of what his friend was about to find out about him.

'Pete didn't give details, but he asked me to speak to you, said you wouldn't listen to him and that I might have more luck.'

'Well, I suppose it was sort of your suggestion,' Paul couldn't quite keep the grin off his face.

'No!'

'Yep, and you're right it is cheaper, and worth every penny. Although I didn't quite stoop to curb crawling, she was a respectable escort.'

'Respectable is an interesting choice of words. I don't know what to say. I mean I should tell you how wrong it is, but part of me understands why, though don't you ever tell my wife I said so, or my boss comes to that.'

Laughing Paul replied, 'I wasn't intending either of them to find out, or my parents either. Pete and Jay were both horrified at me, especially when she was still there the

164

next morning and I sent them both away so I could have a couple more hours of fun!'

Despite himself Abe was laughing. 'You are terrible, Paul. No wonder you were merry when you got here.'

'Abe, I don't want to offend you, or glorify my misdeeds, but she did things I didn't know were possible! I am an educated man. I don't intend to make a habit of it, although,' he paused as though thinking, 'maybe I should compare the English with the French, for purely scientific research reasons of course.'

The two friends laughed together and found that, despite everything they had been through in recent weeks, their usual rapport was still there. They spent a very pleasant afternoon, made even better when Eve came to join them again. The three of them swam, lazed, laughed and relaxed. It was the last part that Naomi and Jen noticed as soon as they returned. Both were relieved to see it. They had had a wonderful day shopping. Jen had bought some things for Eve so that she wouldn't be left out of the fashion show her sisters were planning that evening. In fact, between all the women, there were things for everyone. Naomi had enjoyed buying for her husband and her three boys just as much as she had enjoyed buying things for herself.

Eventually the men returned, having had an equally happy day. Greg had won the game and as such had been nominated the chef for the evening. 'I don't know how that works though,' he moaned. 'Surely the winner should be waited on all evening, with his wife as his main servant.'

Leah laughed at the idea, knowing that he didn't mean a word of it, and also knowing that he would claim his prize later that night. She was so happy, and so glad that she and Greg were married. It was everything she had dreamed it would be. Although she wanted a baby she was willing to wait, partly because they needed to save some money first, and now because of her sister too. She wasn't sure how she would be able to tell Eve when the time came that she was pregnant, it would seem so unfair. Greg saw the cloud cross her face and came over to hug her. 'I was only joking honey,' he whispered into her ear.

'I know, I was just thinking about other things.' He pulled her close, guessing as he saw her look towards Eve what had gone through her mind. Although they had not been married that long, he understood his wife very well, and often guessed what she was thinking. He hoped she was planning the same end to the day as he was. He hadn't been sure about being on holiday with his in-laws, he got on with them very well, but wasn't sure how Leah would feel about making love with her parents in a room nearby. He needn't have worried though. Leah was every bit as exciting here as she was at home. They had had a perfect honeymoon, and although they were at work all day at home, they still found time for each other almost every night.

Now on holiday, and seeing her in a bikini in the pool or sunbathing, he had plans to enjoy his wife. The bikini clad girlfriend was having the same effect on Adam. He, however, was not sharing a room with Rebekah and was frustrated as a result. He was hoping to get some time alone that evening. He had made a decision on the golf course that day. He had spoken to Bill quietly, who had pumped his hand hard, grinned at him, and promised not to say anything to anyone. Adam just hoped Rebekah was as positive. He thought she would be, but couldn't help being nervous, it was a big decision.

Elizabeth and Thomas were also enjoying the holiday. They loved spending time with their family. The youngsters had a bit too much energy sometimes, but then they would just slip away to somewhere quieter and enjoy each other's company. The heat and the holiday

166

atmosphere was putting a sparkle in Thomas's eye too. Elizabeth giggled as he winked at her. Just lately she had noticed that he was slowing down. Once or twice she had been a little worried, as he was becoming forgetful, or even confused. She was glad that the holiday was bringing him back to the man she knew and loved.

Greg proved to be a very good cook and the barbeque was a huge success. The girls then decided that there was to be a fashion show by the side of the pool. Everyone in turn was sent to try on the new things and come to show everyone. The evening was one full of laughter. Jason was once more surprised and moved that he was included. It still surprised him that he was now one of the family.

He played his part beautifully, putting on a wonderful display of model poses, which brought the house down. In fact he stole the show, and Peter watched him with pride. He was more in love with him than ever, especially after his support in Paris. He knew that Jason was uncomfortable about the money Paul had insisted he had, but also knew that Paul would not take it back. He had been thinking about it and had an idea that he hoped Jason would go for.

And so it was that the group broke up quite early. Couples disappeared quietly, whether for a walk or for bed. Soon it was just the three that had spent the day at the villa left sitting by the pool. Eve and Abe didn't want to leave Paul by himself and were happy to stay chatting. He appreciated their friendship, but eventually said he was going to bed, leaving them there. The following day was the one Eve and Abe were both dreading. Abe had looked at a map and found a little country town not too far away that would have a church they could go to. They talked about it and Eve said she wanted to leave before the others were up.

They could leave a note, she just didn't want, or rather knew she wouldn't cope with, any fuss.

Having made their decision, the two walked arm in arm to their room. There Abe gently undressed his wife and took her in his arms. Their love making was gentle, but with a depth of feeling that they had never reached before. It was as though they needed to lose themselves in each other. Eventually they fell asleep cuddled together, the two still seeming to be one.

Rebekah was beginning to wonder what was up with Adam. He had been quiet all evening. She wondered if he was feeling ill or, worse still, if being with her family was becoming his worst nightmare and he was wishing he was back home. They had walked quite a way, when he eventually stopped and turned to look at her. He began to kiss her passionately and she responded with relief. Then he pulled away, although he could easily have continued. He held her face in his hands and said gruffly, 'I love you Beks, more than you will ever know.'

She smiled up at him, 'I do know, and I love you just as much.'

'In that case,' he paused and took a deep breath. 'Will you marry me?'

Rebekah's answer was lost in her throwing her arms round his neck and smothering him with kisses. 'I take it that's a yes then?' Adam laughed.

'Yes, yes, yes, yes, yes! Let's go back and tell everyone right now.'

'Let's not!' Adam pulled her into his arms and began to kiss her passionately. He wanted this moment to belong to just them, and anyway he had the impression that the others would all be in bed by now. He wished he could take Rebekah there, but he wouldn't disrespect her parents when they had allowed him to come on holiday with them. Instead he had to make do with a country lane and the thought of a cold shower when they got back to the villa. Eventually he pulled away from her, and they both reluctantly walked back. Adam wished he had decided before they came away that this would be the right time to propose, then he could have had the ring ready. As it was, Rebekah would have to wait until they returned home and go with him to the jewellers.

Back at the villa, Peter was putting his idea to Jason. 'Paul won't take the money back Jay, whatever you say. So how about using it to help your Mum?'

Jason looked slightly confused. 'How? How can it help Mum?'

'It would make a nice deposit on a flat, or pay a year or two's rent on a small place. We could help her start a new, free life. One where you and she could see each other, one where you wouldn't have to worry about what your Dad is doing to her.'

Jason was choked as he said, 'Do you think Paul would mind if we did that? I mean, if she would do it we could help her and see she was ok. It would be so good to know she was away from him, and I'm sure she only stays because she can't see a way out.' He flung himself on Peter, holding him tight. They continued to talk the idea through long into the night.

It was late by the time everyone was sleeping in the villa that night. All of them safe in the love that surrounded them. Rebekah and Jason both looking forward to going home to put their new plans into place. Adam thrilled that Rebekah wanted to marry him, Peter thrilled that he had finally been able to suggest something to pay Jason back for what he had given up for him. Paul contented that his life was moving forward, even if he had a divorce to get through. Naomi snuggled into Bernard, peaceful because all the people she loved most were safe and secure. Jen cuddling Bill, having cried herself to sleep knowing what

169

the next day held for her eldest daughter. Bill sleeping peacefully, knowing that however hard the next day was they would get through it, and possibly have reason to celebrate too. Leah and Greg sated, and her grandparents likewise.

Chapter 23

The sun rose early the next morning with the promise of yet another glorious day. Eve had woken just before sunrise and was lying quietly gazing at the ceiling. Last night she had felt so close to Abe, but now again she could feel the cold hand of fear gripping her heart, filling her with dread that he would leave her. She knew if he did she would die. Losing her daughter, her precious baby had been almost more than she could bear. The only thing that had got her through it was Abe. If he went, she would have nothing left.

Today should have been the day they became parents. Oh, she knew babies rarely came on the expected day, but it was the day she would always think of as Eva Marie's day. She turned her head to look at the photo at the side of her bed. She had brought it with her, being unable to even think of not looking at it each and every day.

That slight movement told Abe she was awake. He too had woken early and lay there lost in thought. He had no idea of the thoughts that had gone through Eve's mind. He would have been horrified if he had. Abe loved Eve with all his heart, had done for years. They had met as children. Then of course, she was no more than the cousin of his best friend. She was often at Paul's house when Abe was there, and it wasn't long before Abe was invited to join Paul when he went to his cousin's home, as the two boys were inseparable. As an only child, Abe had loved being part of this bigger family.

It was at Eve's thirteenth birthday party that they had shared their first kiss. He smiled to himself now, remembering how horrified Paul had been, and how because of that he had played it cool for a while afterwards, much to Eve's distress. By the time she was fifteen she had been constantly by his side. He had known then that she was his soul mate and that he would have done anything for her.

He had explained it all to Paul one day, who, though not fully getting it back then had accepted it, just warning him never to hurt her. And he never would. He still blamed himself for her being injured, and for the loss of their child. Now he gently felt for her hand, and they lay there, neither saying anything. No words were needed, and no words were able to say what they were feeling.

Eventually they rose, washed, dressed and made their way to the kitchen, expecting it to be empty this early. However, Jen and Bill were there quietly drinking tea. Jen rose as they entered and drew her daughter into her arms. 'Don't Mum, please don't say anything,' Eve whispered into her shoulder. The two women just stood there holding each other and Abe, unable to bear the painful scene, walked over to the sink. He rested his arms on it, his shoulders beginning to shake as tears ran down his cheeks blurring the view from the window. Bill walked over and a put a reassuring arm round him. 'It's ok lad, it's ok.'

It took a few deep breaths before he said, 'We're planning to go out for the day, spend some time alone. Can you just ask people not to make a fuss when we get back? It'll be easier for us that way.'

After much hugging and kissing, the young couple were allowed to leave. Bill then suggested that Jen joined him for a swim. He knew she needed to be occupied or she would sit and brood all day. They swam lengths side by side, each lost in their own thoughts.

Rebekah was the next to wake up, and she hugged her knees to her chest in pleasure. Then suddenly her eyes opened wide and she groaned. She jumped out of bed and rushed to Adam's room. It seemed to take ages for him to come to the door in answer to her knocking. The second he did she pushed him back into the room and stood with her back to the door.

'This is a nice surprise,' he said, smiling at her.

'Shhh, listen!' We can't say anything to anyone today.' He looked slightly confused and she continued hurriedly, 'Eve's baby was due today. It would be so insensitive for us to celebrate and expect everyone to join us.'

'Oh babe, I'm sorry, I didn't realise. We'll just keep quiet. We can wait 'til we get home if you want, though your Dad will probably think I've chickened it.' At her questioning look he explained, 'I asked his permission yesterday on the golf course.'

Rebekah threw her arms around him again. 'I love you, you make everything perfect. I'll talk to Dad and ask when he thinks we could say something. Is that ok?' He kissed her in reply, instantly aroused by the feel of her body under her pyjamas. The kisses became more and more urgent, both of them wanting more.

Eventually he pushed her away. 'Get out of here before I do things to you that your Dad certainly wouldn't think were alright!' She giggled as she left the room, wishing she had stayed, but knowing Adam was right and loving him for respecting her parents' feelings. She showered and dressed quickly, then went into the kitchen.

Her parents had just returned from the pool and she went over to hug her Dad, getting slightly damp in the process. 'I love you Dad,' she said simply.

'Thought you might,' he grinned his reply. Jen looked slightly confused at this exchange and Bill winked at her.

'I know we can't say anything today, but do you think it would be alright to say something before we go home?' Jen's heart sank slightly, she guessed what this was all about, and she wasn't ready to hear it. She liked Adam,

173

he was a smashing lad, but Rebekah was her baby, and she was still recovering from Leah's wedding.

'Button,' Bill resorted to her childhood nickname, 'You are a wonderful girl to think of your sister like that. I am sure we can arrange something before we go home.' He looked over her head to see if Jen had regained her composure, having noticed her initial reaction. He could have kicked himself, he should have warned her. She had recovered and she walked over to hug her daughter.

Bill left the two women gushing over the romance of the proposal and went to shower and dress. Life was so bitter sweet he thought. One daughter so happy, another so sad. He sighed.

It was a quiet group that sat at breakfast. Elizabeth looked around the table as the meal was ending. 'I know it's a hard day for us all,' she said quietly, 'but let's just take a moment or two to ask God to be with Eve and Able.' The family bowed their heads as she prayed.

Paul, having spoken to Abe and Eve the evening before knew they did not want to come back to misery that evening, so he suggested they all go to the beach for the day. Jen smiled gratefully at him, and Bill patted his arm as he passed him saying, 'Good idea!'

It didn't take long for everyone to be organised and off they went to spend a pleasant, if slightly quieter than usual day. Paul disappeared for a while during the afternoon, borrowing Peter's car and saying he had things to do. He returned in time to help pack everything up and return with the others to the villa. Abe's car was there when they got back, but they weren't anywhere in sight. Paul went to see if they were inside, gently knocking on their door. Abe called to come in and he found them sitting on the bed. Both looked drained.

'I know you wanted no fuss,' he began, 'but I couldn't let the day go without doing something.' From his pocket he produced a box from the jewellers he had visited earlier. He handed it to Eve, who opening it found a delicate gold chain with a tiny diamond droplet on it. Her eyes filled with tears at his kindness.

'You two are so alike sometimes,' she said gently holding out her hand to show Paul the delicate eternity band Abe had given her at the church that day.

'Probably because he loves you almost as much as I do!' Paul said gruffly. He then produced another box which he gave to Abe. 'I love you too you know. Thought this might help you write a decent sermon now and then.'

Though he was making light of his gestures they all knew the feeling behind them. Abe opened his gift to find a gold pen. He rose from the bed and hugged Paul. The three of them then went to join the others. Eve was hugged by both of her sisters, but then made sure everyone treated her as normally as possible.

She went back to her room after a while, not quite coping with everyone's efforts at normality. Rebekah went to see her. She wasn't sure whether to say anything, but wanted to tell her big sister, even if no-one else was told yet. She snuggled next to her on the bed, like she had when she was little. The two had always been close, and Eve had always been protective of her baby sister. 'It's ok, Bekky,' she said. 'I know we're sad at the moment, but it will be alright. I appreciate everyone caring so much, and I'm glad we are away from home today, but I can't just carry on as thought it's any other day.'

Rebekah looked up at her shyly. 'Are you up to hearing a secret?' Eve nodded, wondering what her sister was going to tell her and hoping it was nothing bad. 'Last night Adam proposed.' Eve smiled for the first time that day. She hugged Rebekah hard.

'That's wonderful news. Oh Bekky, why aren't you out celebrating? Have you told everyone?'

'Mum and Dad know. Adam asked Dad yesterday whilst they were playing golf.' Rebekah blushed. 'I was planning to tell everyone at breakfast, but then when I woke up I remembered what day it was, and it seemed wrong to be so happy. I'm sorry Eve, I know I'm selfish, but I love Adam so much and I was so excited when he asked me to marry him.'

'You're not selfish at all. You have gone all day without telling anyone and I know you well enough to know how hard that must have been.' She hugged her tight again. 'But I won't have you missing out on all the excitement of telling everyone. Come on let's go. It will take the attention off of me and Abe, and to be honest, that will do us a favour.'

Rebekah shook her head. 'Can we just stay here for a bit? I wanted to talk to you.' She was blushing again, and Eve guessed this was personal stuff. 'I love him so much Eve. When he kisses me I really don't want him to stop, and I want to sleep with him.'

'I cant' tell you what to do honey. I know how you feel, I was the same with Abe, but how far you go is between you and him. If you are ready, and sure, then I'm not going to tell you it's wrong. I should because I am a vicar's wife, but I am also human and I know how hard waiting can be. Just make sure you are careful, and that it's planned not just that you get carried away one night.'

Rebekah was still blushing, and Eve laughed at her. 'I know, I'm acting like a baby, not like a woman of the world, but I can't help it, it's not easy talking about such personal things. That's why I haven't talked to Mum.'

'Talk to Adam then, it involves him. I take it you can talk to him?'

176

'All the time, about everything. He feels the same way.'

'Then let's go back to the others and the two of you can make your big announcement.' Eve pulled her to her feet and walked out of the door. The news had brought her out of herself and she was glad. The two went laughing out to the others who were still sitting by the pool. Bill saw them and raised his eyebrows. Eve went over to stand by him. 'It's fine Dad, I want her to tell everyone. I've had time to mourn today and so has Abe, but something happy to concentrate on will stop this holiday becoming morbid.' Her father hugged her close.

She beckoned to Abe to come over and whispered in his ear. He nodded and so she cleared her throat loudly. It took a while, but eventually everyone went quiet and looked at her. 'Right, now that I have your attention,' she began, 'I, no we, would like to thank you all for your thoughts today, but enough is enough, and there are other people to whom today, or rather last night, was very special. I don't want to steal their thunder so I'll leave it to Bekky, who bless her, has managed to keep quiet all day for my sake. Bekky?'

Rebekah was blushing furiously now, and it was Adam who, arm around her, spoke. 'Last night I asked Rebekah to marry me.'

There was excitement from everyone. Each had something to say. Her parents, Aunt and Uncle and Grandparents offered their congratulations with hugs and kiss all round. Then Leah grabbed her sister. 'I really can't believe you managed to go all day without saying anything!'

'And you moaned at me for not telling you about Jason!' was Peter's comment as he hugged her.

'I hope I am getting to marry you,' said Abe.

'Keep up mate, she's just said she's marrying Adam,' Paul quipped. Then he added, 'You should have said Adam, you could have come with me to the jewellers this afternoon.'

The laughter carried on for quite a while, Paul producing the two bottles of champagne that he had left from Paris and toasting the young couple. He then suggested that they all went out for a meal to celebrate. Everyone liked the idea, and went to change.

Alone in their room Abe checked that Eve was really alright with the idea of going out. 'Yes. Bekky was so sweet when she came to talk to me. She was prepared to wait until we got home you know, though how she would ever have managed that I don't know. I'm glad she told me though, it's helping everyone to move on, otherwise I think tonight would have ended in tears all round and that wouldn't have helped me at all. Are you ok with it?'

'Yep. I'm wondering if it's a record, marrying three girls from the same family.' Eve laughed at him. He had been honoured when Leah and Greg had asked him to marry them, and was sure that Rebekah would want him to do her wedding as well. 'But I am glad you are the one I am married to.' He kissed Eve, and then they hurried to get ready so as not to keep everyone waiting.

It was a really good meal, the restaurant coping well with such a big party turning up without having booked. Everyone enjoyed themselves, and although they were quiet Abe and Eve felt the stress of the day seeping out of them as time went on. Paul insisted on paying for the meal as an engagement present, which earned him lots of hugs from Rebekah.

It was late by the time they returned to the villa and most of the group went straight off to bed. Rebekah and Adam wanted to have some time together. They sat in the moonlight just holding hands at first. Then Adam moved over to join Rebekah on her lounger. Their passion grew and this time neither of them could stop. There, in the moonlight , they made love for the first time.

Chapter 24

The rest of the holiday was great. Everyone enjoyed themselves, and it was a relaxed and tanned group that returned to England. Abe had teased Paul about not stopping in Paris on the way home, and although he was tempted he resisted, knowing his mother would have panicked if he had. On the journey Peter filled Paul in on his idea of how they should spend the money. Paul thought it was a great idea, and generously offered to give them more if they needed it. Jason was choked by his kindness and once more thanked the day he met Peter.

Naomi rushed to the cattery first thing the next day. She couldn't wait to see her two little darlings. She got them into the baskets and home as quickly as possible. She was hurt that they both then ignored her for the rest of the day. Bernard cuddled her and reassured her that their behaviour would soon change, but it did little to cheer her. She went out and bought all their favourite treats but it wasn't until that night, when they both settled on her bed, that they forgave her.

Adam and Rebekah went to a jeweller that day and she chose a simple ruby ring. They then set about planning an engagement party. Adam's mum was thrilled and was making them a cake. She and Jen got together to plan the catering and Rebekah worked hard on the guest list. In no time at all everything was planned, and Rebekah got more and more excited.

On the day of the party she ran around all day, until Bill made her stop. 'Look you are not going to enjoy this party if you carry on. You will be asleep in the corner. Go upstairs and lie down for a while until it's time to get ready. I'll call you when Adam gets here.' Rebekah dutifully did as she was told; convinced she wouldn't be able to rest, but actually falling asleep within minutes. It was Adam who woke her up, having been sent up by Jen. Rebekah decided it was the nicest way to be woken.

The two of them had been even closer since that night at the villa, both relieved not to have been caught out. Rebekah had been to the doctor, keeping the tablets well hidden in her room. Now Adam had woken her with a kiss and he smiled at the sleepy smile that spread across her face. 'Come on sleeping beauty, time to go to the ball.'

'That's mixing up two stories.' She laughed.

'Well even if it is, it's true for you. You are a sleepy head, and it is time to go to the ball, so shift yourself. I'll be downstairs.'

Rebekah moved slowly from the bed, but within minutes she was in the shower, out of the shower, dressed and stressing that her makeup was going wrong. Why oh why were her sisters all married before her and not here to help her get ready? Hearing the yells Jen appeared at her door, saw the look on her daughter's face and came to her rescue. Soon she was ready, looking beautiful, which Adam commented on as she came downstairs.

The party was in full swing and going well by the time Rachel and Nigel arrived. Something made Paul turn towards the door, and his heart sank as he did. With them was Felicity. She was dressed in a simple black dress, and was obviously going for the innocent victim look. He heard Rachel speak to Rebekah. 'I hope you don't mind Felicity being with us. She is so fond of you and it's awful the way the family are treating her as though everything is her fault, when actually she is the innocent party in all this.'

Poor Rebekah really didn't know what to say. She didn't want to cause a scene, but she really didn't want Felicity there. Felicity had never been fond of her, and the feeling was mutual. Adam came to her rescue. 'It's fine Rachel, as long as she doesn't make a scene. I don't want anything to spoil this evening for Rebekah.' He put his arm protectively around his fiancé. Rachel just glared at him and walked away to the table Nigel and Felicity were now sitting at. Knowing that Rebekah was beginning to fret Adam led her to the dance floor.

Paul had watched from a distance, and was pained to see how it had upset Rebekah. He got up and walked across to where she and Adam were dancing. 'I guess they don't do "excuse me's" anymore, but would you mind terribly old chap if I stole your dance partner for a while.' He bowed to Rebekah who was laughing at his mock posh voice. Adam gracefully handed her over to Paul and he whisked her off across the floor. He waited a minute of two and then said what was on his mind. He reassured her that he knew Felicity hadn't been invited and tried to encourage her to enjoy the rest of the evening. 'You look too beautiful tonight to let a frown or a worried look spoil it.' She smiled up at him.

'You are teasing me, and you shouldn't. I know I am not beautiful. Pretty maybe, but definitely not beautiful. And you know that full well. You are married to Felicity, and *she* is beautiful.'

'Beg to differ. Oh yes she has classic good looks, but she is not beautiful. She is an ugly person on the inside, and I don't intend to be married to her any longer. I fell for the looks, but having grown up with three beautiful young women I should have known that beauty comes from the inside.'

'Three?'

'Well, strictly between you and me,' he leaned forward and whispered in her ear, 'I don't count Rachel.' Rebekah almost choked with laughter. He winked at her and then manoeuvred her across the dance floor back to Adam. 'Just be warned,' he told him, 'Rebekah is, to me, the baby sister I never had, hurt her, and you will have me to deal with.'

182

'I don't have any intention of hurting her, but thanks for the warning,' Adam smiled as he took Rebekah off of Paul.

'Good. Now if the two of you don't mind, I am going to call it a night. No Rebekah, please don't make a fuss, I've danced with you and what more could any man want? Oh and by the way, I know I said the meal was your engagement pressie, but there will be a cheque for you to add to your savings.'

Rebekah hugged him and Adam shook his hand. Then stopping just to speak a word to his Mum and Dad, Paul left the party, not seeing the victorious look on Felicity's face.

The next family celebration was exam results. Peter and Jason both had reason to be proud. Peter having always excelled at exams took it in his stride. Jason, on the other hand, was stunned to get a first. Bernard and Naomi bought a convertible for their son, knowing that he had his heart set on one. For Jason they bought a small hatchback, with Paul buying him the driving lessons he would need to be able to drive it.

The only shadow on his horizon was the fact that, as of yet, he had failed to convince his Mum to move. She was scared of leaving his father, scared of what he might do. He rang her during the day to tell her how well he had done, and asked her once more to think about getting out. 'If you were you could have come out with us tonight to celebrate,' he said. Brenda's heart sank. She would have loved to have been with her son today of all days.

'You know he will come looking for me if I leave,' she answered. 'But I do think about it love, every day, and I wish I was there with you, though I am not sure I would fit in to go out with you tonight.'

'Don't be daft, of course you would! They are great; well you've met Naomi so you know.' In the end they agreed that she should come for lunch the next day.

Naomi saw the look of disappointment on his face as he came into the kitchen. Drying her hands on her apron she went over to him and held his shoulders as she looked him in the eye. 'You can't make her decisions for her love. It's a big thing and she needs time.' They talked for a while about how bad things were for her, and Naomi agreed to offer her some encouragement the next day. She was thrilled that Jason had invited his Mum, especially as he hadn't asked if she minded as he once would have done.

The family went out to eat that night. Peter insisted on going in his new car, with the top down. Jason laughed at the pleasure on his face as he drove along. Paul drove his parents, giving him the chance to talk to them. He had started divorce proceedings and had heard from his solicitor that day. Felicity had decided that she would not agree to divorce him, and Paul was furious.

He didn't want to take the shine off the day for the others, so hadn't said anything until he was alone with his parents. He intended to speak to Felicity about it, but not without witnesses present. He asked Bernard if he would be one of them. He didn't want Naomi to be there as it would be too distressing for her. Bernard agreed at once. Paul intended the other witness to be Felicity's father. He would be on her side, of course, but he was a shrewd business man, and Paul intended to put a business deal forward that she would be stupid to decline.

Once in the restaurant no-one would have known that Paul was anything other than happy for his brother and Jason. Naomi's heart went out to him, and more than once she patted his hand, or touched his knee to show her support. The atmosphere was light and full of laughter.

184

Both men were on a high. Peter had a couple more weeks before he started his new job, Jason was starting the following Monday.

They were the last group to leave the restaurant, Paul tipping the manager handsomely for not rushing them out. They drove home, Naomi then putting the kettle on to make coffee. Her two babies almost tripped her up such was their urgency for supper. She laughed, bent down to pet them both, then gave them some Pate out of the fridge. Bernard caught her in the act and stood with his hands on his hips trying hard to look cross. He failed miserably, and Naomi putting her arms round his neck kissed him, putting any other thoughts out of his mind.

Eventually the family went to bed, most to sleep peacefully, Paul to lie looking at the ceiling making plans for his future. He was first up the next morning, and was showered and ready to go when Naomi came downstairs. She was horrified that he was leaving without breakfast, but he assured her he had made some toast, and was having a breakfast meeting with his solicitor. Dropping a kiss on the top of her head and telling her not to worry Paul left.

He was in his office with ten minutes to spare before Andrew Franklin arrived. Andrew had been Paul's solicitor since he started the business and the two had gradually become friends. Today Paul greeted him with a smile, but not the usually wide friendly one Andrew was used to.

'So, she wants to be difficult does she? Well from what you've told me that's nothing out of the ordinary.'

'True! But I will have the divorce, and I intend to meet with her and set out an offer she would be stupid to say no to. I just wanted to run it past you first to make sure I am within the law.'

The two men sat for over an hour discussing the details. Andrew was as straight as they came and would not suggest any of his clients broke the law. He could see Paul was willing to be more than fair for a quick finish to a marriage that should never have been. By the time Paul's secretary arrived he was ready to leave. 'Well good luck, let me know how it goes, and if you need to use plan B definitely phone me first.' They shook hands and he left.

Peter was the last to get up that day, but once he was up he was hoping that he and Jason could spend the day trying out his new car. The sun was shining and he was longing to be out on the open road. He said as much as he ate his very late breakfast. Jason looked downcast and, after some pushing from Peter, reminded him that his mum was coming for lunch. Peter had only met Brenda once, and had liked and felt sorry for her. Now he reassured Jason that they would go out later.

Brenda arrived at twelve on the dot. She had been very punctual every time she came. It was almost as if she had been waiting at the end of the road for it to be time to knock on the door Jason thought, not knowing that that was exactly what she did. She was desperate for every moment she got to spend with her son. There wasn't a day she didn't miss him, and didn't wish things were different.

Today she almost fell on him as he opened the door to her. Jason laughed at her as he struggled free from the hug and kissed her. 'I am so proud of you Jason! My son, with a degree and such a good one at that.'

'A First, Mum, and the first in the family to have one,' he was still laughing. Together they walked into the lounge. Peter was waiting there and he hugged Brenda and agreed with her that Jason deserved praise. She had liked him the first time they met, and now, as they shared their love and pride in Jason, she liked him even more.

Naomi called them through to lunch. She understood Brenda's need to be there on time and had made sure that lunch was ready. The two women hugged and again the greetings were of how proud of Jason they were. Jason was beginning to get embarrassed about the fuss and told them so. Laughing the group sat down to lunch. Brenda's eyes hardly left Jason the whole time.

Eventually the conversation turned to the idea of Brenda having her own flat somewhere. She still claimed she couldn't possibly do it. 'I've told you Jason, it's a lovely thought and I would love to, but he would find me and I'm scared of what he might do.'

'I can understand you being frightened, but you could always get an injunction out against him if he tried anything.' Naomi was trying not to interfere, but she too wanted Brenda to be free of that man.

'There's an apartment just around the corner from here,' Peter said, 'why don't you at least come and look at it with us.'

'I couldn't live round here,' Brenda seemed bemused at the very idea. 'The likes of me don't belong in this part of the town!'

'Mum! You are as good as anyone else. I know he makes you feel worthless, goodness knows he did it to me long enough. But you are a good person, and you deserve the best.'

'It can't do any harm to look can it?' Naomi was gentle as she prompted Brenda to take the chance. In the end it was agreed that she would go to look, although only if it could be viewed during the day as she wouldn't be brave enough to come out of an evening.

Brenda stayed as long as she dared, and she hugged Jason hard before she left. She thanked Naomi yet again for taking care of her son, and hugged Peter and kissed his cheek. After she had gone Jason seemed subdued as he always was when she left. For him it was as though she was leaving him, a worse feeling than his first day of school.

187

Peter guessed how he was feeling and tried to cheer him up. He said how positive it was that she was willing to view the apartment. He then phoned the estate agent, making the appointment for the following day at noon. Jason smiled and crossed his fingers, hoping against hope that she would do it.

The two then went off for a long drive in the new love in Peter's life. 'I think I am going to be second best now,' Jason joked. Peter just laughed, and squeezed his knee. They drove for miles, and Jason couldn't help but smile at the look on Peter's face. This car really was all his Christmases come at once. They eventually stopped to eat at a country pub, then drove home. Jason was glad he had put a jumper in the car as it was quite chilly driving in the dark with the top still down. Peter couldn't bear the thought of driving it without lowering the top just yet.

Their weekend was spent driving. Peter was in his element, and so was Jason after his Mum fell in love with the apartment and said yes to moving into it. She had 'oohhed' and 'ahhed' over everything, hardly able to believe that she could have the opportunity to live somewhere so lovely. The fitted kitchen had brought tears to her eyes, the bathroom left her speechless and the size of all the rooms left her saying, 'who would have believed they could make so much space in an apartment.' It was light and airy, newly refurbished, and beyond her wildest dreams.

They put down the deposit the same day and started planning her escape. Every day Brenda was going to remove a few of her things from the house. Naomi would meet her in town and take them from her. She knew she wouldn't be able to do this with everything, but was just taking the things that meant most to her. Jason had enough left from the money Paul had given him for her to be able to buy any new clothes and things she needed for the apartment. Naomi was looking forward to taking her shopping, although Brenda was saying she wouldn't let him spend all that money on her.

She hadn't told her daughter that she was leaving in case she let anything slip. She intended to phone her once it was done, but wasn't sure yet whether she would be able to tell her where she was living. Her son-in-law was so like her husband, and she was sure he would tell him where she was. Although she was about to leave her abusive husband she was still very scared of what might happen when she did.

Chapter 25

Monday morning found Jason feeling sick. He was nervous beyond belief at the thought of starting his new job. It was better than he had ever hoped he would get and he was desperate to do well. Naomi insisted he sat and ate a cooked breakfast before she would let him out of the door. Peter had got up ready to run Jason to work. He was also insisting on picking him up at the end of the day. Jason loved him for it.

The Drive there went all too quickly for Jason, and soon they were pulling into the car park. Jason's stomach was doing flips and his breakfast was threatening to make a quick exit. Peter gave his arm a squeeze. 'You'll be fine. They are lucky to have you, never forget that.'

Jason smiled at him. 'I'll try not to. Just hate first days, once I'm in and working I'll be fine. I'll text you later to confirm what time I get off.' With a quick kiss he was out of the car and heading towards the doors. Peter watched him go and wished him well. Jason deserved some luck, and although Peter didn't know a lot about design, he knew you didn't get a first in a degree without being good at the subject!

As he walked through the glass doors at the front of the Hamilton Fields building Jason felt his mouth go dry. It didn't help that he was followed in by the other new member of staff, Brandy, who pushed past him as though he didn't matter at all.

She walked confidently up to the girl on the reception desk. 'Good morning, Brandy Rice, designer, could you direct me to my office?' The girl had been in the middle of something and looked up in disbelief at the way she was being spoken to. The tone of voice clearly showed that Brandy thought it was beneath her to have to deal with a receptionist. She checked her computer screen.

'You and the other new designer are to wait here for Mr Hamilton. Sit over there.' She pointed to a couch in the corner of the reception area. It was where they had sat when they arrived for the interviews, before being taken through to the offices.

Brandy tutted at the lack of respect she seemed to be getting. Clearly the girl didn't realise who she was. Jason smiled and winked at the receptionist, who smiled back and blushed slightly, and then he went to join Brandy on the couch.

'And you are?' Brandy asked, with a slight wrinkle of her nose.

'Jason, the other new designer,' Jason replied, trying to look as disinterested as her. He would play her at her own game. He had already decided he didn't like what he saw, but guessed he would be a fool to make an enemy of her.

Cedric Hamilton walked through to the reception. Brandy leapt up greet him, almost knocking Jason off the couch in her hurry. 'Mr Hamilton, how lovely to see you. I've been so looking forward to today. I have so many ideas I'd like to use on projects here.' Jason had now stood and waited behind her. Cedric Hamilton shook her hand murmured something about it being good to be keen and then moved on to Jason.

'Jason, good to welcome you on board. Fantastic result! Congratulations. You'll find a bottle of champagne at your desk, just a little token. A first should always be recognised.'

Brandy stared at him in disbelief. 'You got a first?' Jason smiled and nodded. They were led through to the offices and shown to their design areas. Brandy was to be working with Claudia Boxer, another young designer. Jason was with Trevor Jones, the top designer under Cedric Hamilton and Macalister Fields themselves. He felt really honoured as he had long admired Trevor's work. Brandy automatically presumed it was because Jason wasn't to be let loose on his own, whereas she fully intended to have Claudia following her ideas within days.

Trevor closed the door to his office and invited Jason to sit down. 'It's great to have you onboard Jason. I especially asked for you to be on my team. I loved your design ideas at he interview. Not surprised at all that you got a first. Strictly between you and me, I haven't taken to miss iceberg out there. Too fond of herself that one!'

Jason smiled, and relaxed. The two chatted for a while and then Trevor showed him to his desk. He talked through the project he was working on and gave an area of it to Jason. He then left him to study the file and begin to work. Never happier than when working on designs, Jason was soon lost in thought and before he knew it Trevor was looking over his shoulder admiring his work and telling him it was lunch time.

The two men went together to the canteen. Trevor groaned as Brandy approached them in the line. 'Not found it too taxing this morning I hope Jason,' she said with a smile that somehow didn't reach her eyes. Before Jason could answer, Trevor had jumped in.

'Wouldn't know it was his first day. Fits into the team brilliantly. Had to force him to stop for lunch.'

At this Brandy shot daggers at Claudia who quickly responded with, 'Same with Brandy. Don't know how I survived without her. She has such fantastic ideas.' Trevor grunted, collected his lunch and moved to a table with only two seats. Jason joined him.

'Hamilton Fields will rue the day they employed her,' he commented, 'that bitch is determined to get to the top and she won't care who she steps on in the process. What's her name? Brandy Ice?'

Jason choked and replied, 'It's Rice!'

192

Trevor returned his grin, 'Think I was right the first time, definitely ice in her veins!' They both laughed but then went on to discuss work. Trevor was a dedicated designer. He could, by now, have started his own company, but was happy to continue working for the two designers who had given him his first break. He was now a partner in the firm, and his opinions were usually respected. Jason knew he would learn a lot from working alongside him, and that the more important projects would come his way. He was glad he was on Trevor's team, rather than with one of the younger designers who only got to handle small projects.

The afternoon passed all too quickly for Jason. He was still working when his phone rang. It was Peter saying he had been in the car park for fifteen minutes and was wondering whether to stay and wait or go and come back later. Jason looked at his watch in disbelief. He quickly packed up and got ready to leave. He remembered to pick up the champagne, called his goodbyes to Trevor and was out of the building.

All the way home he gushed about his day. Peter had to smile at him. Once they were home Jason started all over again, describing everything in detail for Naomi. He leaned against the counter in the kitchen and chattered to her as she prepared dinner. The champagne was put on ice to be enjoyed later in the evening. Paul came in and asked about his day and Jason had to tell it all over again.

Bernard arrived home just as Naomi was dishing up. 'So was it a good day?' Bernard asked and Peter groaned. 'Ignore my rude son, I want to hear all about it.'

Jason laughed, 'I think having heard it all three times already he was hoping you wouldn't ask. Yes it was a good day. I am working with Trevor Jones.' Bernard looked blank. 'You must have heard of him! He's one of the top designers in the country. Anyway he is great to work for, and I will learn tons from him. The other new designer is a bit frightening though.' He went on to describe Brandy and left them all laughing at Trevor's adaptation of her name.

Naomi was at her happiest. She loved nights like this, with all her men folk at home and everyone so relaxed, herself included. So much so that she let Paul load the dishwasher for her and went to sit in the lounge next to Bernard. She had met with Brenda again that morning and had some more of her things to go to the apartment. Jason and Peter decided they would take them over. Peter suggested they took the champagne with them.

They arrived at the apartment within a couple of minutes; it was that close to home. They went in and Jason put his mum's things in her room. Peter was beginning to wonder if coming here was a good idea. The furniture they had ordered hadn't yet arrived, so there was nothing to sit on. It also depressed him slightly being here, as Jason was going to be moving in with his mum and Peter was dreading it. He had become used to Jason being there every day, and didn't want him to move out, even though he understood his reasons for doing it.

Peter sat down on the floor and leant against the wall. Jason came and joined him. 'We forgot to bring glasses,' he said. Peter shrugged but said nothing. Jason looked at him, feeling his hurt. He pulled him into a hug. 'It'll be ok you know. Just because I am going to live around the corner, it doesn't mean we won't see each other every day. And mum goes to bingo every Monday, so we are guaranteed one night alone.'

Peter held on to Jason, but still couldn't bring himself to speak. He couldn't believe the strength of the feelings inside him. He loved Jason more than he had ever thought possible. He pulled back from the hug and kissed Jason long and hard. Eventually the two of them pulled apart and just sat holding hands. 'I know I am being unfair, but I've got used to you being there.'

'I still will be there. Outside of working hours the two of us can be together either here or at your parents'. Try to think of it making the time we spend together more special. Now are we going to drink that champagne? Or will it make you even more maudlin?'

Peter laughed, 'No, champagne makes me daft, but we will be drinking out of the bottle like a couple of old winos. Sure you don't mind that?'

'The winos I've seen in the past have never been drinking champers, but we could start a new trend.' The mood had lightened again and the two shared the bottle, sharing their dreams, enjoying each other's company, and ignoring the fact that the wooden floor was hard and rather uncomfortable. By the time they had emptied the bottle they were both giggly. Jason was doing impressions of Brandy, and Peter was howling with laughter. 'She sounds a real dream to work with,' he said.

'I'm just glad I'm in Trevor's office, he has seen straight through her and won't have her working on any of his projects whatever she tries.'

'I wish there was a bed here, we could stay the night,' Peter's voice had become husky with longing. 'How do you think your mum will feel about me staying over?'

'I don't know to be honest,' Jason sounded intrigued by the idea, 'I mean, it's not something we ever discussed. I am sure she knew I was gay, but in that house it wasn't something you could mention, and the idea that my dad would ever have let my boyfriend stay over, well!' Suddenly they were both laughing again. Jason was sure he was going to have a bad head the following day and knew it was time they went home and he hit the black coffee. He said as much, and reluctantly Peter agreed. They stood and made their way to the door. Jason pulled Peter into another hug before they left, 'I love you Pete. You do know that don't you?'

'Yep,' Peter sounded smug and it made Jason laugh again. 'But you had better get me out of here now, or you won't get out tonight, furniture or no furniture!'

The two walked back home, Peter knowing he wasn't in a fit state to drive. He also found it a little difficult to get his key in the lock, which just caused the two of them to start laughing again. Naomi was shocked at the state of them, but Bernard told her to relax. 'What did you expect when they've downed a bottle of champagne, choir boys?' was his comment as he went through to the kitchen to put the kettle on.

Three cups of coffee later, Jason decided he had better get to bed. He left the rest of the family in the lounge and went upstairs. He felt contented: a boyfriend he loved and was loved by, a lovely welcoming, safe home, his dream job, and soon he would have his mum back. Peter was going to wait for the furniture to arrive the next day, and then the day after that, his Mum was finally going to be free of that brute she had been forced to marry.

He was sorry he wouldn't be able to help her move, but he didn't feel it was right to take time off in his first week, and she wouldn't be able to leave at the weekend when her husband was there. She was going to go out as though just going shopping, so none of the neighbours would know anything if asked.

Downstairs, the family sat enjoying each other's company. Bernard and Paul were discussing the politics programme they had watched earlier, and Peter, still slightly drunk, was snuggled up next to Naomi, who was making the most of his soppiness. Peter too was feeling very contented. He hated the thought of Jason living elsewhere, but was hoping Brenda would be ok with him staying over. He liked her, and was pleased that Jason would be reunited with her and would worry less.

Eventually everyone went up to bed, and soon Paul was the only one left awake. He was thinking over his meeting with Felicity the next day. She hadn't been keen on meeting him, but he had managed to get her father to persuade her. They were meeting in her house. For over two years it had been his house, but it had never felt like home and he didn't miss it one bit.

Bernard was taking the afternoon off to be there with him. He had had papers drawn up ready and was hoping her father would see the sense of her signing them. As far as he was concerned the sooner his marriage was over the better. It was as though the scales had fallen from his eyes when he found out about the abortion. Suddenly he wondered what he had ever seen in her. He knew it was her beauty that had captured him, the idea of the perfect wife to complete his image as an up and coming business tycoon, and yet now all he saw was the ugliness within.

He shook his head as though to clear the thoughts. He needed a good night's sleep as he wanted to be fresh tomorrow. He tried to think of something nicer to drift off with and then smiled as the French woman came into his mind. Now that, he thought, was a sure way to have good dreams. Smiling to himself he fell asleep, his dreams those of a happy man.

Chapter 26

Closing the file he had been studying, Paul pushed back his chair and rose. He stretched, pleased with his morning's work. He just hoped the afternoon would prove as profitable. He let out a sigh, but, never one to put off what had to be done, he set his shoulders, and with a determined air left his office. In the outer office he took the time to speak to his secretary, who didn't know what his appointment was that afternoon, but guessed it was something serious from his manner.

He then drove to collect his father. He had dropped him at the hospital that morning to save time now. Together they went to the house that had brought Paul nothing but misery. His father-in-law's car was already on the drive. One of the neighbours was mowing the lawn in front of their own house, and called out a friendly greeting to Paul. He walked over and made polite conversation for a minute or two and headed back to join his father and walk to the door. 'That's probably the friendliest conversation I will have here today,' Paul joked. Bernard smiled back at him, and squeezed his arm as the door was opened and Felicity allowed them in.

Paul nodded at her father as he entered the lounge. They didn't bother with polite conversation, both knowing any niceties wouldn't be meant. The three men remained standing until Felicity walked back in and invited them to sit. The atmosphere in the room was cold and all four of them seemed to have the same set line to their mouths. This was not a meeting of friends.

'So, you don't want a divorce then?' Paul started the conversation in a tone that whilst not rude was certainly not welcoming. When Felicity didn't answer he just raised an eyebrow and stared at her. Still getting no answer he shrugged and continued, 'Well once we have been apart for

198

two years, I can have one anyway, but two years will give me plenty of time to become bitter. Whereas, at the moment, I am willing to be more than *reasonable*. The choice is yours Felicity, but if you want to keep this house, its contents, your standing in the neighbourhood, I suggest you try to be a little *reasonable* in return.'

His voice never rose, but stayed steady and calm, although inside he was boiling with rage at having to be willing to compromise with her. 'I should also say that, so far, I haven't told anyone outside of the immediate family the reason I left you, but it wouldn't take much for me to become very open about our marriage and the reason I want it ended.'

The colour drained from Felicity's face at that. She opened and closed her mouth a few times without saying anything. Eventually her father spoke up. 'I think Fliss was hoping you would come to your senses and come back. There is nothing that has happened that can't be rectified, now is there?'

Paul laughed. 'Well I could answer that, but as I said, at the moment I am trying to be nice.'

'And what is that supposed to mean?' The other man was not being as successful at holding his temper and Paul watched as his face began to redden and that nerve in his cheek begun to twitch.

'Felicity? Would you like to explain our marriage to your father? No? Well then, let's be sensible shall we?' Felicity nodded her head. Her parents had been shocked to learn that she had had an abortion, and she wasn't sure she would cope with them knowing how bad things had been ever since their honeymoon.

'Good, that's more like it! Now, as I said, I am more than willing to be *reasonable,* though I am beginning to hate that word. I will let you keep the house and the contents. I will pay seventy-five per cent of the balance of

199

the mortgage off as well, and pay you a monthly allowance for as long as the company is in profit, but with a minimum of two years. There are, obviously, no offspring to consider and my solicitor assures me that this is a more than fair offer.

You have the option of keeping the house and paying the rest of the mortgage yourself, a remortgage on the little left wouldn't be beyond your means, if you get a job.' Felicity looked horrified at the thought of having to work. 'Or you could sell this, pay off the mortgage and have enough to buy a very nice apartment outright. That would, of course, be up to you. Buy one with three bedrooms and you would be able to use one as the breakfast room you always longed for.' This last sentence was the only time that Paul's tone became bitter.

Felicity still didn't speak, but her father did. 'Fliss, that seems a fair offer. Obviously more went on between you than you have told us, and let's be honest you couldn't stay married to him now; look at how he is with you. You would be miserable darling, and this way you will be free to find someone who can love you the way you deserve.' Paul laughed again at this. He was finding this easier than he had thought. 'You will let her keep the car as well I presume?'

'It's hers. I bought it outright and it's in her name. I am not trying to be difficult about this at all. As you say, this marriage is beyond help. Truth is it should never have happened. We clearly had different views of what makes a marriage. I just want it ended. And no, before you ask, there isn't anyone else. Once bitten, twice shy, as they say. I will not be rushing into another relationship, but I don't want to sit for two years with this one hanging over me. I want a clean break, finished, put it behind me and get on with being me.'

'Alright, you win, I'll sign the papers, but you have to agree not to go telling everyone our business. I don't want people knowing about the baby.'

'Can't say I am thrilled with the idea of everyone knowing you murdered my child either.' Both fathers flinched at Paul's harshness.

'Paul! Don't speak like that, however hurt you feel.' Bernard was stern and the look he gave Paul made him apologise.

Felicity said in a soft voice, 'It's alright Bernard, I know how angry he is with me, and there are moments when I wish I had made different decisions. You would never have left me if we had a child would you Paul?'

Paul looked her straight in the eyes and answered equally as softly, 'No Felicity. You would have had me as a prisoner for life. Whatever else I had to put up with I would have. Really, I should have stuck to my guns and had the marriage annulled straight after the honeymoon. We both knew then it wouldn't work. But hindsight is a wonderful thing. Let's just get it over with and move on.'

'Annulled? You can't do that after you've had the honeymoon.' Paul looked his father-in-law straight in the face and watched the realisation slowly dawn on him. He cleared his throat a few times, then said, 'Felicity, read the papers carefully, then sign them.' He walked over to the mantelpiece and stood with his back to them all. He had clearly learned more about his daughter that day than he was able to deal with, least of all in front of Paul and Bernard.

Felicity read the forms, asked her father to check them for her, and then signed them. 'Thank you.' Paul rose from the chair, shook his father-in-law's hand, wished him all the best, and together with Bernard left. Neither of them spoke until they were at least half way home. Even if his

201

marriage had been a sham, both were still saddened to see it end this way.

At the same time, Naomi and Peter were arranging the furniture in the apartment. Jason had chosen well. He knew Brenda would feel uncomfortable with anything too expensive, but he wanted the apartment to look good. His choices had been simple, which was his normal style in design unless directed otherwise. Naomi thought he had done a wonderful job. She had been out that morning and bought bedding. Both rooms had double beds, and Naomi had made them up ready.

The lounge had two couches, a coffee table, a television and a shelving unit. Naomi was intending to take Brenda out shopping to buy a few personal bits and pieces and had seen a lovely figurine she thought would look wonderful in the lounge. Perhaps a couple of pictures for the walls too. She was determined to make sure Brenda felt happy and settled as quickly as possible. She couldn't imagine being married to a man who thought nothing of giving you a black eye, or being verbally abusive. It would be so different for her to live with Jason in a peaceful, happy home.

Satisfied with their work the two returned home. Bernard had just finished making a pot of tea and poured them one too. Naomi was relieved to learn that Felicity had agreed to the divorce. She had been glad to have something to keep her occupied that afternoon, or she would have fretted. Now she could make the evening meal feeling at ease.

The three men smiled at each other as they heard her humming as she worked. You could always tell when things were fine in Naomi's world by the activity in the kitchen. They heard her open the door to let her two treasures in and then listened to the conversation she had with them. 'One day they will answer her you know,' Bernard shook his head slightly, but smiled as he spoke.

Peter went in to remind his Mum that he and Jason wouldn't be in for tea. After he collected him from work he was taking him to see the apartment and sort his things. Jason had already moved most of his things across, and had decided to stay there tonight so that he could make sure everything was perfect for Brenda's arrival the next day. Naomi was disappointed as she wanted him there for his last evening meal, but Peter pointed out that it wouldn't be his last anyway. The two of them were planning to eat together at one or other home each night. She knew she would have to get used to it, and knew that Brenda deserved time with Jason, but Naomi wasn't looking forward to the nights when Peter was not eating at home.

Peter drove to collect Jason from work. On the way he stopped at the supermarket and picked up some bits and pieces for a meal. With a skip in his step he returned to the car, happy at the thought that he and Jason had a whole evening alone ahead of them, and a new bed to Christen. He was a couple of minutes late arriving at Hamilton Fields and Jason was waiting for him. Brandy saw him get into Peter's car and raised her eyebrows and both men saw the sly smile appear on her face. Ignoring her totally, Jason kissed Peter, leaving her in no doubt as to who he was.

'Whilst that was a very nice hello, I am wondering if it was wise. She looks like nothing would give her more pleasure than to cause you trouble at work.'

'Oh I have no doubt what she is planning, but it won't do her any good. Her little followers, I know its only two days in but she already has followers, will no doubt agree with her that it's disgusting, but what most of them don't know is that Trevor is gay, and so is McAlister Fields!'

Peter laughed loudly and drove away. 'How did you discover that, if most of the workforce doesn't know?'

'Trevor told me. I was talking about you this morning, saying how merry we were on that Champagne. He was just asking general questions about where I live etcetera, and somehow he got the whole story out of me. He was pretty angry that I had had it so rough, and amazed that, even with all that to deal with earlier this year, I had managed the first. He told me he has been with his partner for over twenty years. He keeps it quiet in the office, only a few people know, but he has said he will invite us over for dinner soon. He was really sweet about Mum, and glad she is escaping.'

They soon arrived at the apartment and Jason was pleased to see it looking like a home at last. He tweaked things a little, making Peter laugh. He had to admit that, although the differences were only slight, they somehow made a big difference to the look, and made the rooms look perfect. Peter served up the food he had bought and the two chatted while sitting at the breakfast bar in the kitchen. They went from there to Jason's bedroom, and it was a very reluctant Peter that left him there and returned home.

Jason lay in bed listening to the strange sounds around him. It felt weird being alone in a room he wasn't used to. He looked at the room, which he loved, and felt the tears prick his eyes. If anyone had told him a year ago where he would be today he would never have believed him. He only hoped his Mum didn't lose her nerve in the morning and that she was here waiting when he got home from work. He had arranged for flowers to be delivered in the afternoon.

Peter was also lying in bed. His thoughts were much more mixed. He was contented after an evening with Jason, but saddened that he was no longer living here. He wasn't seeing him at all the next day, the first time since Jason had arrived at his home that awful night. They had agreed that Brenda would need Jason there, and that they had a lot of catching up to do. Peter had arranged to go to the pictures with Paul, just to keep himself occupied. He was hoping there wouldn't be many evenings like that.

Before he had got together with Jason he had never felt at a loose end. There was always something going on. He had his studies, family life, his acting, nights out with friends. He realised suddenly that he had neglected some of his friends, and knew that he should make it up to them. His closest friends knew about Jason, and were pleased that Peter had found someone so special. Some were surprised to learn he was gay, but a few realised it explained a lot about his indifference to the many girls who had made a play for him. His female friends seemed to have taken it hardest of all. Determining to make more effort with friends once he started work, Peter drifted off to sleep.

Brenda had not yet got to sleep. She was lying looking at that patch on the ceiling. All day she had been having doubts about leaving. She was sure he would come looking for her. Then when he came home from work this evening his dinner had not been to his liking. He had called her all the names under the sun and thrown the plate against the wall. His violence was increasing and as she had wiped up the food, Brenda had known she had to get out. Now she lay worrying that somehow he would sense something was up.

She only had to put her clothes in her shopping trolley in the morning and go. She was leaving almost everything behind. He hadn't noticed the old photos she had taken, but then, he wasn't sentimental enough to look at photos. The ones on the wall she had had copies made of, and they were already at the apartment. She smiled to herself as she thought of it. She had never in her wildest dreams thought she would ever live somewhere like that. It was new and modern, clean and simple. She could hardly wait to see the furniture Jason had chosen for it.

She finally fell asleep thinking of the new life that lay ahead of her.

Chapter 27

Brenda woke early the next morning. She lay still so as not to disturb the snoring man at the side of her. She would wait patiently for the alarm to go. Her eyes looked around the tired room. It had been like this for as long as she remembered. It needed decorating, but he hadn't seen it as important. She would have loved some new furniture, but he didn't want to spend 'his hard earned money' on new stuff when this was still ok. She had done her best to keep the house nice, but it was not easy.

She wondered how he would manage without her there. He never cooked, she wasn't sure if he knew how. He certainly had no idea how to clean up after himself. Brenda just hoped her daughter wouldn't be lumbered with him. She would stay herself rather than have that happen.

She had been with this man since she was fifteen. He was nearly twenty and had seemed so grown up and wonderful. She was pregnant at sixteen and her parents had insisted she marry him. How she wished she had run away then and brought up her daughter by herself. The only good thing that came out of her marriage was her son. If she had run away she would never have had Jason. She smiled as she thought of him. He was such a wonderful son. Her daughter was special to her too, but had followed in her footsteps and had married at sixteen, Brenda was sure it was to escape from her father.

She was a good girl, but her life was not much easier than her mother's. Her husband also expected his wife to be at home, seen but rarely heard. He was also racist and homophobic but, as far as Brenda knew, he had never lifted a finger to her daughter for which she was thankful. He was also a better dad, loving his children, even if he did stereotype them.

Brenda went through her plan for the day. She would get up as usual and make breakfast. After he had gone to work she would clean up and then prepare him something for his tea, even though it would probably hit the wall when he realised she had gone. If, by chance, he didn't throw it, all he would have to do was pop it in the microwave. She had a feeling he and the microwave were about to become really good friends.

After making the meal, she would write the note. She had planned in her head exactly what she intended to write. Short and sweet as anything more would be a waste. 'Your dinner is in the fridge, just put it in the microwave for a couple of minutes. I have left you and will not be returning. If you want someone to blame just go and look in the mirror.'

She smiled to herself as she thought of his reaction when he read it. He would be so angry, but there would be no-one here to take the brunt of it. She hadn't said anything to her daughter, so she wouldn't be able to help him. She had asked Jason to get her a new mobile phone so once she had transferred the numbers she wanted the old one would be turned off. None of the neighbours knew anything of her plans, so none of them would be able to let anything slip. She didn't speak to many of them anyway. There were few friendly people when you were married to a man like that. Those that did speak to her mainly did so because they felt sorry for her.

Since her own parents had both died, Brenda had little family to tell. Her brother thought she was stupid to stay for so long, so maybe she would let him know her new address. Maybe they would even become closer once she was free. She hoped so, she missed him.

The alarm brought her back to the present. Sighing deeply, she got out of bed and went to the bathroom. Then she went down to start getting his breakfast. It was just ready when he walked into the kitchen. She placed it in front of him and he grunted. 'Hope you are planning something more edible for tea tonight.' She mumbled a reply and turned away so he wouldn't see her cheeks redden.

'Stay calm,' she told herself, 'stay calm. He mustn't suspect anything.' She busied herself at the sink, and before long he was gone to finish dressing. Never again would she have to share a breakfast table with a man in his vest. Brenda wrinkled her nose at the thought of him. Not long now. Soon he would leave for work and she would be on her way to freedom.

He called 'bye' as he left. He didn't come to kiss her goodbye. The only time he would kiss her was in his awkward advances when he wanted sex. Brenda shuddered. Never again would she feel the weight of him pressing down on her and making it so hard to breathe. Never again would she lie there with tears spilling down her cheeks after he had finished with her. He never asked if she enjoyed it, never tried to make it wonderful for her, he just satisfied himself at her expense.

Brenda went upstairs to wash and dress. She wasn't intending to take her dressing gown with her, it would remind her too much of breakfast here. Neither did she bother to shower, just a quick wash then dress. She was intending to buy herself some posh bubble bath on her way to the apartment, and then she was intending to have a long luxurious soak in that new bathroom.

Downstairs she prepared a shepherd's pie and boiled some peas to go with it. That done, she washed up for the last time. She put the meal in the fridge, having covered it with cling film. She then collected the last of her things, managing to squash them down so the shopping trolley didn't look full and left the note on the table for him to find when he returned home from work.

At ten twenty-five exactly she closed the front door behind her for the last time. There was quite a spring in her step as she walked to the bus stop and caught the bus into town. She saw no-one she knew. She was meeting Naomi at eleven so she had just enough time to buy some new toiletries. She chose some lavender bubble bath, a pink toothbrush, pink flannel, even a pink shower cap. She laughed as she looked at the pinkness of her basket. Well, she felt feminine, young even, for the first time in years and she intended to relish every minute of it.

Naomi was already waiting in the café when she arrived. 'I'm so sorry I'm late,' Brenda was slightly breathless from having rushed down the road.

'It's fine,' Naomi smiled at her, 'It's only a couple of minutes.' She didn't tell Brenda that she had already started to worry that she hadn't managed to get away. They ordered coffee, and Brenda couldn't resist showing Naomi the things she had bought.

'I know it's a bit silly, but I had such fun choosing things I wouldn't normally have chosen.' The two women laughed together and Naomi noticed that Brenda was already looking younger and less down trodden than she had. They finished their coffees and then went out to Naomi's car. Brenda got in and let out a big breath as they drove away. Naomi parked in the parking place belonging to the apartment, and reached in her bag. She pulled out some keys and handed them to Brenda.

'I hope you liked what we've done with it. If not, I'll help you rearrange things as you want them. I am under strict orders to make sure you have everything you need before I leave you to settle in.' Together they made their way to the entrance. Brenda found the right key and they entered the apartment block. Her new home was on the first floor, so they went up the stairs and she unlocked the

210

front door. 'Welcome home.' Naomi pulled her into a big hug and led her inside.

Brenda gasped as she saw it furnished for the first time. Naomi noticed the subtle changes Jason had made the previous evening and smiled. He really did have an artistic flair. Brenda moved from room to room, unable to speak but loving everything she saw. Tears fell freely, and finally, she just sat on the end of her bed and wept.

Naomi left her there and went to put the kettle on. There was milk in the fridge and tea bags in the jar marked tea. Jason had left everything tidy before he went to work this morning. Laying a tray, Naomi took the drinks and a plate of biscuits into the lounge and called out that tea was made.

Wiping her eyes Brenda went through to join her. 'I'm sorry Naomi, what must you think of me.'

'Don't be silly. You are entitled to be emotional; it's a big day for you. I'll just drink this tea and then I'll get out of your way and let you settle in. There is bread and some cheese and ham in the fridge, and Jason said he would be bringing things in with him tonight for your evening meal. You've got my number so if you think of anything else you will only have to call.'

The two women sat in a comfortable silence and drank their tea. Brenda was still feeling tearful, but managed to control it. She saw Naomi to the door and hugged her again as she left. She then made the phone call she was dreading. She kept it simple and to the point, refusing to be led into saying anything she didn't want to. 'I won't be available for a couple of days dear, but try not to worry. I am fine, just going to be busy. I will call you after the weekend.'

She hung up, leaving her daughter very confused and slightly uneasy. She wondered if her Dad had hit her again. It had happened a couple of times before, this phone call to say she was going to be busy, and then when she had seen her Mum again there had been the tell tale signs of fading bruises. She wished she would leave him, but that would never happen. She would go round tomorrow and try to talk to her.

Having made that call, Brenda went into the bathroom. She found herself humming as the water ran and she watched the bubbles appearing. She undressed and climbed into the deep bath. She wasn't sure how long she lay there; she just closed her eyes and revelled in the warmth and peace. It was the buzzer sounding that brought her out of her reverie. Panicked Brenda climbed out of the bath and wrapped herself in a large towel. Had he found her? 'Be sensible girl,' she chided herself, 'He doesn't even know that you've left yet.' She went to the receiver and carefully lifted it. 'Yes?'

She then pressed the buzzer to let the caller up. Flowers. She smiled to herself. Trust Jason to think of flowers. When she opened the door she was amazed to see not one but three bouquets waiting for her. Not only had Jason sent her flowers, but so had Peter and his brother Paul. Brenda found herself once more in tears. She thanked the delivery man and took them all inside.

Jason's card read, 'Welcome home Mum.' Peter had written, 'Hope you and Jason will be very happy here.' Paul had written, 'Wishing you every happiness in your new home. If you need anything just ask the landlord!' she laughed at that. He was her landlord. She wondered how many people got such a welcome from a landlord.

She quickly dried herself and dressed, then rang Naomi. 'Help, I need vases and we haven't a single one here.' She went on to explain about the flowers. Naomi promised to pop over with a couple straight away. She arrived shortly after and together they arranged the flowers. Naomi was secretly pleased with both her sons and with

Jason too for being so thoughtful. She then left, with a kiss and a promise to pop over the next day.

Just a few minutes later the buzzer went again. Brenda jumped once more and chided herself for being so scared of everything. Her voice was still slightly shaky though as she said, 'Hello?'

'Hi, it's Bernard. Just thought I'd pop by and check you had arrived safely.' Brenda buzzed him in and went to open the front door to him. He had a bottle of claret in his hand. 'Housewarming! Can't tell you how good it feels knowing you are safe.' She invited him and in and he walked through to the lounge. 'Wow! Jason has done a wonderful job. No wonder Naomi keeps hinting to me to let him do our dining room.'

'He is so clever at all this. I know he's my son so I am probably biased, but he is gifted.'

'You have every right to be proud of him, he is a wonderful lad. We are going to miss having him around, well except that he will still be around quite a bit I imagine.' They both smiled.

'I expect Peter will be here quite often too,' she replied.

'Well, I'll be off home. Just wanted to drop the wine off. Hope you both enjoy it.'

Brenda went to put it in the fridge, then remembered that you didn't do that with red wine. At least, she didn't think you did. She went to unpack the things from her shopping trolley and then stored it in the hall cupboard.

She started to make a list of things they would need. She was glad that Naomi was going shopping with her tomorrow. She wasn't sure she would manage it all on her own. Jason had told her he had money left from the deposit on the apartment, the balance having been paid by Paul as an investment. He was charging a minimal rent, not really wanting that, but Jason knowing she wouldn't live there otherwise.

She was determined to pay Jason back for anything that she spent, but was glad that he had some funds she could use in the meantime. She would begin to look for a job as soon as possible. She had noticed that José had had a notice up requiring a waitress, perhaps she would try there. She would discuss it with Naomi the next day. She seemed to know him well, so maybe she could put in a good word for her.

Before she knew it Brenda heard a key in the door and Jason was calling hello. She ran out to meet him, and the two of them hugged. Then laughing they went into the lounge arm in arm. They kept talking at the same time, and laughing. Some tears were shed, and lots of hugging took place. Eventually Jason went to make them something to eat. Brenda had tried to tell him that was her job, but he was having none of it. 'I will do my share of the work in this home, so get used to it woman! You are no longer the slave, but a joint partner in this adventure.'

They enjoyed the wine with the meal. 'One thing that family have taught me is good wine,' Jason commented.

'I don't think I've ever tasted anything so lovely,' was Brenda's reply. 'Now you have to let me do the washing up. Are you going out to see Peter?' She was touched when he said he had arranged to spend the evening with her. She cleared away, then they spent the evening together watching her choice of programmes on telly. It was the best evening Brenda could ever remember. Snuggled up with her grown up son beside her, in a peaceful environment, not having to worry about something being said or done that would cause a row.

Eventually both of them went off to bed and both slept soundly.

214

Chapter 28

On the other side of town things were not so peaceful. Debbie was lying in bed worried sick. Having spent the afternoon trying to think of a way to get through to her Mum that you did not have to stay with a man that beat you, she had been shocked when her father had phoned. Apparently her Mum had left him. He had yelled and shouted and cussed down the phone until Debbie hung up on him.

It wasn't long after that that he had arrived on her doorstep. He had become very abusive. He would not believe that she didn't know about this. He would not listen to her saying she had no idea where her mother was. Brett too, had assumed she would know something, and told her to say if she did. Inwardly she wanted to cheer that her Mum had left, but outwardly she was being bullied and was scared.

Then her father had crossed the line and things changed. When, once more, she said she knew nothing he lifted his hand to hit her. Brett saw red. He caught hold of his hand and manhandled him out of the door. There he told him never to come by again. The shouting went on for a while, the neighbours looking out of their windows to see what was happening. Debbie's two children, Sandra and Keith, were becoming hysterical; Debbie herself was crying and shaking.

Eventually the door slammed and Brett came back in. 'The nerve of that man, coming here and raising his hand to my wife,' he fumed. Seeing the fear in the eyes of his wife and children he sat down and fumed silently for a few minutes. Then he pulled the children to him and reassured them. 'It's alright, Daddy made him go away and he won't be coming back. Stop crying now, stop it. Why don't you both go and get an ice-lolly out of the freezer while I talk to your Mum. Go on. It's alright, we aren't going to shout or fight.'

The children dutifully went out of the room. Debbie looked up and across at him. 'Thanks,' she whispered. 'I honestly don't know where she is. She rang me today, and said she was busy and wouldn't be available for a few days. I just thought he had hit her again. I was going to go over tomorrow and see how bad it was.' She shrugged her shoulders at a loss to know what to think or say.

'Come here,' Brett was unusually gentle. 'I know your Mum thinks I am just like your Dad and I suppose in some ways she is right. I have no time for gays, hate all that multi-cultural rubbish the kids learn at school. I think a woman's place is in the home. But I have never laid a finger on you and neither would I, and I certainly wasn't going to let him touch you. I don't agree with women leaving their husbands, but if he is hitting her, well that's another matter.'

Eventually she had managed to get the children settled, but now she was lying in bed far from settled herself. Where was her Mum? How had she managed to keep her plans a secret? Brett had said it would be so that she hadn't been able to say anything, however much pressure her father had placed on her. He was probably right, but she was worried. She didn't know how to get in touch with her. She would just have to wait and hope she phoned after the weekend like she said she would.

A tear slipped down her cheek. She felt alone. She needed her Mum. She knew things hadn't been easy since Jason had been thrown out. She felt guilty that she hadn't given her more support, but with two young children she had her hands full. She was also pretty sure another was on the way. She hadn't done a test yet, but she knew the signs.

The following morning any doubt was taken away when Debbie was sick. Brett had gone to work and she

216

needed to get Sandra to school. Why had her Mum chosen now to disappear? She groaned as another wave of nausea flowed through her. She tried her Mum's mobile, but it was still switched off. She had no choice but to dress herself and the children and go out on the school run.

She then went home and spent the rest of the morning on the couch. She dropped Keith at nursery for the afternoon and then decided to get some groceries before it was time to pick him and Sandra up. It was in the supermarket that she bumped into Brenda.

Brenda was with Naomi. They had had an eventful day. Naomi had picked Brenda up after breakfast. On the way into town Brenda had commented on seeing the advert in the café window the day before. Naomi made that their first stop. She had walked in, taken the card from the window and walked over to José. 'I have the answer to your problem,' she started. 'This is my friend Brenda. She needs a new job, and would be perfect for here.'

José smiled at them both. 'Do you have experience?'

Before Brenda could say a word Naomi answered him. 'She has years of experience of waiting on a family, what more could she need?' She raised her eyebrows, and José unable to resist this wonderful woman laughed.

'OK. Naomi's recommendation is enough for me. When can you start?'

Brenda wasn't sure what to say. It had all happened so quickly. Eventually it was decided that she would start the following week. The two women then stayed for a coffee before moving on to begin the shopping. Brenda had quite a long list. Jason had thought of the basics, like crockery and cutlery, but there wasn't an iron, an ironing board, and only two saucepans. The women had laughed about the things men just didn't think about. Brenda also wanted an alarm clock, a new dressing gown, and now some work shoes.

All of that meant that it was the afternoon before they went to the supermarket to pick up some groceries. Naomi was surprised when Brenda was suddenly engulfed in a hug from what seemed to be a slightly hysterical young woman. It took a while for Brenda to extract herself and to be able to introduce Naomi to her daughter, Debbie. Naomi suggested they made use of the coffee shop in the supermarket as Debbie obviously needed to talk to Brenda. She sent the two of them to a table and she collected the drinks.

Over coffee Debbie told her mother what had happened the previous evening. Brenda was upset and apologised again and again. She was pleased to hear how Brett had behaved and told Debbie so. She then explained where she was living and how it had come about. Debbie was pleased to know that Jason was fine, and impressed with his job. Another wave of nausea then reminded her of the news she had to share. 'I'm pretty sure I'm pregnant again,' she murmured, then rushed off to the toilets. In the end, Naomi gave her a lift to pick up the children, dropped her at home and then took Brenda back home.

By the time Jason got home Brenda had a meal ready, but only just. As they ate she filled him in on the day's events. Jason smiled as he listened. Everything seemed to be working out well, and with a sister providing grandchildren at regular intervals he didn't have to feel guilty about not providing any of his own.

Peter arrived just as they were finishing eating. Jason let him in and the two hugged as though they had been apart for much longer than a day. They went into the lounge and Brenda greeted him warmly. She hugged him and thanked him for the flowers. She then went to clear up

218

after the meal, leaving the two alone. She intended to keep herself out of the way for as long as possible.

Brenda smiled as she heard the easy laughter coming from the lounge. It did her heart good to know that Jason was so happy. She had been so frightened when he had been attacked by her husband. She wasn't sure he would ever recover from it. Oh she realised that there were still some scars that must run very deep, but he was better than she had dared hope.

After a while Peter came through to the kitchen. He had come to find her and bring her through to the lounge. 'I don't want you hiding yourself away every time I come over you know. I would feel uncomfortable if you did.' He pulled her into a big bear hug that left her breathless.

'Put me down,' she managed to gasp and he laughed. 'I won't always be staying in the kitchen, but I thought you could do with some time. I appreciated having Jason to myself last night, but I am more than willing to share him with you. I can't tell you how much I feel I owe you and your family for taking him in.'

Jason walked in as she was speaking. He pulled both of them into a hug. 'My two favourite people,' he said. 'Now, what are we going to do for the evening?' Peter had brought some house warming gifts with him which he went to get from the car. Amongst them was a scrabble set and so they settled down to a game, which involved much laughter and talk of cheating. Brenda won in the end and said on that note she was off to bed.

'Subtle, I'll give her that,' Peter winked at Jason. The two of them cuddled up on the settee. 'I've missed you. It seems strange you not being at home.'

'Yesterday was the first day I wasn't there. Have you really had time to miss me?' Peter pulled him into a long passionate kiss that left him in no doubt that he had. It was late when Peter finally went home, Jason having assured him that he would sound his Mum out about him staying over.

After closing the door he gently tapped on her door. As she invited him in Jason went and sat on the end of her bed. 'Mum, what do you think of Pete?' he began.

Brenda patted the bed next to her and Jason moved up. 'He is lovely,' she smiled, 'but I guess that is not what you are really asking me is it?' Jason blushed. 'I am guessing you will want him to stay over?' She raised her eyebrows. Jason nodded and held his breath.

'That's fine with me love. I don't know what arrangements you had there, but this is your home as much as mine, and I want you to feel more comfortable here than you ever did in your father's house. This is a new start for both of us and it has to be good. We are lucky to have this chance and I don't want anything to spoil it. So you invite him over whenever you want, and if he stays that's fine, and if he goes home that's fine too, as long as it is what you want.'

Jason hugged her. 'Thanks mum. We had separate rooms there. When I first arrived Bernard asked us to be circumspect. He needed time to get used to the bombshell Pete had just dropped on him. I was so glad that he was willing to consider accepting us that I wouldn't do anything to rock the boat.' He grinned as he continued. 'It drove Pete mad at times, but I wouldn't budge.'

'Well then, he will be glad I am happy for him to stay won't he,' Brenda smiled. 'I'm glad you respected Bernard's wishes. I'm sure he respects you for it. It can't be easy for a man to learn that his son is gay. But not many are as disgusting as your father. How are you coping with what he did? I have been scared to ask until now.'

'It's late. Let's talk about this tomorrow shall we? I am coming home for tea before going out with Pete. We can talk then.' He kissed her cheek and left her. As he lay

220

in bed he thought about how he would explain it the next day. He didn't want to cause her any more hurt, but he wanted to be honest.

In the end it was easier than he thought. Brenda knew the emotional scars could not have gone. 'It hurt, but it was what I expected. I tried to ring Pete from a call box but he wasn't home. Naomi came and got me and took me home.' He briefly told the story of the next few days and then how Naomi had told him about her past. 'The strange thing was, the more I became a part of that family, the more it hurt in some ways. I guess it was being shown what a family should be like. Because of him, ours was never like that was it?'

Brenda shook her head and pulled him close. 'I'm so sorry Jason. You and Debbie missed out on so much. Even if we weren't well off, you should have had the security that comes from a loving home. I will spend the rest of my life regretting not getting you both away from that.'

'Mum, I don't want you to regret it. It wasn't your doing. You ask Debbie, she will say the same thing. You loved us and we knew it. We also knew how much you suffered. If Debbie had been in a position to get you out of it she would have. As it happens, luck came my way. I don't regret what I've been through.'

He Paused and thought, before adding, 'Like Naomi says, it makes you who you are. Maybe one day I too will be given the opportunity to help someone else the way she has helped me. And every punch was worth taking to be with Pete. That sounds soppy I know, but it's how it is. The more you get to know him, the more you will realise how special he is, so are all the family. You will love being a part of it you know. And now, I had better be getting over there. I promised Pete I wouldn't be late, but don't wait up,

I will probably be late back. Are you sure you are going to be alright?'

Brenda assured him she would be fine and sent him off. She had a book Naomi had leant her, and was intending to spend a long time soaking in the bath. She loved the bathroom here, and spending time luxuriating in a bubble bath was her new pleasure. She took Jason's CD player in with her and put some gentle music on. For her, this was heaven and like Jason had said earlier, it was worth everything she had been through to get this.

Naomi answered the door to Jason and looked at him in surprise. 'Have you lost your key?'

'Well no, but it didn't feel right using the key when I don't live here any longer,' he explained.

Naomi pulled him into a big hug and tutted at him for being so silly. 'This will always be your home now you know,' she said. 'You just come in and call out that you've arrived same as always.' She pulled back and held him at arm's length. 'You'll do.' She hugged him once more. 'I have missed you, you know.' He kissed her on both cheeks told her he'd missed her too and together they went into the lounge. 'Look who thought he had to ring the bell!' There was teasing all round with Peter and Paul both pretending to be dreadfully offended at that and Bernard asking the same question as Naomi had.

Jason loved being back there. He grinned at them all. 'Oh I've missed this.'

Peter exclaimed out loud, 'Oh and I was being daft when I said that yesterday. I don't know why I put up with you.' Everyone laughed again at his indignation.

'It is great being with Mum, don't get me wrong, but it's good to be back here too.'

Naomi was thrilled to hear that. She patted his arm and went off to the kitchen to put the kettle on.

'Well that's the mother lady crying! See the effect you have on her son number three!' Bernard went off to see if she was alright. As he suspected she was shedding a tear. He held her close, loving her for being so soft about their adopted son. 'Come on now, don't go all soppy on me.'

'I know it's daft, and I know Brenda needs him and he needs her, but I am missing him and it's so nice to know he misses us too.' She blew her nose on the hanky Bernard offered her and set to making the tea.

The boys all pretended they hadn't noticed she had been crying when she walked back into the lounge and together they spent a very pleasant evening. Jason had spoken to Peter earlier that day and told him the good news about Brenda being happy for him to stay over. So after Jason had gone that night Peter managed to get Bernard on his own and asked his advice on how to tell his Mum he was planning to stay over the following evening.

'I'll tell her, don't worry. We knew it would happen so it isn't going to be a complete surprise, but be prepared for her to be as bad as when you went off to scout camp.' Peter groaned at the memory. Naomi hadn't coped at all, and it was before mobile phones, which had made her worse. She had phoned the camp site multiple times a day to check he was alright, until Bernard had hidden the phone. 'Just come home for tea before you go, and ring her before you go to bed, and first thing the next morning and she will be fine.' Bernard hugged him and patted his shoulder.

Chapter 29

Life soon fell into a routine. Brenda and Peter started their new jobs and both loved them. Jason was more and more in love with his job and spent many hours working on design ideas at home. He also redid Naomi's dining room, as a thank you for all she and Bernard had done for him. She loved it, and so did everyone else who saw it. Before any of them had realised autumn was upon them. The days grew a little chillier and shorter, the leaves fell from the trees and life somehow calmed down a little for everyone.

After such an eventful year it felt strange to have what could only be described as 'normality', but here it was happening on a daily basis. Naomi was the only one who seemed unsettled. She still found it hard that some days Peter did not come home for dinner. His hours at the hospital were long, which was bad enough, but his free time was shared between home and the apartment. Sundays had become the day when Brenda and Jason always came for lunch and she loved that, having everyone together.

Bernard was a little worried about her. He had a feeling it went back further than Jason moving into the apartment. He thought it was maybe since her fall. That was back in the summer and she should have been over it, but something was still not right. He wondered if he should suggest she went back to the doctor, but didn't want to worry her so was trying to think of a careful way to word it.

He waited until they were snuggled up in bed one night. The cats had refused to come in and Naomi had got very upset about it. 'Darling, I know you don't like them staying out all night, but they are cats, it's what they do!' She didn't answer, but turned her back on him and pulled the duvet up tight around her neck. This was such an unusual move that it floored Bernard for a minute or two.

Then he pulled back the duvet, turned her to face him and saw she was crying. 'Oh baby, what's up? It has to be more than the cats being out. I'm worried about you. I have a feeling it goes back to that fall you had. I know you said the doctor said the bloods were fine, but you aren't keeping anything from me are you?' This just made Naomi cry even more. Suddenly Bernard was worried. 'Naomi, stop crying and tell me what is going on.' His voice was stern and that was so unusual that it stopped Naomi in her tracks.

'It's nothing. I'm ok. Really I am. The bloods were fine. At least, for a 'woman of a certain age', as he so delicately put it.' She watched the light dawn on Bernard and then turned away again. She hated the way she felt. He turned her back towards him once more. He looked deep into her eyes and kissed her. Despite herself, Naomi felt her body responding. She tried to resist, but Bernard knew her too well. He knew exactly how to get his wife aroused, and he left no stone unturned.

After they were both satisfied he held her tightly. 'Well, Mrs Smedley, for a woman of a certain age, you sure know how to have a good time, and how to give one too.' She smiled at him and hit him gently on the chest.

'It's not funny! I hate it. I seem to have no control over my emotions at all, and before you say I never have had, it is worse now. I cry for no reason, I get angry over nothing, I can't do things without feeling tired, my brain doesn't want to work and so the list goes on. I know we've had a difficult year and that probably explains some of it, but Bernard I hate this. I hate feeling I'm getting old.'

Bernard kissed her forehead. He tried to reassure her. 'Naomi, it happens to every woman at some point. If not now, then next year or the year after that. It will pass, and you can get help from the doctor or a herbalist or even a reflexologist if that's what you want. There is no need to suffer in silence. And,' he emphasised the word, 'you can share how you feel with your husband. I am here for you darling. I will cope with you being bad tempered, and will do more to help in the house, whatever it takes. It won't make me love you any less because you are a woman 'of a certain age'. I am not getting any younger either. I am kind of looking forward to us growing old together.'

Naomi hugged him tightly. Somehow Bernard always made things better. She wondered why she hadn't said anything before, but knew it was because she hadn't wanted to admit it to herself. She was feeling old for the first time in her life and she didn't like it. Perhaps if she had grandchildren it would be easier. She would have a new role instead of being redundant in the one she had loved so much.

Thinking of grandchildren just made her sad again. She thought of Paul and how hurt he was. She then thought of Eve and suddenly she was crying again. As though he knew what she was thinking Bernard pulled her close. 'It's been a hard year for our family, Naomi, but it's passing. Things are looking up. Who knows what next year will have in store? Perhaps Eve and Abe will adopt. Paul will eventually be ready to move on, and let's be honest the next one can't be as bad as the last. Then we will have the grandchildren we dream of. Life is just entering a new phase, but that doesn't make it bad, just different.' He kissed the top of her head gently.

Eventually she fell asleep in his arms, and after that night she seemed to cope better with the changes taking place around her. She discussed it with Jen the next time they met for lunch. Jen too, had noticed things changing and, like Naomi, she didn't like the way they were going. 'It seems only yesterday that we were at school and dreaming of boys, marriage and children. Now all our children are grown up and our hormones are a law unto themselves.'

Naomi agreed. 'It seems so unfair. Just as we are enjoying life it throws something else at us.' They laughed together. Brenda came over to take their desert order. They both ordered the pavlova, their regular and absolute favourite desert. 'We are bemoaning getting old,' Naomi told her.

'Neither of you are old!' Brenda seemed shocked that they thought it of themselves.

Jen laughed. 'Tell that to our hormones. You wait; before you know it you will be saying the same thing. We didn't think we would be feeling it but we are.'

'You are only as old as you feel,' was Brenda's comment.

'She's right,' Jen mused. 'Why don't we book a couple of days away? We can do some shopping, enjoy some pampering and reassess ourselves.' The two women laughed, but the idea had taken hold and they went from the café to a travel agent and booked that very afternoon.

Bernard was surprised when Naomi told him, but pleased. He was sure it was just what she needed. Paul also thought it was a good idea. He suggested his Dad joined him on a golf holiday at the same time. 'Pete can cat sit,' he said. Bernard liked the idea of a few days away with his eldest son and told him to get it booked the following day.

So the next week Peter found himself home alone. He fed and watered the cats, but ate at the apartment every night. Brenda thoroughly enjoyed having him there. She was fond of him, and loved seeing him and Jason together. The two were bound together in a way that took her breath away. Sometimes it was hard to see where one ended and the other started. They were so clearly two halves of the same whole.

Some nights that week they stayed at the apartment and some nights Jason stayed with Peter. Both of them dreaded going back to normal at the weekend, and the realisation came that they would have to think about moving in together sooner rather than later. 'We can't say anything this side of New Year though,' Jason as always urged caution. 'It wouldn't be fair on Naomi or my Mum.' Peter agreed with him. They decided to wait until then, but also agreed they wished it could be tomorrow.

While they were away, Jen and Naomi did most of their Christmas shopping. Both of them liked to be ready early. They had done ever since the children were little. This time was no different. Soon the car was filled with bags. Both of them were good at choosing just the right thing for people, probably because they loved the people they shopped for so much.

Jen searched for ages to find the right thing for Eve this year. She knew that Christmas was going to be hard for her. She and Abe had told both sets of parents that they wanted to spend the day by themselves. Whilst she understood why that was, Jen was hurt by the thought that Eve wouldn't be surrounded by her family. So she shopped for something extra special. Eventually she found a simple gold locket. Both she and Naomi admired it and she went in to buy it.

Naomi found just what she wanted for each of her men folk. She also found a lovely necklace for Brenda. The only ones she didn't buy for while she was away were Jen and Bill. She would take that shopping trip alone.

Besides the shopping the two enjoyed all the treatments the hotel spa had to offer. They had their nails and hair done, and then had aromatherapy massages. They also used the pool and sauna. They enjoyed lovely meals, and each other's company. Both considered themselves blessed to have such a good friend and sister.

At the same time Bernard and Paul were also enjoying themselves. Paul had booked an expensive hotel with great facilities. 'I could get very used to having a wealthy son you know,' Bernard told him.

'Get used Dad, get used. I have plans to be wealthier than this within the next couple of years. I had planned to expand the business, but as the profit from it would make me have to pay Felicity forever, I am selling up. I will pay her the allowance we agreed for two years, but then it will end.'

'It's a bit drastic to sell up isn't it?'

'I have plans for an alternative. It's what I would have done with the current firm, but now it will be a separate enterprise. I will take my best workers with me, make sure the rest still have jobs and I won't be employing the current accountant, so no-one that I don't want to find out will know my business.'

'Life has hardened you son and that's a shame. I understand it, but wish you could have been spared it.'

'Dad, please don't worry. That marriage stopped me from being myself, but I am back, and intend to make sure I never disappear again. I won't be rushing into another relationship, but hopefully, one day, the right woman will come along.'

It was on the golf course the next day that Paul really opened up. He talked to his Dad as he hadn't for years. He told Bernard just how bad his marriage had been. Shocked Bernard told him he must be a saint to have stuck with her so long. 'It's true what she said that afternoon we were there, if she had had the child I would never have left.' Bernard nodded.

Paul then became very pensive and said nothing for the next couple of holes. Bernard thought he was thinking of the child he had lost, and so concentrated on the game. That wasn't what was on Paul's mind though. He was thinking of Paris. He was wondering what his father would think of him if he knew. Eventually he could cope no longer. 'It's a shame they don't have a greenhouse around here,' he joked.

'This is more open than any greenhouse, and whatever you tell me will be in confidence, you know that.' So Paul opened up and told his Dad everything. To say Bernard was surprised would be an understatement. 'Well I thought your brother had shocked me more than anything ever would, but you've beaten him today son.' He did, however leave Paul sure that he understood, and whilst he didn't recommend it he did manage to make a joke or two.

It brought the two men closer together than they had ever been, and they had always been close. Somehow a closer bond was created and both of them treasured it. They spent the rest of their trip enjoying the company, the good food and the golf.

It was a happy band that came back together that weekend. Everyone had benefited from their week. Naomi, because time with Jen always did her good, and being pampered had made her feel better in herself. Bernard, because he was always happy on the golf course and because he was now even closer to his eldest son and understood him better. Paul because he had opened up to his Dad, and he too treasured that bond. Jason and Peter, because they had had each other and time alone.

Bill was also glad to have his wife back. He was pleased that she looked so well and had clearly enjoyed her time away, but he had missed her. He suggested an early night and Jen laughed at him. 'You are so predictable you know Bill, but yes I would like an early night.' She teased him by adding, 'I am quite tired after the journey.' Bill picked her up and carried her up the stairs. Laughing they tumbled onto the bed and rediscovered one another.

Chapter 30

Christmas arrived with all the glitter it always brought. The shops were full of decorations and present ideas. Brass bands were playing carols in the town centre and people could be heard humming them as they tried to get their shopping finished. Everywhere you went people seemed to be rushing.

Naomi was glad she was ready early. Every year she was amazed at people who left it until December. She had written all her cards, posted those that needed posting, and had wrapped all her presents. These were hidden away, lest anyone should be tempted to feel them or peek inside the wrapping. She smiled as she thought of how the boys, when they were little, would search high and low and never find her hiding places.

Brenda was an excited as any child. This was the first year that she would have a wonderful Christmas with her children without someone spoiling it. She had gradually stopped worrying that he would try to find her. She knew that Debbie still saw him, Brett having relented on letting him visit, but it wasn't something they talked about and she trusted her and Brett not to tell him where she was. She had been invited to spend Christmas day with the Smedley's. She was then going to spend Boxing Day at Debbie's. She had bought all her presents, being able to spend what she wanted without having to explain herself.

Jason was also excited. He had bought the biggest tree he could find and then made Peter help him get it into the apartment. He had gone overboard on the decorations, and for once he had ignored the designer within him and everything was gaudy and mixed. Peter had laughed at him, but he loved the way it looked. He also bought every singing Santa, reindeer, and toy he could find and every evening he would set them all off until Brenda and Peter begged for mercy.

Paul was looking forward to a family Christmas. He was now in the countdown to getting the decree absolute. Early in the New Year he would be a free man. He also had a buyer lined up for the firm. It was someone he had done quite a lot of business with and he was happy that he would take care of the workers. Paul felt an obligation to make sure that no-one suffered through his desire to start again. The buyer also knew about the new firm Paul was intending to start. He was happy that it was a sideline he didn't want to go into and so Paul wouldn't be stealing work from him.

Paul had also decided that a chunk of the money he made from the sale would go to a children's charity in honour of his lost child. In his mind he was sure it would have been a son, and he thought of him as Caleb. It still hurt to think of him, but he was gradually coming to terms with what had happened.

The only people dreading Christmas were Eve and Abe. She had gone and bought vouchers for everyone. She knew it was a cop out, but she couldn't cope with going into town at the moment and seeing all the lovely things on sale. All her groceries were being delivered, or brought in by Jen. Every time she came she would hold Eve close and together they would shed a few tears. Jen wished she could somehow make it easier, but knew this first Christmas without their daughter would be harrowing.

Abe had services to plan for Christmas but his vicar was keeping his load as light as possible. Instead he had him concentrate on visitation, especially to people he knew would also be dreading Christmas. Abe was grateful to him, but did want to feel that he was pulling his weight. He wasn't sure Eve would make it to the Christmas day service, but he would be taking it before they spent a quiet day together.

He had bought Eve a couple of books he knew she wanted to read, a cashmere shawl, and had a star named after their precious daughter. He had then bought DVDs of all their favourite films. That way they could avoid the TV programmes and adverts all day long. He was determined that they would come through this, and next year it would become easier. The first of everything was the worst so they said.

Bernard was, as always, leaving most of it up to Naomi. This was partly because she was at home and he was busy at work, and partly because, since he introduced her to Christmas, she had become a great fan of the season and he wouldn't deprive her of the pleasure it gave her. The only present he bought each year was the one for her. This year he wanted it to be something special. He knew it had been a hard year for her one way and another. So far he had found nothing that seemed right and he was beginning to doubt he ever would.

The main problem was he didn't know what he was looking for. Jewellery seemed too predictable, anything too big and she would be cross, and clothes were something he had never been comfortable buying. He was still trying to come up with an idea with just a week to go. He decided to go out in his dinner hour and risk the crowds. Then suddenly, as he walked along, he saw the perfect gift. It was a painting, a landscape and it was of the coast they had gone to on their honeymoon.

Smiling he walked into the shop. The artist was pleased to have the sale and Bernard was pleased to have solved his problem. He carried the wrapped parcel back to the car and hid it away in the boot. He then had another idea. He went back to the shop and asked the artist if she could make up a book of prints of that area for him. She said she could, she had painted the area often over the years and had taken many photos to use for her paintings.

She agreed to do copies of these and to put them into a book with blank pages in between.

It would be ready on Christmas Eve, which wouldn't give Bernard time to do what he had planned with it before Christmas. So he decided that instead of filling those pages himself he would suggest that he and Naomi filled them together. It was to be a memories book. Each page was to remind them of one year together. They could pick out the most memorable events of that year and record them there. He was very pleased with himself at coming up with such a wonderful idea, and Naomi noticed it when he got home.

'What are you so pleased with?' she asked.

'Being married to a wonderful woman,' was the only reply he would give. Naomi was sure it was something to do with her present and tried every trick she could think of to get him to tell her. Experience should have told her that this never worked, but she still tried every year.

On Christmas morning Brenda and Jason arrived first thing. Brenda had been sure it was too early, but Peter had insisted he wanted them there first thing and Jason had taken him at his word. The two of them had been on the phone at midnight wishing each other a happy Christmas, but no-one seeing them now would have known that. As Jason let them in with his key Peter was there waiting. The two hugged as though it was ages since they seen each other, and then pulled Brenda into the hug as well.

She complained, as though she didn't want to be hugged, but they both knew this was no more than bluster on her part. Eventually Paul came to the lounge door and asked them if they were coming in. He claimed he couldn't wait another minute for his presents. Laughing the group went in.

As was the custom, Naomi would only allow them one present each before Church. They then took a present with them to open during the service. Naomi always thought this was a wonderful idea. Bernard made her take the book of prints. Brenda was pleased to be invited to join them for Church. This was another thing that was new and special this year. God had never featured in her husband's idea of Christmas. Together they all walked to Church, greeting friends on the way.

Carols were sung, presents opened, a short message given by the vicar and it was time to go home. Naomi slipped her arm into Bernard's as they walked. He made sure they dropped slightly behind the others so that he had the chance to explain how the book was to be filled. Naomi reached up and kissed his cheek. 'I am so lucky to have you,' was all she said, but he knew how much was meant by those simple words. He patted her hand and they walked on home.

Bernard then poured them all a drink, purposely taking his time as he always did. His sons reacted the way they always had, right from being small. They tried to hurry him, and the more they tried the more he slowed down. Brenda laughed at the show. Jason squeezed her arm. This for them was the start of many Christmases of fun, love and laughter.

Eventually all the presents were open. Everyone was pleased, both with those presents they had received and the joy that their presents had brought to others. Perhaps the biggest response had been to Peter and Jason's present to Paul. They had bought him a weekend away in Paris. Naomi was horrified, much to their amusement. Peter noticed a look pass between his Dad and his brother and knew instantly that Bernard knew what had happened there this summer. He raised his eyebrows at Paul who nodded slightly.

'If you don't trust him to go on his own, we could always go with him,' Peter said to Naomi.

'Fat lot of good that would do, judging by last time,' she replied, and then added, 'maybe I should send your Dad with him to keep him in check.' Neither she nor Brenda understood why this made the men all howl with laughter.

Dinner was a marvellous affair. Brenda had offered to help in the kitchen, and Naomi had let her. The clearing up they left to the younger members of the family while Bernard phoned his sister to wish them all a happy Christmas. Naomi went on the phone as well. They had gone to Abe's church that morning and Jen said he had coped very well. Eve had gone with them and sat in between her parents, tears streaming down her face throughout the service.

Abe had told her parents what he had planned and they were relieved that he had been so thoughtful. Naomi agreed that it would be good for them to avoid the day as much as possible. Bernard and Jen's parents were also with her this year. They took it in turns which of their children they spent the day with. Rebekah was there, but was anxious for Adam and his mother to arrive. Leah and Greg were with his parents but were coming by later. Rachel and Nigel always went away for Christmas and Jen was annoyed to tell Naomi that she hadn't even phoned them yet.

After the clearing away was done, the phone call made, Peter decided they should have a game of charades. It turned into a riot and time flew by. No-one was hungry at tea time, which was no surprise after all they had eaten and drank that day. Bernard put the TV on for a film he wanted to see, and the group sat happily munching on chocolates and nuts as they watched.

Eventually, Brenda said she thought it was time they left. Peter tried to talk her out of it, but she insisted. Jason looked like a child being pulled away from a party. Bernard felt sorry for him, and for the first time suggested that Peter went too and stayed over. The two of them were intending to have their own mini Christmas day the next day anyway, while Brenda was at Debbie's. Jason wasn't going with her as Brett wouldn't have him in the house. It hurt, but he understood and had met with his sister a couple of days earlier to give her the presents he had bought for his niece and nephew. They were the only two presents he had bought. All his other presents had been handmade pieces that he had designed especially for the person he gave them to.

Debbie had also received one of these and had been over the moon when she opened it. She had phoned him to say thank you, and even Brett had managed to come on the phone and say, 'happy Christmas.' It was a small thing, but it had meant a lot to Jason. Not, however, as much as it meant that Bernard was openly suggesting Peter and he spent the night together.

Naomi also noted the fact that Bernard was openly giving his blessing to them. She squeezed his arm, before he stood to receive the hug Peter wanted to give him. 'Thanks Dad,' he whispered as they hugged. Bernard nodded at him, and then moved on to hug Jason and Brenda before they left. She hugged him, Paul and Naomi, thanking each of them in turn for giving her such a wonderful day.

The group of three left and walked home comfortable in each other's company. Naomi went through to the kitchen and made a very light supper for Paul and Bernard. She had enjoyed the day but it was twinged with sadness. She shook her head to get the sad thoughts away and went through to join her husband and eldest son. Both of them could read her thoughts and so made the effort to lift her spirits.

237

They succeeded. By the time they decided to go to bed, Naomi was once more counting her blessings. She sent them up ahead of her, saying she just wanted to give the cats some supper. Both of them had received presents from each of the younger members of the family, all carefully wrapped as though the cats would notice. Naomi smiled as she remembered the solemn way the gifts had been given, and the indifference with which the cats received them.

She bent down to stroke them both. Basil, her tabby cat, with the wonderful way of knowing when people needed him, and Alfred, her black cat, the smallest of the litter and still smaller than his brother. 'I love you,' she whispered into their fur. They purred back, and then turned their attention to the pate she had put down for them. Naomi went to the sink and washed the last few pots of the day. Suddenly she realised again that she had forgotten the dishwasher. This time though, it wasn't because something was wrong, but because everything was right.

Lightning Source UK Ltd.
Milton Keynes UK
UKOW04f1050230815

257358UK00001B/9/P